forever with you

by ROBIN JONES GUNN

Christy & Todd

THE MARRIED YEARS

BOOK 1

ISBN 978-0-9828772-1-0

This novel is a work of fiction. Names, characters, places, and incidents are either products of the author's imagination or are used fictitiously. All characters are fictional and any similarity to people living or dead is purely coincidental.

Published by Robin's Nest Productions, Inc.
P.O. Box 2092, Kahului, HI 96733

Edited by Lisz Mast
Cover Images by Jenna Michelle Photography
Cover and interior design by Taylor Smith, Ringger Design,
Nicolas Ace Wiinikka, and Ken Raney

Printed in the United States of America by Believers Press
Bloomington, Minnesota 55438

*"LORD, You have been our dwelling place
throughout all generations."*

~ PSALM 90:1 NIV

one

*C*hristy was ready.

Todd wasn't home yet but she was ready to surprise him and make her grand announcement the minute he entered their apartment. She'd gone all out and made Ritzy Chicken, Todd's favorite. A cluster of candles were gathered in the center of their small kitchen table giving the room a romantic glow. Two places were set, complete with folded paper napkins under the forks.

Todd is going to be so happy about this. The timing is perfect. I can't wait to tell him!

Christy pulled the hair tie out of her long, nutmeg brown hair and gave her mane a quick shake. She reached for the pitcher of homemade lemonade in the refrigerator and filled two tall glasses. On this warm September evening in southern California, lemonade sweetened with frozen strawberries seemed like the perfect, festive way to get their evening of celebration started.

Through the open windows of their vintage style apartment Christy heard someone approaching the front door. She hurried to undo the lock, feeling her heart flutter with anticipation. Christy pulled the door open and her exuberance came to a screeching halt as the last person she expected to see was standing on her doorstep.

"Rick?"

"Hey. How are you, Christy?"

"Good. I'm good. How are you? It's been awhile since we've seen you."

They exchanged an awkward hug and Rick looked past her into the apartment. "Is Todd home yet?"

"No. He should be pretty soon. Do you want to come in? Is Nicole with you?"

"No." Tall, dark-haired Rick's abrupt reply about his fiancée caused Christy to look at him more closely. He was disheveled, which was not a look Christy remembered ever seeing on him.

"Are you okay?" She motioned for him to come inside.

Rick didn't answer. He seemed intent on catching another whiff of the casserole that Christy was keeping warm in the oven. His eyes fell on the table where the candles were flickering with promise.

"You have plans," he said more to himself than to Christy.

"Yes. Well, sort of." She didn't want to say another word. The last thing she wanted to do was slip and end up telling Rick her good news before she had a chance to tell Todd. She quickly covered by adding, "I decided to surprise Todd and make a nice dinner for once."

"I'll come by another time." Rick retraced his short steps to the open front door. "Tell Todd I'll text him later."

"Okay. Are you going to be in the area for a few days?"

"I think so."

For decisive, always-on-an-agenda Rick, that was an unexpected answer. He turned to go and then paused. Giving

Christy an odd glance at her stomach he said, "I hope you guys have a good night."

"Thanks. You, too." Christy closed the door and frowned. That was strange.

It was moments like this when Christy tried to remember why she'd ever gone out with Rick when they were in high school. He was nothing like Todd. Never had been, never would be. If anyone would have told her then that she, Todd and Rick would all be such great friends now, she never would have believed them. Their forever friendship was a rare gift and she appreciated it. However, tonight was not a night for catching up with old friends. Christy wanted her husband all to herself.

She returned to the kitchen and pulled the salad from the refrigerator, anticipating Todd's arrival any minute. The sound of the key turning in the lock prompted another round of flutters in her heart. She hurried to the front door and greeted her husband with an exuberant kiss.

Todd pulled back, surprised. "Whoa! What's the occasion?"

"I made dinner for us. Did you get my text?"

Todd's tussled, sun-bleached blond hair had been growing out the last few months and now fell across his forehead. He took in the sight of the table and drew in the aroma. "Ritzy Chicken?"

Christy nodded proudly. "With salad and green beans."

Todd's silver blue eyes focused on hers as he tilted his head and asked, "What's the big occasion?"

"I . . ." Christy paused, feeling her face turn rosy. "I thought it would be nice to sit at the table for once and talk about things."

"Things?" Todd looked skeptical.

She knew she was enjoying drawing out her big announcement way too much but it was too fun to stop now.

"About our future."

Todd leaned over and gave her another kiss. This time she was certain she detected a hint of taco flavoring on his lips.

"Did you eat already?"

"Yeah, I grabbed a taco on the way home." Todd put his keys and his phone on the counter and washed his hands in the kitchen sink.

"You didn't get my text, did you?"

Before Todd could answer, his cell phone chimed an alert. He reached for it and read the screen. Typing a quick reply to the text that had just come in, he set his phone to mute and said, "Remind me to set an alarm tonight. Rick's in town. I'm meeting him for coffee in the morning."

"Yes, I was going to tell you. He came by right before you got home. He doesn't look like he's doing very well."

"What do you mean?" Todd took the seat at the kitchen nook table.

"I don't know. He seemed kind of spacey. Like he hadn't slept for a week."

"That's not good. Do you think we should invite him to come back and eat with us?"

"No!" The answer popped out way too quickly so Christy added, "I mean, I was hoping that . . ."

"Because I have a feeling things aren't going well between him and Nicole. She wasn't with him, was she?"

"No, she wasn't." Christy lowered herself into the chair across from Todd and felt a sense of empathy for Rick. She'd only been around Rick and Nicole a few times but they seemed like a good match. Even her best friend, Katie, who dated Rick in college and had introduced him to Nicole, thought they were the ideal couple. Christy hoped Rick and Nicole weren't breaking up.

Todd got up from the table and went for his phone. "I

think we should have him over. There's plenty of food and if he's hurtin' the way I think he is right now, and if I were in his place, I'd need to be with my friends."

Christy knew Todd was right. She was okay with waiting on telling him her big news. People in need always came first with Todd. His position as a Youth Pastor gave him plenty of opportunities to reach out to teens and their parents and so far Christy had never regretted any of those times.

Todd paused and looked over at Christy. "Is this okay with you? Sorry I didn't ask."

"It's okay. Go ahead. Give him a call. I'll set another place."

Apparently Rick hadn't gone far because it took him less than five minutes to return. Todd opened the door and Christy watched the two of them give each other their typical manly sort of hug as they clasped hands and leaned in to bump shoulders.

Rick hesitated before stepping into the small kitchen area where Christy stood. "Are you sure I'm not crashing your party?"

"No. It's okay." Christy motioned for him to have a seat at the table. "You're welcome here any time, Rick." She took a seat at the end and make sure they had everything they needed on the table.

Instead of praying, as Todd usually did before they ate, he raised his glass of lemonade and Rick and Christy followed his lead.

"To the King and His kingdom," Todd said with winsome sincerity. "And to His mysterious ways and His perfect timing. We are grateful, Lord, for good food and good friends and this chance to enjoy them both. Amen."

"Amen," Christy echoed as their glasses clinked.

"Mysterious ways," Rick repeated quietly. "That's for sure." He picked up his fork and moved the steaming green beans around on his plate but didn't take a bite.

Christy looked at Todd, wondering if they should ask Rick any questions or just let him eat.

Rick put down his fork and lifted his chin. He had tears in his eyes. Stubborn tears. They rose to the rim and then belligerently refused to spill over. He blinked a couple times and said, "Nicki gave me the ring back last night. She said it's over."

Christy's hand instinctively reached over and gave Rick a comforting squeeze on his arm. Todd placed his hand on Rick's shoulder and said, "Really sorry to hear that, man. What happened?"

"She said she's not ready. Not ready to marry me; not ready to get married. She's not even willing to stay engaged and try to work this out. She said it's over."

Christy didn't know what to say. Todd kept his hand on Rick's shoulder as if infusing him with courage to say everything he needed to say.

"It's my fault." Rick stared at the untouched food on his plate. "I pressed her to get engaged too soon. She wanted us to take our time and go slowly. I'm the one who wanted to get married in October. Then last month, when we moved the wedding back to January, I thought that would give us the time she kept saying we needed. But last night she said she couldn't marry me. Not next year, not ever."

The tears spilled over his lower lids and he quickly wiped them away with his napkin and drew in a courageous breath. "Man, this really bites."

"You didn't see this coming?" Todd asked.

"No. Not at all."

Todd pulled his arm back and started eating, which seemed to put all three of them more at ease.

"What about you?" Todd asked. "Did you have any doubts about marrying Nicole?"

Rick looked up. His eyes were clear, focused. "No. No

doubts at all. I love her. We make a great team. I love everything about her. We're so much better together than we are
apart. At least that's how I saw our relationship. I thought she
felt that way, too."

Christy wanted to say that maybe it was a case of nerves
and Nicole would change her mind. Things could still work
out for them. But she didn't know that and it felt cruel to offer
Rick false hope at a time like this. She wished she knew what
to say.

"It doesn't make sense," Rick said. "It just doesn't. We
could have worked this out. I know we could have." He looked
down and took his first bite of food. That bite was followed by
another bite and then another. Christy was glad to see that at
least he was eating and that should help somehow.

The guys managed to put away two-thirds of the Ritzy
Chicken casserole before they leaned back and drew in a
deep breath as if they'd finished a race. Christy felt a quiet
sense of satisfaction knowing they liked dinner so much.

Rick talked about how he'd spent the whole day trying to
figure out what he did wrong and what he could do to win
Nicki back. He ended by saying, "The conclusion I keep coming to is that I have to let her go."

Christy nodded. She and Todd both knew what it was like
to release an emotional hold on someone you love. Christy
also knew that as much as she wanted to jump in and give
him advice, perhaps the best gift she and Todd could give
Rick right now was this time of gathering around a candle lit
table, sharing good food and offering their prayers and their
listening ears.

Todd's cell phone began to vibrate on the kitchen counter.
Christy glanced at it as she cleared the table and placed the
dishes in the sink. The screen showed that Todd had missed
four calls and three text messages.

"Do you need to check any of these?" Christy handed

him the phone. "It looks like you have quite a few."

Todd scrolled through his messages. As he did, his eyebrows seemed to cave in.

"Everything okay?" Christy asked.

"I've gotta go back to church tonight." He looked up at Christy. "I just now saw your text. You said to come home because you'd made dinner and had some good news. Sorry I didn't see it earlier. What's the good news? Is that what you wanted to talk about tonight?"

Both Todd and Rick looked at her expectantly.

Christy felt her face turning rosy again. "It can wait," she said haltingly. "We can talk when you get back from church."

"Are you sure?"

Christy nodded and tried to look as if she meant it.

"Okay. I'm gonna go, then."

"Me too," Rick said.

Todd got up and gave Christy a quick kiss. "Later."

"Yeah. Later," Christy repeated.

Rick followed Todd out the door and called to Christy over his shoulder, "Thanks again for letting me hang out with you guys."

"Of course. Let us know if we can do anything, okay?"

He nodded and left, closing the door behind him. Through the open window she heard Rick ask if Todd knew what Christy's big announcement was.

"I think she's up for a raise at work," Todd said. "At least that's what I'm hoping it is. Hey, do you still want to meet for coffee tomorrow?"

"Sure, if you've got time."

"Of course. Like Christy said, we're here for you, man. You'll get through this."

Christy folded her arms over her stomach and stood alone in the vacated apartment. She hated the way she felt in that solitary moment. She was not getting a raise at work.

And truth be told, she wanted to be the one who was being invited to meet Todd for coffee in the morning. Unfortunately, she'd agreed to fill in for a few hours at work tomorrow, even though it was Todd's day off. Not that he actually took a day off very often.

Christy could feel her jaw clenching.

As genuinely concerned as she was for Rick and what he was going through with Nicole right now, at the same time, she felt chewed up inside with her own set of emotional woes. One of the most difficult adjustments for Christy in their less than two years of marriage had been fitting into her husband's erratic schedule and finding her own sense of place and purpose as well as not feeling as if she had to compete for his attention.

Hopefully, all that is about to change.

Christy unfolded her arms and gave them a shake. She refused to slide into a swamp of discouragement. She put on some music and started cleaning up the kitchen. Instead of using the dishwasher, she filled the sink with hot water and added a squeeze of lavender scented dish soap. Tiny bubbles floated upward, catching a luminous twinkle from the candles still adorning the table.

Plunging her hands into the soapy water, she looked at her wedding ring. In her heart she'd always known this was what her life would be like when she married Todd. She also knew that it was important for her to admit the truth to herself and not bury it. And the truth was that deep in a dusty corner of her heart, the high school version of herself was still mad. Mad at Rick Doyle for hijacking her dinner plans, and mad at Todd for having to go back to church that night.

Why is it that I can be an understanding, grace-giving ministry woman one minute and an hour later all I want to do is eat ice cream and feel sorry for myself?

"Ice cream!" She said out loud.

Leaving the clean dishes to dry, she opened the freezer and took out the carton of Tahitian Vanilla Bean ice cream that she'd forgotten to offer to the guys for dessert. She reached into the refrigerator for the sauce pan filled with a hot fudge concoction.

Christy warmed the hot fudge on the stove and scooped a generous serving of ice cream into a mug. She slowly drizzled the hot fudge over the top, drawing in the yummy scent of dark chocolate. With a spoon in one hand and the mug of happiness in the other, she headed for the bedroom where a good book waited on her nightstand next to her phone.

She coached herself to relax, enjoy the sweet treat, read a little and hope that Todd would come home soon. Even though her great news would alter their lives significantly and even though it was killing her that she hadn't been able to tell him yet, she could be patient.

Christy let the first spoonful of ice cream melt in her mouth and thought, *No, I can't. I'm not that patient. I want to tell him now!*

Reaching for her phone, Christy typed out her announcement in a text. She paused before sending it and immediately changed her mind. This was news that had to be delivered in person.

Quickly deleting each word, back-spacing letter by letter, Christy thought about what she wanted to say instead. She smiled to herself and playfully typed her eager message:

HURRY HOME TACO LIPS!

two

*T*urning on her side, Christy reached over to the vacant side of the bed. Todd wasn't there. She squinted in the darkness and tried to read the time on the alarm clock: 2:07.

Did he ever come home from church last night?

She noticed the strip of light seeping through the bottom of the closed bedroom door and guessed that Todd must be in the living room. She'd given up on waiting for him to come home and fallen asleep a little after eleven.

Christy tossed back the covers and got up. She found Todd asleep in the recliner in the living room with the laptop open on his midriff.

"Todd." Christy went to him and gently shook his shoulder. "Hey, Sleepy Head. Wake up."

He looked at her and then closed his eyes again.

"Come on." Christy leaned over and kissed him on the forehead. "Come to bed."

"Okay. Yeah. Okay. I'm coming." He stayed as he was, unmoving.

Whenever Todd fell asleep in the recliner it was as if he'd been siphoned into a worm hole. It took great effort to pull him back into this dimension. Christy moved the laptop to the floor and put her hand in his. She pulled him to an upright position and walked him to the bedroom with his brawny arm looped over her shoulder.

More than once Christy had mused that if this was what Todd was going to be like as an old man, their future would be pretty comical. She had never been especially grateful for her 5'7" frame or for what her aunt had once called her "wide berth" in reference to her hips. Both those features were advantages when it came to rousing her sleepy, nearly six foot tall, broad shouldered husband and ushering him to bed.

Todd went straight to the bed and fell in, still dressed. At least he was bare footed. Christy urged him to roll over so she could get him under the covers. He complied and as she looked closer she thought she detected a slight grin on his handsome face.

"You're sleep-smiling, you know."

His grin widened just slightly.

Christy considered turning on the light and rousing him so that he'd wake up all the way. That way they could finally have a chance to talk. She'd done that once, a few months ago when they needed to discuss some charges on their credit card. The conversation did not go well. They both were so exhausted that it ended with Christy in tears and Todd shut down in silence. Neither of them had slept much during the few hours that remained that night.

Christy wisely opted to wait until the morning. She turned off the light and crawled into bed, cuddling up to his back and resting her chin on his shoulder. "I love you," she whispered.

"A-lug-u, oo," he murmured with about as much energy as a tortoise.

Christy gave his shoulder a kiss and could tell by his steady, deep breathing that he was on the express train to dreamland. Unfortunately, now that she'd gotten up, Christy found it impossible to get on the same train. She turned on her side, on her back, on her stomach. No position felt comfortable. No amount of breathing in through her nose and out through her mouth slowed down the roar of thoughts that tumbled over her like an invisible waterfall.

Exasperated, Christy rolled out of bed and quietly slipped into the living room, closing the bedroom door behind her. Going for the laptop on the floor beside the recliner she opened to the screen Todd had left open when he fell asleep. He had been on the website for their bank account. The session had timed out but Christy could see that Todd had paid their electric bill and water bill online before he dozed off. The balance in their checking account was now $214.96.

Oh man. That's less than I thought we had.

Christy logged back in and checked the balance in their savings account. That balance was much less than it had been the last time she'd checked. Leaning back, she tried to do some quick calculations in head of their total monthly income and their rising monthly expenses.

Her middle of the night math quiz was too stretching. She and Todd needed to talk through their finances later. For now, it would be much less stressful to check her email. Especially if there were any notes from Katie.

Ever since Christy's best friend, Katie, had moved to Kenya last spring, the two Forever Friends had managed to keep up a consistent stream of emails in order to stay in close contact. Even though they'd tried to carve out times to call each other, the time change and their work schedules made it too challenging to be consistent. Emails were their lifeline.

Each time Katie sent an email Christy expected to see an announcement of her wedding date. Katie and Eli had only been engaged a few weeks and Katie had explained more than once that things were different in Kenya. Their wedding date needed to fit into the schedule of everything else that was happening at the mission center where they lived and served. She seemed to think they wouldn't need to do a lot of advanced planning.

Christy didn't know if that was true or if Katie was naïve as to all the details that go into putting together a beautiful wedding. Christy's desire was that her friend have a beautiful wedding. It was also Christy's desire to get the date on the calendar so she and Todd could start figuring out how they would make the long trek to Africa. How they were going to pay for it was another issue, and something else for she and Todd to talk about soon.

Christy clicked on the email from Katie waiting in her inbox and frowned as she read the opening line.

I had a meltdown yesterday. It was because of you, just so you know.

Poor Eli! I don't think he'd seen one of my hysteria shows before. Not like this one. I'm fine now. Really. But it wasn't pretty. What happened was that reality caught up with me. I finally faced the truth that I am here and you are there. Many, many miles apart from each other.

The thing is, I always thought that after you and I got married we'd live on the same cul-de-sac and do life together as we have since we were fifteen. In the perfect world in my little head, you and I were going to have our babies together and raise our kids to be best friends.

Yesterday I realized that's never going to happen. And that tragic realization rocked me to the core. You are family to me, Chris. How can we live our lives on the opposite ends of the globe? I'm pretty much not okay with that. Everything else in my life right now gets an A+.

Knowing that this is my life – the rest of my life – and you're not a daily part of it is just wrong. Unbearable, basically.

So? How are you?

A slow tear traced a curve down Christy's cheek. She missed Katie more than ever now. She, too, had not given full space in her thoughts to the reality of how their lives would be, living on separate continents. Christy had been too happy for Katie to let in sad thoughts for herself. Katie loved Africa. She loved living at the conference center where she worked. She had fallen deeply in love with Eli, the guy who had patiently pursued Katie her senior year of college. Together, she and Eli were molding a new life, nestled in the hills of the Rift Valley outside of Nairobi. They were surrounded by tea fields as well as good friends and Eli's caring parents.

All of that was good for Katie. So good.

But now, five months after Katie's relocation to the place she called, "the home of her heart", the reality of what the future held for she and Christy had settled on her; settled on both of them.

Christy hit reply and started typing her response. She had to keep blinking because the tears were flowing freely now and she knew she couldn't stop them.

I know exactly what you're saying! I feel the same sadness, Katie. It comes at me in waves. I miss you terribly. I mean, of course, I'm happy for you and Eli and how you're settled in there in the home of your heart. But not being able to be in and out of each other's everyday lives has left such a hole in my heart. I really wish you were here. I have so much to tell you. Some really big news! But I want to tell Todd first and I was all set last night but then Rick came over and . . .

Christy stopped typing. She thought about how Katie and Nicole had become good friends last year when they worked together as Resident Assistants at Rancho Corona University. In the crazy way that all their friendships overlapped, Katie had the closest friendship with Nicole, Todd had the closest friendship with Rick, and Christy had the closest friendship with Katie. It was an amazing circle of camaraderie when everyone was getting along with everyone else in the circle.

But if Nicole hadn't told Katie yet that she'd ended her relationship with Rick, Christy knew their smooth circle could quickly turn into a pointy-edged triangle if she was the one who shared Rick and Nicole's private news.

She deleted her last few lines and ended her email with, "I have some big news to tell you. I'll write you tomorrow after I've had a chance to tell Todd."

Hitting send, Christy pushed herself out of the recliner and set the laptop aside. With light steps she went into the kitchen and looked through the cupboard to see if she had any herbal tea to settle her churned up stomach and make her sleepy. Tea always reminded her of Katie. The most prevalent memory was Katie's attempt at blending her own variety of herbal tea when they were college roommates and how it caused Christy to break out in a rash.

Christy found only three bags of tea in the basket in the cupboard. All three were Earl Grey. Not her favorite and not sleep inducing. She turned out all the lights, and went back to bed. The closeness of Todd, his rhythmic breathing, the cool breeze through the open bedroom window all comforted Christy like the familiar refrain of a lullaby. She soon drifted off to sleep.

When Christy awoke to the annoying buzz on the alarm on her cell phone, she immediately noticed that Todd's side of the bed was vacant once again.

"Todd?"

She padded her way to the bathroom and saw a sticky note on the mirror that had become their central communication board over the last few months. Their notes were usually short and sweet, like the messages found on Valentine candy hearts.

Call me. Love you.

Christy realized she must have been sleeping deeply if she didn't even hear him get up and leave. She called his cell and left a voice message before getting in the shower. The warm water made her yawn and realize how tired she was. She wished she hadn't agreed to take the extra hours at work today but she knew the income would help.

When she arrived at The Ark bookstore her new manager, Rosalyn, waved her over to the register and said, "Did you see the sewing machine?"

"Sewing machine? No. I just got here."

"It's in the break room. I'm cleaning out my mother's closets now that we're moving her to the retirement community. She hasn't sewed in years. It's a good machine. Portable. I thought you might want it."

"Oh. Thank you." Christy wasn't sure why Rosalyn thought she would need a sewing machine. She didn't exactly sew.

"If you don't want it, I'll offer it up to the rest of the staff. But I wanted to let you have the first chance if you're interested."

Somehow Christy felt she should accept the offer and be grateful even though she guessed she'd probably end up giving it to someone else who could make good use of it. "Sure. Thanks, Rosalyn. I'd love to have it. I appreciate you thinking of me."

"My mother always offered her unused items to people in the ministry. Since you and Todd are doing youth ministry, I know you're more in need than the rest of the women who work here."

As soon as the explanation for her generosity spilled out, Rosalyn looked as if she wanted to take back her words. She blinked behind her round rimmed glasses and parted her lips as if trying to find an antidote for her awkward explanation.

Christy's spirit bristled at the insinuation that she and Todd were a charity case. But it was true. She and Todd were more in need than any of the other women who worked there and more than Christy would ever admit to anyone.

With a smile that was calmer than what Christy felt inwardly at the moment, she reached over and lightly touched Rosalyn's forearm as a gesture of appreciation. "Thank you. I really appreciate you thinking of me."

Rosalyn checked her wristwatch and said, "You're welcome. Be sure to take it with you when you leave today."

For the next two hours Christy kept going at an even pace as she helped a few customers, answered the phone and stocked books. It was unusually slow, which added to her anticipation of getting off at one o'clock instead of at five o'clock since she was only filling in half day.

At a little after eleven o'clock, Christy looked up and saw Todd walking into The Ark. He had a wild grin on his face and held a big bouquet of white carnations. When he spotted Christy at the register he practically sprinted across the store, went behind the counter and scooped up Christy in his arms.

Before Christy could say a word, Todd's lips were on hers, the bouquet of carnations were pressed against the side of her face and she was overcome with the fragrance that connected her heart to every single romantic memory she and Todd had shared, starting with their first kiss when she was fifteen.

For a moment everything around Christy fell away and she was lost in the secret corner of her heart where she had quietly stored every wish and every prayer she'd ever whispered for the man whose happy tears were now mingling with their kiss.

As beautiful and wonderful as the moment was, Christy didn't understand why her husband would rush in like this and shower her with such lavish attention. As soon as she found her voice she murmured through her still-tingling lips, "Todd? What is going on?"

Todd could barely speak. He touched the side of Christy's face and brushed back a strand of her hair.

With tears glistening in his eyes, he whispered, "Kilikina, why didn't you tell me?"

three

$\mathcal{C}$hristy studied Todd's flushed expression and asked, "Why didn't I tell you what?"

"About the baby. Why didn't you tell me about the baby?"

"What baby?"

"Our baby." Now Todd was the one tilting his head and trying to reassess the moment. "We are having a baby, aren't we?"

Christy's eyes grew wide. In a small, convincing whisper she leaned close and said, "No. Todd, no. I'm not pregnant."

He pulled back, stunned. His expression caved in. "What?"

Christy looked apologetically at the customer who had approached the register and was watching the interaction between Todd and Christy with great interest. "I'm sorry. Someone else will be here to help you in just a minute."

Rosalyn stepped up to the register and Christy quickly led Todd over to the area where the theology books were shelved. It was the least active part of the store and she hoped no one would follow them there.

"Todd," she whispered. "Who told you I was pregnant?"

"Eli."

"Eli!"

"Yeah. He sent me an email and wanted to know if they should set their wedding date for some time during the next few months."

"Why was he asking you that?"

"He said they were guessing that it would be safer for you to travel that far in the earlier stage of your pregnancy."

Christy's hand went to her forehead. "I didn't tell Katie I was pregnant. I just said I had some good news."

"So, you're not pregnant." Todd looked confused.

"No. I'm not."

"You're sure."

"Yes. I'm sure."

Todd rubbed the back of his neck. "I saw Eli's email and remembered that you said you had good news last night. I thought I'd really messed up and that your big announcement was that we were pregnant."

"You didn't mess up anything. I do have big news. But we're not pregnant. Honest."

"Okay." Todd still looked befuddled. "So, what is it? What's going on?"

Christy looked around. She noticed one of the other women who worked at The Ark had conveniently decided to start doing an inventory count on Bibles in the next row over. In a low voice Christy said, "I can't tell you here. Not right now."

"What do you mean you can't tell me?"

Christy tried to get him to lower his voice. "Let's go somewhere."

"Okay. Should I go grab us a booth at The Dove's Nest?"

"No. Let's go home. Can you just take me home? It's okay

if I leave. I'm going to tell Rosalyn I need to go home. It'll be fine. I'll grab my purse and meet you at the car."

Todd's jaw flinched. He muttered, "Okay." Christy handed the carnations back to him.

She had no trouble finding Rosalyn. It seemed everyone in the store had found a reason to gather close in hopes of catching a hint as to what was going on.

"I wonder if I might be able to go home early since it hasn't been very busy," Christy asked.

"Certainly. Yes. You should go home and get some rest." Rosalyn's motherly smile made it clear that she'd picked up on the "baby" part of the exchange between Christy and Todd. As much as Christy wanted to set things straight with her manager, she knew she could do that later. Right now Christy just wanted to get out the door and set things straight with her poor husband.

Christy grabbed her purse and saw the sewing machine on the lunch table. It was a portable machine that came in a case with a handle. Even though it was heavy, Christy decided to lug it to the car instead of leaving it and inviting any further awkward exchanges with her manager.

Todd was waiting in the car with the engine running. The carnations were on the back seat, tossed aside like a forgotten gym bag. Christy opened the back door and hoisted the "gift" in next to the carnations.

"What is that?"

"A sewing machine." Christy got in and closed her door.

Todd pulled out of the parking lot and gave her another confused look. "Is it just me or does nothing make sense today?"

"It was a gift. Sort of," Christy said. "From my manager."

"Why?"

Christy knew she didn't want to try to explain the sewing machine right now. It was more important to tell Todd her good news and get this whole knot untangled. "She was try-ing to be nice. But let me tell you my big news"

"Okay."

"I was offered a new job."

Todd glanced at her in surprise and then back at the road. "I didn't know you'd applied for anything."

"I didn't. Not exactly. Do you remember when I told you last spring about Dr. Swanson in the English Department at Rancho Corona and how she was applying for a grant so that she could do extensive research on Harriett Beecher Stowe?"

"No."

"Well, I hardly remembered, either. It was months ago when she asked me. The point is, she called yesterday and said the grant came through. She's able to hire a research as-sistant and she asked if I wanted the job."

Todd looked straight ahead. "So, the job doesn't involve the sewing machine."

"No. Forget the sewing machine. The job involves lots of typing and organizing. Most of the work I can do at home but I'll go on campus at Rancho a couple days a week when Dr. Swanson needs me to do some of the work there."

"Is this something you want to do? Be a research assis-tant?"

Christy was stunned at his flat line reaction. She thought Todd would be much more excited for her. "Dr. Swanson was one of my favorite professors. It's an honor to be asked to work with her. The best part is that I'd be able to work my own hours so I'd be able to arrange my schedule better. That's what I'm most excited about. It'll free me up to go to more youth events at church with you. We can plan to be together on your days off."

Todd didn't give any indication that he thought that was a bonus.

"And the salary would be more than what I'm making now."

Now she had his attention. "Really? How much more?"

Christy told him the hourly wage that Dr. Swanson had quoted her. Todd look impressed but not that impressed. It wasn't a huge pay increase. For Christy, the fact that she'd be able to schedule her own hours was as much of a bonus as the additional income.

"Is the job permanent?" Todd asked.

"Not exactly. The project is only funded for two years so when the grant ends I'd be out of a job. Unless she's able to renew it or something else happens."

"Do you get benefits? Health insurance?"

"No. But I told her we have all that covered through your position."

Todd drew in a long breath as he turned down the street where their apartment building spread down the length of the city block. "Did you tell her you'd take the job?"

"No. I told her I needed to talk to you about it and pray about it and I'd give her my decision next Tuesday."

"Why Tuesday?"

"I don't know. She was the one who asked me to call her and tell her next Tuesday."

Todd pulled into their parking stall and turned off the engine. He stared at the steering wheel, deep in thought.

Christy didn't know how she expected Todd to respond to the news but she thought it was pretty great news and she was hoping for at least a "congratulations" or "good for you for being selected" or something.

Todd kept staring at the steering wheel.

"So? What do you think?"

"I think," Todd scratched the side of his head and turned the engine back on. He put the car in reverse and pulled out of their apartment complex before finishing his sentence.

Christy assumed he was headed to Joe's Taco Truck since that seemed to be his favorite hangout lately. She guessed it would take him awhile to digest her news and once he did, he'd be happy for her and excited about the benefit of them being together more if she took the job. He just needed a little more time to process and for some reason he seemed to process better with a taco in his belly.

They were almost to the freeway when Todd said in a steady voice, "I think we should go to the beach."

"The beach?"

"Yeah, you know that place where they have all that sand and lots of salty water?"

"Yes, I know that place. Todd? What's going on?"

"Well, I hardly remember what it looks like. You're off for the rest of the day. I'm supposed to be off today so we're going to the beach."

Christy leaned back and smiled. This was unexpected. She caught a glimpse of the neglected flowers in the back-seat. Reaching for them she said, "I didn't thank you yet for the carnations, Todd. They're beautiful."

She buried her nose in the fluffy flowers and drew in their spicy sweet fragrance. Christy couldn't help but give way to a smile as she thought back to the summer when she met Todd and he had given her the very first bouquet of white carnations. That was the day he sealed their summer prom-ise with a kiss – her first kiss, their first kiss. The memory of that exhilarating moment in the middle of the intersection in Newport Beach now seemed like a lifetime ago.

A cascade of her favorite memories of their dating years came over Christy as they got on the freeway and headed west with the windows open and the southern California breezes tugging at the wisps of hair around her face. Her memories were the stuff of fairy tales and golden innocence. The Forever ID bracelet Todd gave her, cooking breakfast on the beach and shooing away the seagulls, driving the Hana road on Maui, the day Todd returned from surfing on the

North Shore, Carnforth Hall in England and the train ride to Spain, Rancho Corona days, pastries and promises at the bakery in Basel, the Gus the Bus crash and the day she knew, really knew that she loved him.

It had been a long time since they'd taken a spontaneous getaway. Both of them had been working very hard and doing everything they could to help build their future together.

"You know what?" Todd said over the roar of the wind and the traffic zooming past them. "Let's make an agreement that we won't do that again."

"Do what?"

Todd rolled up the windows and turned on the air conditioning so they wouldn't have to yell to be heard. With evenly spaced words he said, "The next time I go crazy telling people we're pregnant, let's be sure we're really pregnant."

Christy wanted to laugh. But she could tell that Todd wasn't trying to be funny. He seemed upset and still processing what had happened.

"I promise I'll tell you right away," she said. "Immediately. You'll be the very first to know. I'll even let you be there with me when I take the home pregnancy test, if you want."

"I'm not sure I have to be right by your side, exactly. Just tell me, right away. Okay?"

Christy repressed her grin. "I will. I promise." She thought of how the words "I promise" had always meant something sacred to them. When they knew without a doubt that they were going to get married their warm-hearted whispers to each other included the term, "I promise" and they meant it. At their wedding they chose to seal their vows with those two little words, instead of "I do" because those words went deeper for both of them.

Reaching over and putting her hand on Todd's neck she massaged his tight muscles and rubbed the back of his head. He definitely wasn't his usual easy-going self.

"Are you okay?" Christy asked.

Todd didn't answer. He kept driving and Christy's instincts told her something significant was going on at church. The meeting he'd been called to last night was the main clue. His posture and expression were even bigger clues.

Todd drew in a deep breath through his nostrils. He paused before saying, "The leadership at church is making their final decisions on the necessary budget cuts."

"Budget cuts?"

"The term they used was downsize. They want to downsize my current position in order to accommodate the budget. They asked last night if I'd be willing to go part time and make better use of volunteers."

Christy was stunned. "Didn't they go through all this last spring? They decided then to keep you on full time."

"It's up again for discussion. They meet next Tuesday and they'll take the final vote."

"Tuesday."

"Yeah, Tuesday. The same day you're supposed to give Dr. Swanson your answer."

Christy knew it would difficult for her to make a two year commitment to the research position if Todd's position and income was about to be cut in half.

They drove in silence for a while before Todd said, "And I need to tell you that I think there's a chance I could be let go all together. It's just a feeling I got after the meeting last night. Things have been unstable for almost a year now."

Christy was beginning to feel a clammy sort of panic creeping up to her throat. "What should we do?"

"Pray."

Praying was the last thing Christy felt like doing. Her mind was spinning with how they could possibly get by if Todd was let go from his position. She stared out the front windshield, lost in her dismal thoughts.

Todd reached over and covered her hand with his. "It's going to be alright, Kilikina."

For many years, whenever Todd had called Christy by her Hawaiian name, just the sound of the syllables in his deep voice softened her heart and comforted her. This time she didn't feel comforted. She felt anxious and very low on the hope scale.

Todd turned to her for a moment and she tried to offer him an optimistic smile. It seemed to her that Todd had always found it easier to trust God more whole-heartedly than she had. But she was getting there. She had seen too many times when everything should have fallen apart and then God did one of His God things and all the right pieces came together. Her Heavenly Father had given her plenty of reasons to trust Him.

But she had never seen Todd looking this somber or quietly concerned before. The only thing she could find to be grateful for at the moment was that they weren't expecting a baby anytime soon.

four

By the time they arrived in Newport Beach, Christy and Todd were both hungry so they stopped at a grocery store and picked up some deli sandwiches and a few other picnic goodies.

Todd drove the few remaining blocks to the beach and turned down the street where his dad's two story beach house was located. The plan was to park in front of the house or in the narrow driveway, but when they arrived they were surprised to see that three cars had filled all the usual spots. Loud music blasted from the open windows of the three bedroom beach house where Todd grew up.

"I thought your dad wasn't able to find anyone to rent the house," Christy said.

"That's what I thought, too. He must have found somebody." Todd drove down one of the short alleyways between the closely built beach houses and found a place to park a few blocks away. They pulled an old Mexican blanket out of the trunk of the Volvo and grabbed the grocery bags with their picnic lunch.

"It didn't seem right, did it?" Christy asked, thinking about what they'd observed at the house. "Why would there be so many cars? Do you think the renters are having a big party?"

"That would be my guess."

"Why would they have a party in the middle of the day, in the middle of the week? It's odd. We should tell your dad."

"I will."

Todd's cell phone buzzed just then. "It's Rick. You okay if I pick up?"

"Yes. Of course."

They started walking toward the beach by way of the street where Todd's dad's house was located. "Hey, Rick. How are you doin'?"

Todd made all his familiar listening sounds. "Uh huh. Mmm. Yeah. Sure. Sounds wise."

They strode past Todd's dad's beach house and the music was ridiculously loud. Christy noticed that one of the small windows in the kitchen was broken. Todd took it all in but kept walking, still listening to Rick on his phone.

They were two blocks from the house and coming to the sidewalk that separated the oceanfront cottages from the sand when Todd finally stopped. He ended his call with Rick saying, "Let me know how it goes" and then started typing something into his phone.

Christy gazed out at the familiar stretch of beach. She knew she could never grow tired of the view; the long stretch of sand, the even longer expanse of deep blue ocean that kept going until it met the autumn sky at the horizon. This was one of Christy's favorite places in all of God's beautiful earth. This was where she and Todd had shared so many memories.

In a lot of ways, Newport Beach felt more like home to her than her parent's house in Escondido or the apartment where Todd and Christy lived now in Murrietta Hot Springs. She was glad they had settled in the same area as where they had gone to college at Rancho Corona University, but she knew that living inland, a two hour drive from the California coast, had been torture for her surfer boy husband.

Todd looked up. "I sent my dad an email. You're right. Something is way off at the house. You know what it seems like . . ." Todd started scrolling through the contacts on his phone. Finding the one he was looking for, he pressed the button to make the call. He turned around and started walking quickly back toward his dad's house. Christy followed, not sure of what was going on.

"Did you forget something?"

"No. I'm going to try something. Just hang with me, okay?

They were almost at the house when Todd started talking. "Yeah, hi, I'm checking on a beach house you have listed for rent."

The person on the other end responded and Todd looked surprised. He walked a little faster and said, "Really. Because I understood you had a place available at Newport Beach that was just a couple blocks from the beach."

Todd and Christy were now only one house away from his dad's. A short man wearing a tank top had stepped out on the deck. Todd stayed back so that he and Christy would be out of view. The man held his cell phone to his ear and had a cigarette in his other hand. Christy could hear the man speaking loudly over the music at the same time that she could hear his voice coming through Todd's phone.

"We don't have any rental openings right now but check back because it always changes. Especially if you're looking for a single room in a shared rental house. I might have a single room open in about a month. It's a great house. Just a few blocks from the beach."

"Okay. Thanks." Todd hung up, his eyes still on the guy

on the deck.

The man put his phone on the ledge and sat in one of the battered lounge chairs.

Todd turned around and headed back to the beach.

"I can't believe this," Christy said, putting all the pieces together. "That sleaze told your dad that the house hadn't been rented. But there he is, turning your dad's place into a party house and renting out the rooms as if the house was his. I'm sure he's pocketing all the rent money. He must think that since your dad's in the Canary Islands he'd never know what's going on."

Todd's jaw was set. He kept walking.

"What are you going to do?" Christy knew that when Todd was really angry as he had to be right now, he got quiet and clenched his jaw. It usually took him awhile to think through how he wanted to respond. This time he had an unusually prompt reply for her.

"First, I'm going to put my feet in the sand. Then I'm going to get in the water. And then I'm going to have a picnic with my wife."

Christy kept up beside him and spread out the blanket on the sand. Todd was wearing a pair of shorts, Tee shirt and flip flops. He kicked off the flip flops, pulled off his shirt and headed straight for the shore as if he'd been a beached sea creature and needed to feel the salty water in his pores before he could start to think or breathe again.

Christy watched as Todd dove into the first oncoming wave and came up the other side, his bare back shimmering with droplets of the Pacific Ocean that clung to him like old friends who were happy to see him again. He swam out, hard and fast, diving through the walls of liquid blue. His hands sliced through the water and sent a spray of iridescent determination in his wake.

As Christy observed his motions, she thought of something she'd never considered before. This was Todd's art. He played guitar and wrote songs. That was his outlet of worship. But the way he interacted with the ocean was artistic, purposeful and beautiful. It always had been. She had watched him balance gracefully on his old orange surfboard, "Naranja" for years. Todd could carve a pathway through a wall of seawater. He could turn with calm agility on the face of a ten foot wave. He could paddle out with brute strength and then ride the curl all the way to shore as if it were a tamed lion with a great foaming, white mane.

Yes, this was more than just a sport for him. This was where he practiced his artistry and this was where he got his emotional well filled up.

Christy was glad they'd come. Glad that with everything they'd been hit with that day, that Todd had walked right out and plunged himself into the sea. When he came out, Christy could tell by the look on his face that his anger was subdued. He'd have clear thoughts about what to do next.

Todd stood a few feet away from Christy and shook his head, scattering salty drops down her bare legs.

She laughed and held up her hands in sweet protest. "Todd! It's cold."

"It's not cold if you go all the way in." With a playful grin Todd reached for Christy's hands and tried to pull her to her feet.

She squirmed out of his grasp and gave way to a small squeal that made her feel very young again. "Todd Spencer, don't you dare try to pull me out into the water!" More than once during their teen years, when Todd heard that same line it was as good as an open invitation to wrestle her down to the shore line where he'd take her into the water with him, grinning like an eight year old goober the whole time. The more she used to splash him to get back at him for the dunking, the happier he seemed to become.

This time Todd opted for letting her remain seated and giving Christy a more thorough sprinkling as he shook his shaggy mane over her like a happy golden retriever.

"Okay, okay." Christy brushed the salty dots from her cheeks. "I thought you said that after you went in the water you were going to have a picnic with your wife."

"Yeah. I'm ready now."

"Good. Let's eat."

Todd lowered himself to the open spot on the blanket next to Christy. The sun quickly dried them as they enjoyed their sandwiches. Christy thought about how vast and beautiful this beach seemed the first time she put her bare feet into the warm sand. It was a magical thing to be whisked away from her parent's home on a Wisconsin dairy farm the summer she turned fifteen and given the gift of staying with her aunt and uncle here at Newport Beach. She realized now how extraordinary that opportunity was.

She also realized how different her life would have been if she hadn't met Todd that summer. As difficult as her parent's bankruptcy had been that same year, it had turned into the catalyst that brought her whole family to California and opened up the full life they had all been living for almost ten years.

Remembering all that bolstered her courage as she thought about all the unknowns she and Todd were facing now. She turned toward Todd and took in his strong profile as he stared out at the Pacific Ocean that he loved so much.

"What are you thinking?" Christy asked.

"I was thinking about my dad's house. It makes me sick to think about that guy ripping him off and filling the house with short term renters. Did you see the broken window?"

Christy nodded.

"I hate to think about what the rest of the house might look like. It's such a great house. I loved growing up there."

"How did you know that Mr. Sleaze was the guy who was at your dad's house? What made you think to call him?"

"I recognized the BMW in the driveway. I was at the house a couple months ago while Dad was getting it ready to rent. Mr. Sleaze, as you call him, came to the house and said he was a rental agent. He convinced Dad that he could find the right sort of clients and keep the house rented."

"But your dad didn't know him, did he? I mean, he didn't know him personally or have a reliable referral from someone he knew."

"I don't know, but I'm guessing he didn't have any of that. He was in hurry to get the place rented. What gets me is that all this time, since my dad returned to the Canary Islands, he was being told the rental market was so flooded with houses that no renters were interested in a long term lease. I wish I'd come up here sooner and checked on the house for him."

"I wish your dad had talked to Uncle Bob before he started working with Mr. Sleaze. My uncle knows a lot of people in the real estate market in this area. He would have been able to help him find someone reliable."

"I thought the same thing. I'm hoping Bob can help us now. I'll call my dad later tonight. With the time change it will be morning for him. I'm just glad we came today and that I'm able to take the next steps and help him from here."

"What a mess. All this and what's going on at church right now, too." Christy sighed.

Todd pulled his shirt back on and raked his fingers through his dried hair. The afternoon sun had ducked behind a huge, puffy cloud that hung midway between the horizon and the unmarked center point in the ceiling of the vast blue sky. The light around them and even the air took on a softer hue.

"This is how I see it," Todd said decisively. "I can't do anything about what's going on at church. They'll meet next

Tuesday and make a decision. Then you and I will probably need to make some important decisions. Until then, we just have to hold all of it loosely. God is not pacing the courts of heaven right now wringing his hands and saying, 'Oh dear, oh dear. How is all this going to turn out?'"

Christy grinned at Todd's added visual demonstration as he took on the role of looking frantic and panicked.

"God's got this, Christy. All of it. And He's got us. We're covered." Todd slipped his arm around Christy's shoulder and drew her to his side.

She leaned her head close to his and together they watched the waves roll in and roll back, never tiring in their elegant, ancient dance. The sunlight streamed from behind the clouds sending beams of silver radiance into the ocean. She reached for her phone and took several shots of the sunbeams bursting through the clouds.

Content to experience the moment and no longer feeling the urgency to capture it in digital form, Christy cuddled up to Todd and rested her head once again on his shoulder. He leaned over and kissed the top of her head.

Christy smiled. She felt her heart fill with gratitude at the way God had handcrafted such a specific, soul-satisfying afternoon for she and Todd just when they needed it most.

"You know what would be pretty great right now?" Todd asked.

"Nothing," Christy replied.

Todd pulled back and looked at her. "Nothing?"

She turned so he could see the look of contentment on her face. "This moment is golden. It needs no improvement."

"You don't want anything else?"

"The only thing I want," Christy said with a dreamy tone in her voice, "Is to stay right here . . . forever . . . with you."

Todd looked as if her contentment boosted his contentment as well. "I'd like to stay right here forever with you, too."

He returned his arm to where he had it around her shoulder and waited less than a minute before adding, "I was going to say that a couple of Balboa Bars would be pretty great right now but since we're staying right here forever, I guess I'll take that off my wish list."

Christy pulled away and looked at him with instant agreement at the thought of a Balboa Bar.

An adorable half grin lifted the corner of Todd's mouth. "Are you saying our 'forever' moment is about to end? Over a Balboa Bar?"

"It's not ending. We're just expanding it to include other adventures." Christy began gathering up the remains of their picnic lunch. "Seriously, when was the last time we had Balboa Bars?"

"Apparently, it's been far too long, judging by your enthusiasm." Todd started laughing.

"Come on," Christy said, rising to her feet. "I'll race you to the Balboa Island Ferry."

five

$\mathcal{T}$odd stood in front of the order window and leaned in closer.

"Hey, how's it going? We need two Balboa Bars. One of 'em without nuts." He pulled some cash out of his wallet to pay.

Christy watched the girl behind the window as she took from the freezer a rectangle of vanilla ice cream on a stick and dunked it in the melted, dark chocolate. The chocolate quickly cooled and encased the ice cream bar. She handed it out the window and Todd gave the nut-free bar to Christy. Todd's treat followed. This time she immediately pressed the chocolate dipped ice cream into a bed of crushed nuts that stuck to the chocolate.

"This brings back some memories," Todd said as they strolled over to an empty bench and tried to get all the deliciousness into their mouths without dropping any chunks of the chocolate coating or the quickly melting ice cream.

Christy dabbed the side of her mouth with her napkin.

She clearly remembered the first time she and Todd had come to Balboa on a bike ride. They ordered Balboa Bars and she wasn't exactly successful in getting all of it inside her mouth. A wedge of chocolate had turned into a streak mark across her cheek and dried there as they pedaled back to her aunt and uncle's house.

The worst part of that memory was that Todd had obviously noticed the skid mark but he hadn't said anything the whole time. She made the horrifying discovery after he'd gone and she looked in the mirror. Discovering that she'd been traipsing around Balboa Island with a trail of chocolate dried on her face was one of the most embarrassing moments of her teen years. Being with the guy she really liked while traipsing around Balboa Island with a trail of chocolate dried on her face made the experience unforgettable.

Christy turned to face Todd and said, "You'd tell me this time, wouldn't you?"

The way he averted his eyes and grinned mischievously made it clear that he had been silently sharing the same memory. "Tell you what?" Todd teased.

Christy nudged him with her elbow and kept eating. She finished her last bite and repositioned herself so that he had to look at her. "All clear?" She asked.

With just the right amount of maturity that should grace the life of a husband, Todd gave her a scan and said, "Yes. All clear."

Christy chuckled. "You're not. You have a big chunk of chocolate on your bottom lip."

Instead of licking it off, Todd immediately leaned in and pressed a big smacker of a kiss on Christy's cheek, transferring the chocolate to her face.

"Hey!" She was about to press the palm of her hand to her cheek but decided to press up against his scruffy cheek, instead, transferring what remained of the chocolate to the slight stubble on his face.

Todd cracked up.

Christy loved it when he laughed that way. It sounded like a kid who'd just seen his first clown act at a circus or had nailed his friendly opponent in a water balloon fight. To her it seemed that he was experiencing some of the silliness that brothers and sisters grow up with. A common joy he'd not known since he was an only child.

Todd rubbed his face with the palm of his hand, smearing around the chocolate even more. Christy laughed and handed him a napkin. Out of the corner of her eye she was aware that someone was standing beside the bench, watching them as if they were street performers and this was their afternoon clowning around act. The couple seemed to be standing unusually close.

Before Christy could turn to give the couple a "do you mind?" look, she heard the distinct voice of her Aunt Marti shattering their playful moment.

"Christina! What in the world are you doing?"

"Hey!" Todd hopped up and greeted Christy's aunt and uncle with a side hug. "Bob. Marti. What are you guys doing here?"

"Buying sea salt." Marti said it with such an air of matter-of-fact confidence, it seemed as if they should have already known that's what she would be doing there. "The real question is, what are you two doing here?"

"We're having a ditch day," Todd said, sounding equally matter-of-fact.

Marti ignored his half-joking comment and fixed her gaze on Christy.

Christy popped up from the bench and offered her aunt and uncle a hug. "Did you say you're buying sea salt?"

"Yes. There's a gourmet store half way down this street that has the best spices and a variety of sea salts. I always come here for sea salt. Certainly you knew that after all these years."

"I did not know that." Christy also didn't know that sea salt came in a "variety". Variety of what? Flavors?

"Bob, I was going to call you later tonight," Todd said. "I'm going to need some help on my dad's house. He's been trying to rent it out and it looks like the guy he's been working with is ripping him off."

Bob motioned for Todd to take a step aside with him and began to quietly ask a few questions. Christy's petite, stylish aunt asked again what they were really doing on Balboa Island.

"We had the afternoon off so we decided to be spontaneous and go to the beach since the weather is so great. Sorry we didn't call you." Christy wished she hadn't automatically apologized. Even though a lot of the dynamics of her relationship with her aunt had changed after Todd and Christy got married, it was still a struggle for Christy to not revert to how she felt in her vulnerable teen years. That season of her relationship with Marti was marked by Christy's ongoing feeling that whatever she was doing was not the way her aunt would do it.

Dark eyed Aunt Marti scrutinized Christy's answer with a narrowed expression. "Were you planning on coming to our place for dinner?"

"We didn't really have any plans. Like I said, it was spontaneous."

"Your uncle and I would have preferred a little advance notice. But since you're here, you should stay. You came all this way. Besides, you can't go back to that tiny, stuffy apartment of yours. Not on a perfect evening like this. I'll have Bob make something light and quick for dinner. Where's your car?" Marti looked around at the scant spaces that were available for metered parking.

"We left our car near his dad's house and took the ferry over."

"Then come with us. We're parked across the street. We'll drop you off. You can pick up your car and come park it in our driveway. It's all settled. Shall we go? Robert? The kids are coming back to our house. You and Todd can discuss your business there."

As much as Christy didn't like begin swept up in the plans of her domineering aunt, by the time they'd finished dinner that evening she knew it was a blessing in disguise that they'd connected with Bob and Marti when they had.

The first thing the guys did was get on the phone with Todd's dad in the Canary Islands. The three of them worked out a plan for how to get Mr. Sleaze out of the house and press charges for the scam he'd pulled. Bob knew all the steps they needed to take and agreed to "take the bull by the horns".

Their dinner was a large salad with a variety of greens and a colorful sprinkling of diced tomatoes, papaya, blueberries, almond slivers and wedges of ripe avocado. Bob had effortlessly grilled some fresh salmon and asparagus. The meal was delicious and both Christy and Todd embarrassed themselves by saying over and over that it was the best meal they had eaten in a long time.

Todd counterbalanced the effusive praises by saying, "Christy makes some great casseroles."

"Casseroles," Marti repeated with a faint smirk. "I don't remember the last time I had a casserole. Your Midwest upbringing is showing, Christy, dear. You really should try grilling some chicken or focus on fresh fish, like we had tonight. It's so much better for you."

Christy chose to not reply. She didn't want to get into a discussion about the dangers of hidden trans fats or the benefits of omega 3 and flax. That was the direction the conversation had gone the last time she talked to Marti about food.

The truth was, the way Bob and Marti ate was expensive. For them, money never seemed to be an issue, so they lived a much more opulent sort of lifestyle than anything Christy thought she and Todd would ever be able to experience.

"Anyone interested in cheesecake with fresh strawberries?" Uncle Bob asked.

"Oh, Robert. We don't really need dessert tonight. All those extra calories after such a lovely meal."

Bob was already up and on his way to the kitchen. In his usual good natured way he skimmed over Marti's comment and said, "Alright, that's three cheesecakes then. Anyone want coffee? Tea?"

Christy started to get up to help her uncle but he insisted she stay right where she was. "Enjoy the sunset. I'll be right back."

Bob and Marti's beach house had been updated and renovated several times over the many years they'd lived there. One of the best additions had been the improved patio area that faced the broad beach and provided spacious, unobstructed views of the sand and ocean as they dined. The sun was just about ready to make a dramatic statement in orange and pink before taking a final bow and sliding off the edge of the horizon.

It was a perfect, southern California night and once again, Christy was glad they'd stayed for dinner. Todd's phone buzzed. Much to Marti's disapproval he pulled it out and read the text message that had come in.

"Excuse me," he said, pushing his chair back. "I need to give Rick a call back." Todd went inside the house to make his call.

"How is Rick these days?" Marti asked. "Isn't he getting married soon?"

Christy kept her eyes on the stunning sunset, wishing she could ignore Marti's questions because she knew it would turn into a many layered discussion. She tried responding with a neutral comment.

"We saw Rick last night."

"And how is he doing? You know, Robert and I both adore his bride to be, Nicki. We met her at Katie's graduation party, remember?"

"Yes. I remember."

"You know that your uncle and I didn't expect to be invited to Rick's wedding, so I understand about not receiving an invitation, but we'd certainly like to send a gift."

Christy cringed knowing she wouldn't be able to dance her way around this topic.

"Could you give me their address? Or, I suppose we could give their present to you and you and Todd could take it to their wedding for us. When is the wedding?"

Christy reluctantly decided to go ahead and fill Marti in on Rick's broken engagement. She chose her words carefully and gave a shortened version of the facts.

Marti looked genuinely upset. "Oh, dear! That's awful. Why didn't you say something earlier? Poor Rick. Clearly, that fiancée of his was a narrow sighted young woman. She didn't know a good thing when she had it."

Todd returned to the table carrying a tray with a French press of coffee, mugs, spoons and cream and sugar. Bob was right behind with another tray bearing three small plates of cheesecake that were nearly hidden by a mound of sliced strawberries. On the edge of the tray was a small bowl of sliced strawberries.

"Thank you, Robert," Marti said as she took the strawberries from him. "It's a pity we don't have any whipping cream."

Bob placed the tray on the table and produced a canister of whipping cream like a magician, presenting the desired item to Marti by placing it over his forearm as if it were a bottle of fine wine.

"You think of everything."

"I know what you like," he said with a loving grin.

Christy had no idea why her aunt had balked at the suggestion of cheesecake and strawberries but didn't hesitate to be ultra-generous as she squirted the whipping cream onto her bowl of fruit. What Christy did admire, and always had, was the way her uncle navigated Marti's personality and preferences with such kindness and genuine love. She always thought that he was probably the only man in the whole world who could take Marti as his wife and go the distance with the "till death do us part" part of their wedding vows.

After Marti's first demure bite of strawberries and cream she turned to Todd for the dish that interested her more than the strawberries. "How is Rick doing this evening? Christy told me about the devastating break up."

Todd glanced at Christy. She gave him a slight shrug, hoping he would realize she had to say something but that she'd tried her best to be discrete.

Todd took his time, savoring his bite of dessert before offering up his answer. "Rick is doing pretty great this evening, actually. He and Nicole spent the afternoon with both their parents and it looks like they might end up back together."

"Really?" Christy lowered her fork. She had not seen that coming.

Todd nodded. "I didn't get a chance to tell you when Rick called earlier that he met with Nicole's dad and her dad suggested they all meet and talk about what brought Nicole to the sudden decision to pull away from Rick."

"And what did bring her to that decision?" Marti wanted to know.

Todd shrugged and took another bite of his cheesecake.

"He didn't tell you?" Marti asked.

"No."

"And you didn't ask?"

Todd shook his head.

Marti gave Christy an exasperated look. "Men! They fail to grasp the most important elements of a conversation. It certainly would be helpful to know her reason, wouldn't it?"

"Maybe Nicole just needed more time," Christy suggested. "I don't know her very well but Rick said last night that he felt he'd pushed her to get engaged too soon."

"Of course. There it is. It had to be a case of nerves." Marti turned to Uncle Bob. "I was a complete bundle of nerves when I got married. Wasn't I, Robert?"

He nodded and took a long sip of coffee as if trying to keep his mouth busy in order to avoid saying anything else.

"Did Rick say if the wedding date has been re-scheduled?" Marti asked.

"No. One step at a time is what he said. They have both sets of parents giving them counsel, so they're in a good place." Todd took another bite of dessert. Christy thought she caught a squint in his expression that she read to mean that there was more going on but he would tell her about it later.

"Speaking of friends who are getting married," Aunt Marti said. "You haven't said a word about Katie and Eli. Have they set a date yet?"

"No," Christy said. "Not yet. I don't think they're in a big rush."

Todd pushed his emptied desert plate away and said, "I'll tell you who is getting married."

He had Marti's full attention.

"My dad's getting married."

Marti looked stunned. She turned to Bob, then Christy and then back to Todd.

Todd looked as if it was giving him a sense of satisfaction to be able to break this wedding news to Marti. Christy thought it was funny because that wasn't Todd's usual style. But he was pretty excited about his dad's engagement and he should be enjoying this opportunity to tell people the good news. This was a big deal for Todd and a really big deal for Bryan, his dad.

Marti leaned back and placed her hand over her heart as if she couldn't stand the startling news. "When did this happen?"

"It hasn't happened yet," Todd said. "You know that my dad inherited a family house in the Canary Islands and that's why he's been over there most of this year. The house needs a lot of renovation and he's been working on it. He has the ring but is waiting for the right moment to propose to Carolyn."

"Who is Carolyn? And when did all this transpire?"

"They connected in the Canary Islands earlier this year at a funeral or something like that," Todd said.

"I think it was a birthday party," Christy added. "Last spring. Had you guys not heard about this yet?"

"No. Of course we hadn't heard that Bryan was getting married. If you don't tell me, how am I going to know these things?" Marti looked as irritated as she sounded.

"I'm thrilled for him," Bob said. "Your father is a good man, Todd. He deserves all the happiness and blessings that God wants to pour out on him."

Marti put up her hand as if she wasn't ready to offer her blessing until she had the whole story. "How did all this happen? You said they met at a birthday party?"

"They first met over thirty years ago," Todd said. "My dad and Carolyn had a summer romance when they were teens. There, in the Canary Islands. But then they both ended up with someone else and never had a chance to talk about how they felt about each other. That is, until last spring when they saw each other at the birthday party."

"Who would have a birthday party in the Canary Islands? This sounds absurd." Marti looked flustered.

"It's not absurd if you live in the Canary Islands," Christy said. "That's where Carolyn's mom lives. Carolyn lives in California but she went there for her mom's birthday and Todd's dad was there at the same time because of the family house he inherited. That's how they reconnected. It was unexpected and quite romantic."

"It still sounds absurd." Marti folded her napkin and placed it beside the remains of her unfinished berries and whipped cream.

"I'll tell you one thing," Todd said. "My dad is the happiest he's ever been."

"That's great," Bob said. "Really great."

"You still haven't told me. When is the wedding?" Marti asked.

"Probably in the next six months or so."

"Six months? Oh, my. Did they reserve a venue yet? Six months is not enough time to secure any of the more desirable wedding locations. If they need me to make a few calls I'd be happy to check for them."

"They plan to get married in Las Palmas," Todd said. "in the Canary Islands."

Marti looked perplexed, as if she couldn't fathom anyone wanting to get married anywhere other than one of the desirable locations in Newport Beach. "You two certainly aren't planning to go, are you?"

Christy and Todd exchanged glances and then both started nodding.

"Of course," Todd said. "We wouldn't miss it for anything."

They hadn't discussed any of the details yet because there were none to discuss. Now that it looked like their lives were headed into some big changes with jobs and schedules, Christy had no idea how they'd find the money for the airfare. Not to mention trying to get time off wherever they were working whenever the wedding day rolled around. But she definitely agreed with Todd. Their attendance was mandatory. They couldn't miss Bryan and Carolyn's wedding.

"Sounds like we better give Bryan a chance to propose, first, before we ask you kids about your travel plans." Uncle Bob poured a second cup of coffee and stirred in a teaspoon of sugar. "If there's one thing we all have seen in life, love takes its own sweet time."

Bob gave Christy a wink and somehow she felt a little more hopeful about all the unknowns in their future. She wondered if Todd had told Bob about what was going on with his position at church while the two of them had been in the kitchen.

"Well, consider your airfare covered," Marti said with a wave of her hand. "Whenever your father does get married, Robert and I will buy your tickets when we buy ours. I've always wanted to go to the Caribbean."

Todd, Christy and Bob all exchanged glances. Marti didn't seem to realize where the Canary Islands were located. Christy kept her lips together and let Todd respond this time.

"That's really gracious of you guys. We'll let you know if we need to take you up on the offer. And, since you suggested it, I suppose it would be fairly easy to stop off in the Caribbean on your way back from the Canary Islands since the Canaries are located off the coast of West Africa. I mean, why not visit two sets of islands located on the opposite sides of the Atlantic? That would make for an interesting trip."

Christy put her last bite of cheesecake and strawberries in her mouth and gave her husband a look of tender admiration and appreciation. If she'd been the one to enlighten Marti on the location of the Canary Islands it would not have come out as delicately or without embarrassment to Marti.

Marti didn't miss a beat. "Yes. Of course. The Canaries are off the coast of West Africa. I knew that. I was thinking why not stop in the Caribbean on the way there. Or the way back. Either way."

"Either way," Todd repeated.

Or no way.

Christy hoped Todd could read in her look the firm message that regardless of the generous offer to pay for the airfare, the last person Christy wanted to travel across the world with was her aunt. She'd done that once already, before she went to school in Switzerland. Once was enough.

Forever With You

six

$\mathcal{T}$he next few days clicked along like a train that was determined to get to the station on time. For Christy and Todd that "station" was Tuesday. They'd know by Tuesday night what was going to happen with Todd's position at the church.

Wednesday was the next stop. After a short email exchange, Dr. Swanson had agreed to wait until Wednesday for Christy's decision. All Christy felt she could do was go along for the ride and try to not think about what the worst possible outcome might look like in their lives.

She kept whispering prayers with familiar phrases such as, "I trust you, God" and "Accomplish Your purpose in all this". But her heart felt fearful and not at all brave and trusting.

On her way home from work on Saturday, Christy found herself mentally packing up their apartment. There was no concrete reason why she should believe that they would be moving soon, but she found it strangely therapeutic to think through what they would take with them and what they would give away.

The only problem with her organizing exercise was that she had no idea where they'd go next or what they'd need. Mentally sorting their belongings was the only thing she could actively participate in at the moment. Somehow it seemed to help her feel as if she was doing something.

And then again, nothing could change.

Christy pulled into the covered parking area at their apartment and sat for a few moments in the car. She thought about how Mr. Stanley, one of the church leaders, had contacted Todd the day before and said he was going to fight for the budget to stay as it was because his own children had benefited so much from all that Todd had poured into their lives over the past few years. He seemed determined to make sure that Todd stayed on full time staff.

The meeting on Tuesday could be nothing more than a blip and they could vote to keep Todd's position the way it is. And who knows? Dr. Swanson could tell me she's found someone else and I'll just keep on working at the bookstore. By this time next week our lives might be exactly as they are right now and all this anxiety would be for nothing.

Christy got out of the car and found that she was biting her lower lip. She knew her optimism was unrealistic. Earlier that day she'd heard Rosalyn talking to another employee about how slow sales had been and if the fourth quarter didn't pick up she'd have to make staff cuts. Christy had worked at the bookstore the shortest amount of time so she knew the chances were strong that she'd be the one that was let go.

Last hired, first fired.

Nothing on the horizon looked secure for them at the moment.

Christy entered their apartment and found Todd in the kitchen making a salad.

"Hey, you. What are you making?" She wrapped her arms

around his back and kissed him on the shoulder before leaning over to inspect his efforts.

"I'm trying to duplicate that great salad we had at Bob and Marti's. Except I didn't get any avocados. Or blueberries. Or almonds."

"It looks good." Inwardly she was grinning. Todd wasn't even using the same type of lettuce mix that Bob had used. His additions were baby carrots, not cut up, and a not quite ripe tomato cut into four chunky pieces. Todd's version looked a lot like a cafeteria salad that was waiting to be doused in ranch dressing, her husband's long time cure for anything green.

The microwave buzzed and Christy automatically turned to open the door. "What else did you make?"

Todd stopped her. "Go sit down. I was trying to have this ready before you got home. Go on. Let me serve you for once."

Christy washed up and took her place at the table. As predicted, a large bottle of generic brand ranch dressing served as their centerpiece. The table was set with two paper plates and two forks. No fuss dining, Todd style.

"Is water okay for you?" Todd asked.

"Sure."

He poured her a glass of tap water and brought it to the table with the salad, sporting a satisfied grin. Christy smiled back. Todd picked up the two paper plates and took them to the microwave where he loaded each one with a slightly steaming, still wrapped in paper, frozen bean burrito.

"And I got ice cream bars for dessert," he said, taking his seat and surveying his accomplishment. "Actually, they're popsicles. They were buy one, get one free."

Christy was pretty sure the popsicles would be just about as disenchanting as the fare in front of her. But she didn't want to discourage Todd's efforts.

"This is very sweet of you. Thank you."

"You're welcome." Todd reached across the table and covered Christy's hand with hers. He lowered his head and prayed, thanking God for always providing for them and guiding them. Then he thanked God for his amazing wife who had been so supportive and patient with him and ended with a hearty "amen".

For a moment Christy thought about making suggestions about how Todd might shop or cook for them in the future but when she heard his sincere prayer she knew she needed to keep her suggestions to herself and gratefully eat her bean burrito and iceberg lettuce salad. She also needed to keep her anxiety tremors to herself. It would only be for a few more days of living in this limbo of not knowing what their future held. She crunched on a baby carrot and promised her little heart that once they knew something, anything, then she could panic. Until then, she wanted Todd to keep believing that she was being the supportive, patient wife that he had just thanked God for.

Christy managed to keep her panther-sized fears tamed and in their cages. That is, until it was time to leave for church the next morning. She'd gotten up, showered, dressed and was ready to walk out the door on time with Todd. But then the smallest thing happened and she felt the wild, internal snarling increase to untamable portions.

It was the strap on the back of her favorite pair of shoes that opened the emotional cages. The narrow strap broke off just as she was ready to walk out the door and she could tell right away that it was irreparable.

In an untypical move, Christy yanked the shoe off her foot and threw it through the open bedroom door, just missing Todd as he rounded the corner.

"Whoa! What's going on? You haven't thrown a shoe at me since your fifteenth birthday when we got back from Disneyland." He looked like the memory was a humorous one for him.

For Christy, there was nothing humorous about that distant memory or this enflamed moment either. She wrestled the other shoe off and kicked it over by the wall.

"What are you doing?" Todd looked befuddled.

"My shoe broke!" She stomped past him toward the bedroom closet.

Todd followed her into the bedroom where she started rifling through her limited replacement options. Christy reached for a pair of old sandals that she knew would hurt her feet but they were the only pair she could see through her tear-blurred vision. A big ball of frustration rose to her throat, causing her to gasp for a breath in quick, staccato gulps.

"Hey, hey." Todd came up behind her and put his arms on her shoulders. "It's just a pair of shoes. You can get another pair."

Christy turned to him. The tears streaked down her face. "We don't know that." Her voice wobbled. She felt her chest constrict and realized this was going to turn into the ugly cry at any moment.

"Hey, it's okay. Kilikina. Come here." He tried to wrap his arms around her and draw her close but she pulled away.

"Todd, we don't know if I can buy a new pair of shoes. We don't know if we can stay in this apartment. We don't know if you'll even have a job after Tuesday." She drew in a breath in an effort to try to calm herself but it was too late. Her latest fear lunged from her lips. "And after January I probably won't have a job unless I take the research job but I don't know if I can even accept that job yet."

The tears fell in rivulets and she used her forearm to try to blot them. As soon as she put her arm down she saw that she'd gotten a big glob of mascara on her pale yellow sweater.

Now she was mad at herself for not thinking through that maneuver and yanked the sweater off, throwing it into the laundry basket.

Todd took a step back and seemed to be trying to figure out what to do with this wild person in front of him. Christy was aware of Todd's gaze. In an odd way, she felt as if she, too were standing outside the moment looking in on someone she barely recognized.

One more walloping sob galloped out of her gut and then it felt as if the worst had passed. Christy tried to calm herself with every last sane emotional neutron left in her body. She couldn't remember the last time she'd been this emotional.

"Come here," Todd said, reaching out his hand for her to take. His forehead was creased with worry lines as he gingerly led Christy over to the unmade bed. He motioned for her to sit down while he stood in front of her.

"Why don't you stay home this morning." It was one of his statements. Not a question. It was a decision.

Christy rose to her feet with Joan-of-Arc-maiden-warrior-like defiance. "No. I can go. I just need some tissues. I'll be fine."

Todd stood his ground as she reached for several tissues and blew her nose. He didn't say anything until after she'd drawn in a choppy breath and looked at him with determination.

"I'm sorry. I'll be fine. We better go. We're going to be late."

Todd took her hand in his and said, "You need to stay home."

This time his statement felt like she'd been handed a "Get out of jail free" card just when she needed it. She didn't know what the difference was but she could feel her spirit calming and her tears subsiding. Christy lowered herself back to the edge of the bed and felt exhausted. "I didn't sleep well last night," she said in a small voice.

"I know. It's okay. Get some rest." Todd waited until she'd gotten back under the covers before leaning down and giving her a kiss. "If I could, I'd stay right here with you, you know." He smiled.

Christy rolled on her side. Part of her felt embarrassed. Another part felt relieved. This was where she needed to be right now.

Todd kissed her again on the side of her head and said, "Call me if you need me." He stroked her hair three times and leaned down for one more kiss.

Christy turned to him and met his lips with hers. "Thank you for understanding," she whispered as he drew back. "I love you."

"And I love you. Get some rest, okay?"

Christy nodded.

Todd left and as she heard the door close behind him an unexpected second wave of tears made their entrance. This time it was more like a slow rain of tears and not a rushing river. It was as if all the emotions she'd compressed over the past week had risen to the surface in the upheaval and all she could do was give them room to spill out.

Christy could not remember the last time she had such a meltdown. It angered her and humbled her and made her feel a little sorry for herself all at the same time. She pulled the covers up to her chin and curled up in a more comfortable position, remembering the email from Katie that she'd read the night Rick came over. Katie had written that she'd had a meltdown in front of Eli and that he didn't know what to do with her.

Well, Katie girl. You're not the only one who can't hold it all together in front of the man you love. I can't believe I crumbled like that. I am so tired. So, so tired.

Christy closed her eyes. She fell into a deep sleep. When

she awoke she thought she'd been out for hours. It was more like a half an hour but it had been a good, restorative rest. She tried to go back to sleep but now her mind was awake with thoughts of Katie and all the heart to heart conversations the two of them had shared ever since they first met at a sleep over their sophomore year in high school. She missed her best friend dearly and wished she could talk to Katie now about everything she was feeling.

That's when Christy realized she could pull out the laptop and call Katie. Sunday nights in Kenya were one of the times when Katie was available to talk but it rarely worked out for Christy because with the time difference, Christy was usually at church during this time.

She went to the bathroom first and muttered, "oh, brother" when she saw her disheveled appearance in the mirror. With a quick fix up and a change into her favorite lounge-around outfit, Christy returned to the bed with the laptop. She got comfy, clicked on all the right tabs to place a call to Katie and to her surprise and delight, Katie answered.

"Christy! Really? Are you kidding me? I was just thinking about you. Hello? Are you there?" Katie's voice came through nice and clear.

Christy swallowed a lump in her throat. She could see her favorite redhead on the screen. Katie wore a wide, colorful headband that looked like it was holding back her hair right before she washed her face. She had a piece of dental floss dangling from her lower teeth.

"Turn on your video camera, Chris. I can't see you yet. I can't believe you just called me. I mean, seriously, this is such a total God thing! You have no idea." Katie kept talking as if she was oblivious to the string hanging out of her mouth.

Christy found the right button and clicked it so that her image now appeared in a small box at the top of the screen.

"Hey! There you are! *Rafiki! Jambo!* You're at home. You're in bed. Are you sick? Christy?" Katie leaned in closer. "You've been crying, haven't you? What's wrong?"

Christy couldn't help it. She started blubbering all over again. This was such a gift. To know and be known by a best friend, a "rafiki" who could immediately read her and assess the state of her heart. There was no other feeling like this in the world. She felt such a sudden sense of relief. Such a deep-hearted happiness.

"I've missed you," Christy blurted out. "So much."

"I know! Me, too. Stop it. You're making me cry."

The silly piece of dental floss was still hanging from Katie's mouth and the sight of it dangling there made Christy start laughing. She grabbed some tissues and blew her nose in a less than dainty fashion. The enhanced sound of her nose-blowing echoed back through her computer and she knew it must have sounded just as hilarious on Katie's end.

Katie started laughing. "Yikes! I thought we were having an elephant stampede for a minute there. You have been crying your little heart out, haven't you?" Katie's face appeared larger in the screen as if she was trying to move in for a closer look at Christy. The motion seemed to alert her to the trailing piece of dental floss and she quickly gave it a tug, cracking herself up.

"Did you know that was hanging out of my mouth?"

Christy nodded, still laughing.

"Why didn't you tell me?" Katie tilted her head back and laughed a great belly laugh. "Look at us!" Katie's green eyes were now rimmed with chuckle tears as she looked into the camera. "We are still just a couple of Peculiar Treasures, aren't we?"

"Yes, we are," Christy said, dabbing her eyes and feeling as if all was right in the world once again. "Always have been. Always will be."

Katie pulled off her headband. From all the sudden jostling of the picture on the screen it appeared that she was carrying the laptop into another part of her room. Her face came back into focus and Christy could see the cement block wall behind Katie's bed and the soft amber glow from the lamp on the end table.

"There. Now I'm ready. Spill. I want to hear everything. What's going on? Tell me of you."

seven

*C*hristy's hour and a half conversation with Katie on Sunday morning had been a strategically placed gift from God. She was sure of it.

Renewed and feeling steady once again, Christy got up, made the bed, tidied the bathroom and went to work in the kitchen. She opened the shades and discovered that the early afternoon sky had clouded over and the temperature had cooled significantly. It finally felt like autumn was coming and might even bring some rain their way.

The cooling weather inspired her. This was meatloaf weather and Christy was convinced that her mom's meatloaf recipe was the best in the world. One of her favorite childhood memories was of getting off the school bus on crisp, snow flurry days, walking into the kitchen of their Wisconsin dairy farm and drawing in the fragrance of mom's meatloaf. She knew the scrumptious scent had a lot to do with the way her mom would bake big, russet potatoes in the oven along with the meatloaf. It also helped that the glaze her mom added to the top of the meatloaf for the last fifteen minutes as it baked was a mixture of ketchup and dry mustard that was spiked with just enough brown sugar to make every little taste bud in her mouth wake up and take notice.

A hunting and gathering mission in the freezer and refrigerator produced all the necessary ingredients for the simple recipe. She didn't have any big, chunky russet potatoes but she had five small, red potatoes and prepped those so they'd be ready to go in once she had the meatloaf mixed and in the muffin tins. Christy's mom started baking her meatloaf this way, like big meatballs in muffin tins, when Christy was little. She didn't remember ever eating it as a slice from a traditional meatloaf baked in a bread pan.

Christy put on some music and hummed along, eager to keep her domestic mojo flowing. As the meatloaf baked, she made oatmeal cookies, soaking the raisins in a half a cup of orange juice the way her grandmother used to do while she mixed the dry ingredients. She set the table with dinner plates, knives, forks and spoons and lit the vanilla scented candles and arranged them on a ceramic dish that had a pattern of leaves around the edge.

All of the extra efforts felt important to Christy. She wasn't sure why but as she began to think about it, she could see how her subconscious steps around the kitchen were turning into a dance of acquiescence to the change of seasons. It was not only a change from summer to fall but also a change of heart and quite likely a change of jobs for both she and Todd. This was her simple act of worship. It was her way of expressing, by faith, that even though it wasn't so great with her circumstances right now, it was well with her soul.

She was so grateful for the way Katie had tilted Christy's downcast thoughts back up to a much healthier, God-honoring perspective. Katie's off-handed comment at the end of their video call kept rolling over Christy as she loaded the dishwasher. "You're doing good, Chris. You've got everything you need to navigate through the week ahead. Just do what you do best – give Todd a welcoming nest to fly home to. God will take care of the rest."

Katie was right. For Christy, nesting was the best remedy for her when facing the unknown. This was what Christy did best. No wonder she started mentally packing last night on her way home as if she needed to be in preparation for a move. She loved making their sparsely furnished, vintage apartment feel like home. When everything was tidy and fragrant and showed touches of beauty and care, Christy's heart felt light and she felt like she was doing what she was created to do.

She'd never expressed it to anyone in those words before. The fact that her heart and emotions were so tightly strung to her home and her husband seemed pretty elementary to her way of thinking. But Christy was discovering that not every woman was wired that way.

Todd arrived home a little after three o'clock. The meatloaf was ready and waiting in the warm oven with the shriveling potatoes. A salad was chilling in the fridge and all the baked oatmeal cookies were cooling on the counter.

Todd came to her with deep worry lines in his forehead. He took a quick look around and drew in a deep breath. The worry lines began to lift.

"Glad to see you're feeling better," he said.

Christy wiped her hands on her apron and gave him a big kiss. Todd kissed her back with what she read as deep sadness rather than eager passion. With her arms still around his neck as they drew apart, Christy looked into his eyes. They looked red and weary.

"You okay?"

He nodded.

"You hungry?"

"Always."

Christy started to pull away so she could get the food on the table but Todd pulled her back and touched his forehead to her forehead, his nose to her nose. With his eyes closed he drew in the fragrance of Christy and the air around them.

"Thank you," he whispered.

"You're welcome," she whispered back.

"No, I mean it." Todd pulled back and gave Christy a deeply affectionate look. "Thank you for being my haven-maker."

Christy tilted her head and pulled back to meet his gaze. "Your haven-maker, huh?"

"Yeah. You're a haven-maker. You make this small space into a home. I love coming home to you."

In that moment it felt to Christy as if a question she had asked in a dozen ways over the past decade had been twice confirmed. First with Katie's comments on her nesting skills and now with Todd's comment on how she was a haven-maker. This was her gift. Hospitality. This was what came easily to her and made her heart happy. This is the way she was able to best give graciously to others.

It was a small pearl of a gift for her, given so unexpectedly in the midst of their irritating oyster days. She'd ponder what all if it meant later. Right now, she had a hungry husband and a meatloaf that would go dry if she didn't serve it up.

Todd ate two helpings of everything and sat back with a look of resignation. It was as if he would have had three or four helpings if he could have but had resigned himself to the fact that his stomach was at its capacity.

While Todd had been eating, Christy filled him in on her uplifting conversation with Katie. "She and Eli still don't have a wedding date but I told her about your dad getting married in the Canaries and she said for us to let her know what their date is. If we're flying to the west coast of Africa, we might as well go on to the east coast the next week and that's when she said she and Eli would set as their wedding date."

Christy also tried to explain how great it had been to be able to talk to Katie and how their conversation had helped her to bounce back to a more hopeful, trusting mindset.

"I'm grateful for that," Todd said. "Because you definitely had me at a loss this morning."

"Sorry."

"No need to apologize. You're handling a lot right now. And you've been doing it with grace and patience. Sometimes pressure builds up and all you can do is take off your shoe and throw it at someone." He reached over and tickled her on the side.

Christy playfully pulled away and ignored his shoe comment. "What about you? How did everything go this morning? Or should I say this morning and this afternoon?"

Todd rubbed his eyebrows and said, "It's a good thing you didn't go. Several of the parents of the key kids in the youth group have formed a group. They are committed to keeping me there full time. I spent the last few hours listening to them and praying about everything."

"Do you think they'll be successful? I mean, can they change the decisions that the leadership need to make about the budget?"

"I don't know. All I know is that it's escalated to the point where seven main families told me they'd leave the church if I was let go."

Christy frowned. "Where would they go? That seems so disruptive for their kids."

"I know. That's what I said. They started talking about starting a new church."

"And, what? Have you become the teaching pastor of their home church?"

Todd nodded.

"This is getting complicated." She didn't know how she

felt about any of this.

"What did you say to them?"

"I said let's pray and wait until we hear the result of the meeting on Tuesday night." Todd got up and started clearing their dishes. "Do you want anything else?"

"No. I made cookies. Do you want some now?"

"You made cookies, too?" Todd came over and pulled Christy up to her feet. He enveloped her in a tight bear hug and said in her ear, "You are the most amazing, wonderful, beautiful wife in the galaxy. You know that, don't you? Being married to you is far better than I ever dreamed it would be."

Christy buried her face in his chest and felt glad. Glad to be married to Todd. Glad that they were going through all this upheaval together. Glad that she had called Katie and that her Forever Friend had helped lift her up out of the depths of her emotional rubble. And she was especially glad that she had made cookies since that added treat seemed to prompt Todd's extra affection.

Todd kissed her on the top of her head and then on the tip of her ear. She lifted her chin and welcomed his tender, affectionate kisses on her cheeks and eyelids as they touched her skin like raindrops. She heard a soft tapping out the open window and turned to see that it was raining real raindrops outside. The droplets raced one by one to the apartment walkway, leaving polka dots on the cracked cement.

"Todd."

"Um hum?" He continued kissing her cheek and the curve of her chin.

"Todd, it's raining."

Christy's passionate husband had no interest in talking about the weather. His single-hearted interest was in his lovely, curvy, warm and wonderful wife whom he now held in his strong arms. To show her his true feelings, Todd whispered her Hawaiian name in her ear and the sound of his voice resounded through every cell in her body as he said, "Kilikina . . ."

What followed was the most romantic, rain-blessed, this-is-what-married-people-do sort of Sunday evening Christy had ever experienced. The dishes went untouched and the cookies were forgotten as Christy and Todd expressed to each other all the fullness of their abiding love. They had faithfully waited until they were married before giving freedom to the depths of their love for each other and this was one of those times when the gift of their patience was rewarded and blessed in sweetly eternal ways.

Monday was easier for both of them because of their rainy, romantic, robust Sunday evening.

The first thing Todd said when Christy arrived home from work on Monday was that he'd been on the phone most of the day.

"It's turning into an uprising," he said. "All the families who are trying to show their support for me are campaigning to get others to take sides. I can't believe it's turned into this."

Christy had picked up tacos for them from Todd's favorite Joe's Taco Truck on her way home. Todd's phone rang twice but he didn't pick it up. A text message came in. He read it and looked at Christy with an apology building up in his expression.

"It's okay," she said before he even formed the words. "You should go."

"Will you be okay here alone?"

"Of course." Christy had spent lots of evenings at home alone in their apartment when he was involved in youth events that she didn't go to. He'd never asked her before if she was okay being home alone. It was a tender thing for him to ask and she told him so.

"You can come with me if you want, but I don't know how intense things are going to get."

"I'm fine staying here. I actually thought I'd try to set up the sewing machine tonight because I brought home some tablecloths from work. They're still in the trunk of my car."

"Tablecloths? Do they need mending or something?" Todd asked.

"No. They were used for table displays when the store first opened but Rosalyn threw them out because they don't match anything. It's cute fabric. It's just that it has a print on it and she has new ones that are all one color. I thought I'd see if I could make an apron or two out of them."

"Do you want me to get the tablecloths out of your trunk or set up the sewing machine before I go?"

"Sure. That'd be great. Do you have time?"

"For you, I always have time." Todd brushed past her and grabbed her car keys before heading out the door.

She cleaned up the remains of their fast food dinner and cleared the kitchen table in order to make room for the sewing machine. Todd placed the fabric on one of the chairs and then got the sewing machine on the table and plugged it in.

"There you go. Need anything else?" He was already standing by the front door and looked like he was ready to go.

"Just you. That's all I need. Come home in one piece, okay?" She shot him a smile and he smiled back before jetting out the door.

Christy prayed and pondered and tried to not take on any fear or nervousness. Then she prayed some more.

The project of trying to create her own pattern out of the apron that Tracy had given her as a wedding shower gift proved to be a helpful diversion that night. She traced the shape of the apron onto several paper grocery bags that she'd cut open and taped together. Working at it nice and slow, she measured twice before spreading the fabric on the kitchen floor and trying to figure out the best way to get the most use out of the fabric.

All the engineering took a lot of thinking power. Once she had the pieces cut for three aprons, she stacked everything up on the table and headed for bed. She read for awhile and tried her best to stay awake and wait up for Todd. But her heavy eyelids took over and she fell asleep.

When her alarm went off the next morning, Christy found Todd in the recliner reading his Bible. It was Tuesday. The train they'd been on was making its first stop. Today they'd find out what was going to happen to Todd's position and how it would affect their future.

"Did you sleep at all?" Christy asked, feeling a little nervous.

"Not much. I made some coffee if you want some."

Todd never made coffee. At least she couldn't remember him ever making coffee. They'd received a French press from Bob and Marti as a wedding gift but it had only been put to use once or twice when they had company over. Christy knew he must be desperate to stay awake and alert if he was drinking coffee. Especially coffee he made himself.

Out of curiosity and perhaps as one more effort to show her solidarity with him in all things, Christy ventured into the kitchen, poured the remains of coffee in a mug, added milk and sugar and warmed it in the microwave. Stepping back into the living room she lifted the mug to her lips and took a sip. Her eyes widened.

"Todd, this is good. Where did you find the coffee? I didn't think we had any." Christy was not much of a coffee drinker, but this was good.

"It was in the back of the cupboard sealed up in a bag."

"What are you reading?"

Todd started reading out loud without looking up.

"'The LORD is for me; so I will have no fear. What can mere people do to me?'"

Christy's eyes widened. "That verse certainly fits the situation for today. Where is that?"

"Psalm 118. And get this. 'It is better to take refuge in the LORD than to trust in humans.'"

"Keep reading," Christy suggested. She sat down and sipped her coffee, loving the sound of Todd's voice as he read the Bible. He had a different tone than when he talked or taught. When he read God's Word there was always an added sound of reverence. He read till almost the end of Psalm 118 and then his lips began to curve up in a grin.

"'This is the day the LORD has made, let us rejoice and be glad in it.'" He looked at Christy. "Today. This day. Tuesday. The day our lives could change. The LORD made this day."

"Yes, He did," Christy agreed, giving Todd a wide smile. She hoped he could see that she had packed her smile with all the courage and hope and cheer she could muster. "Here's the final verse in that chapter. 'Give thanks to the LORD, for he is good! His faithful love endures forever.'" Todd looked up at Christy. "I believe that. God is good. His love for us will last forever."

Christy nodded. "God's got this." She wondered if Todd would recognize that she was repeating the phrase he'd told her last week on the beach.

"I supposed we should do what that verse says and start rejoicing now," Todd said. "And beat the rush for being glad somewhere down the road when all this makes sense."

Christy tried to smile confidently at his comment but deep down she still felt spurts of anxiety shooting up like toy rockets. The velocity wasn't at jet propulsion level and she hoped it stayed that way. As long as she kept praying, trusting, and not giving way to raw fear, she thought she'd be able to make it through this day-that-the-LORD-has-made without another freak out session.

"I've got to go." Todd lowered the foot rest on the recliner and got up. "I don't know when I'll be back. I haven't heard yet if I'm supposed to be at the meeting tonight or not so I'll call you."

"Okay." She stood and gave him a big sendoff kiss, coffee breath and all. "I love you. I'm praying for you like a crazy woman."

Todd gave her a teasing half grin. "Like the crazy woman who was throwing shoes on Sunday morning?"

"Okay, well, maybe I won't be praying like that particular crazy woman." Christy smiled. "I'll pray like a strong woman who believes God is good and faithful. How's that?"

"I'll take all the prayers you want to pray for me – crazy, strong – I'll take 'em all." Todd ran his thick fingers through her long nutmeg brown hair as it hung down her back. He gazed at her but didn't say anything. Everything that his heart had to communicate at that moment, she could read clearly in his screaming silver blue eyes.

With a smile on her lips, Christy kissed him again and playfully said, "Later."

eight

On Wednesday morning, Christy rode the elevator to Dr. Swanson's office on the campus of Rancho Corona University. She checked the time on her phone and thought it was ironic that at this exact time yesterday she was kissing her husband goodbye and blithely teasing him with his favorite expression of "later".

It was indeed later. A full twenty-four hours later. It might as well be a full week later or even a month for all the ways that their lives had been shuffled and restacked in the last twenty-four hours. Her lungs felt tight and her jaw muscles ached.

The elevator doors opened and Christy made her way to Dr. Swanson's office down a quiet corridor. She was grateful that she hadn't yet run into anyone she knew as she hiked across campus from the visitor parking to the administration building. If she'd been able to put off this meeting with Dr. Swanson she would have, but Dr. Swanson had been insistent in her voice message that morning and Christy felt that meeting with her was the considerate thing to do.

She knocked softly on the partially opened office door.

"Come in." Dr. Swanson stood next to the file cabinet, pouring steaming water from an electric tea kettle into a china tea pot. "Good morning, Christy. Please, have a seat by the window."

Christy chose the padded chair that faced the door and left the tandem chair that faced the desk open for Dr. Swanson. A small table between the chairs was pushed up against the window and was stacked with two, even piles of hardback books. A silver tea service tray was neatly balanced on top of the books. Two china cups with saucers awaited them along with a small dish filled with packets of Sugar in the Raw and a white ceramic creamer.

Christy had forgotten that Dr. Swanson liked the gracious art of serving tea with her conversations. She'd only been to her office once before but that time she'd been treated with this same elegant reception. It was such an expression of comfort, especially this morning.

With tea pot in hand, Dr. Swanson joined Christy and ceremoniously poured the amber elixir into both cups. "It's Irish Breakfast," she said, offering a cup and saucer to Christy. "I tried it after reading about characters in a book that liked Irish Breakfast tea. Isn't that rich? Characters in a novel influenced a life decision for me. That is so like the influence of Harriett Beecher Stowe's novel. A novel that changed the course of history. But then, you've heard all this from me before."

Dr. Swanson lowered her tall, sturdy frame into the other chair and balanced the china tea cup and saucer in her lap, letting it cool. She wore her short, white hair tucked behind her ears and had designer styled glasses that would have looked far too large on most women. On her oval face the glasses seemed to be one of her natural features, as if she came into the world wearing them.

"Thank you for agreeing to meet with me, Christy. I have to be in my classroom in twenty-five minutes so unfortunately, we won't have a lot of time. Here's what I want to know." Dr. Swanson leaned forward. "I listened to your voice message and I understand your choice to turn down the research position. You said that the future is uncertain for you and your husband. Are you able to elaborate on that at all for me? I'd love to find a way that we might be able to still come to an agreement on this."

Christy wasn't sure how to respond. She took a sip of tea, hoping the warm elixir would thaw her stunned and numb spirit and that the right words would come after she swallowed. Looking up, she let the truth tumble out.

"My husband doesn't have a job right now."

It was the first time Christy had said the words out loud and they sent a shiver through her even though she should have felt warmth flowing through her from the tea.

Dr. Swanson looked concerned. "Are you able to tell me what happened?"

Christy cleared her throat. "He was let go from his position as a youth pastor. Well, actually, he resigned. It all just happened last night. I would have given you my answer sooner but we weren't sure what was going to happen."

"I'm so sorry to hear this. It sounds as if it was unexpected."

Christy nodded. She balanced her tea cup on her knee as skillfully as she could and tried to explain to Dr. Swanson what she had not yet been able to explain to herself. "It started with what we thought was just a budget cut meeting but it turned into a mess. I guess the senior pastor decided a few months ago that he was going to resign, but he'd only told a few of the leaders. One of the leaders moved ahead and recommended a replacement pastor. Our current pastor is now ready to resign and the replacement pastor said he's ready to step in as long as Todd would be willing to go to part time."

Dr. Swanson shook her head again. "Anyone who has ever been in ministry knows there's no such thing as a part time position. There are full time positions with part time pay, but when you're a shepherd, you end up being available to your flock around the clock. That's how it was with my husband the thirty-two years he was in ministry."

Christy nodded. Inside, she still felt as if none of this had actually happened. Speaking about the events to Dr. Swanson did not yet make them seem real. Her emotions were locked on automatic pilot.

"Todd was willing to stay on as part time," Christy added. "He said he'd do that, if that's what he needed to do. He's really committed to the students in the youth group and they have a lot going on each week."

"Did he have any support from the families?"

"Yes. And that was part of the problem. He almost had too much support. They turned it into an all or nothing vote last night, saying that Todd had to stay on full time or else a group of them would leave the church and not support the new pastor."

"Oh, dear."

"In the end, Todd stepped back and resigned so that it wouldn't have to go to a vote."

"And now the church doesn't have to pay any severance because he resigned instead of letting them fire him." Dr. Swanson shook her head, looking concerned.

Christy wasn't sure what all that meant. She and Todd had never talked about severance, or about the possibility of him resigning. As he'd explained it to her late last night, the heated discussion at the meeting seemed to dictate the course of action and in his gut he knew that if he resigned it might soothe over the possibility of a church split.

Repressed tears began to well up in Christy. She blinked them back, lowering her head and taking another sip of tea. Her hand was wobbling so she placed the tea cup back on the saucer and tried to sound brave and resolved as she said, "You can see why I needed to turn down the position. We don't know what we're going to do or where we'll be living."

Dr. Swanson gazed at Christy from behind her round glasses as if waiting for any final comments.

Christy had only one.

"I wouldn't want to start something I might not be able to finish. I'd want you to know that you could depend on me. With things the way they are, I don't feel right about taking the position." She hoped that could be the end of it and she could excuse herself and get back to her car before an impending waterfall of tears forced their way to over the edge of her spirit.

Dr. Swanson reached over and sympathetically gave Christy's forearm a squeeze. "Oh, my brave young woman. Your integrity speaks volumes. God will bless you for that. And God will bless Todd for his integrity as well. He will. God pays attention to every detail. Jesus said the peacemakers were blessed and they would be called the children of God. Peacemakers reap a harvest of righteousness. You will both see the reward of righteousness come out of all this."

Christy's hand rose to cover her pursed lips as if she could hold back the sob that begged to be released right then. She bit the inside of her lip in order to force herself to keep her jagged emotions from breaking loose.

Leaning back and placing her tea cup and saucer back on the tray, Dr. Swanson folded her hands in her lap, left hand covering the top of the right hand.

"This might not alter our options after all," Dr. Swanson said with a glance at her watch. "If I turn this into two part time positions, I can take you on as an offsite research assistant. All the work would be done on your own time with your own computer. You wouldn't have to be on campus. It will involve a lot of reading and a lot of typing. Would that interest you?"

Christy put her hand back in her lap and composed herself, clearing her throat. She wasn't sure how to answer.

"You might be able to keep your current job at the bookstore and still take on the ten to twenty hours a week for this position whenever it fit into your schedule. I'd be looking for an eighteen to twenty-four month commitment. If you end up moving, you'd still be able to work for me from home."

"I'm grateful for the offer." Christy's words sounded high pitched and not very convincing.

"You need time to think about it, I'm sure. And time to talk it over with Todd. We can wait another week before you give me an answer. Not much longer than that, though. I have deadlines I need to meet in order to keep the research grant."

"I understand." Christy returned her cup and saucer to the tray. "Thank you so much for the tea and for giving me this opportunity."

"I'd love to see it all work out." Dr. Swanson rose to her feet. "Please give it some prayer and thought and I'll wait for your call."

Christy drove directly to work and arrived two minutes before her shift started. She hadn't told anyone about the decision at church last night but word had gotten around. Several people expressed their concern and sympathy. She thanked them as graciously as she could, but when they started asking what was going to happen at church and what was Todd going to do next, Christy had nothing to say. She willed her emotions back into their flat line position and kept her opinions to herself and did the work that was in front of her that day.

All day long she kept thinking about Todd. She sent him

a few texts and his replies were short and lacked any clear indication of how he was really doing. He said he had spent the morning at church clearing out his office. Even though he made it clear that he was willing to stay on during the transition, the decision was made that his resignation would go into effect immediately.

When Christy came home, two storage boxes rested against the wall. Todd was stretched out on the floor in the living room, his face to the ceiling. The TV was on with the volume low and he was texting while his phone was plugged in. She imagined that he had been on his phone non-stop that day with a stream of hurt students and upset parents.

"The new guy starts next week," Todd said, without looking at Christy.

"What?"

"Yeah. They hired a new part time youth pastor. He's the new pastor's son-in-law."

Christy lowered herself to the floor and sat beside Todd, letting the information sink in. "So, it was all arranged from the beginning. You were going to be let go no matter what."

"I've been assured that's not what the leaders intended. When I resigned it presented the ideal opportunity for Jake to step in. And since the position is part time, they don't need to call another meeting for a final vote. It's a done deal."

His voice sounded as if it were stuck in neutral. Christy couldn't believe what had happened.

"I'm having breakfast with him on Saturday."

"With Jake? You're having breakfast with the new guy?"

Todd sat up and twisted from side to side as if trying to get the muscles in his back to relax. "I want to do whatever I can to make this a good transition for the students."

Christy felt as if her husband was going above and beyond on this. She didn't think she'd be able to graciously meet with her replacement if she'd been let go from her position so suddenly and in such a suspicious sort of way.

"Todd, you are . . ."

He interrupted her before she could offer any wifely opinions. "I'm ready for whatever God has next for us."

Christy definitely didn't expect him to say that. How could he? They'd barely begun to process what had just happened. Todd couldn't possibility be so resilient that all he needed was new marching orders and he was ready to go do whatever God asked him to do.

"Todd, we need some time to let the dust settle on all this. It's a big deal."

"I know."

"We need to process everything."

"Okay. We can do that. But, honestly, it's not that big of a surprise. We knew this might be the outcome. And it was."

Christy disagreed. She had hoped for resolution and prayed for it. She wanted peace, not upheaval. She had asked God for direction and not destruction of everything Todd had worked so hard to build over all the years and months as he'd poured himself out for the students in the youth group.

Todd reached for her hand. "Listen. This whole process started last spring. I found out that they held off from letting me go to part time last April because they wanted to get through the summer program. I appreciate that. It was a great summer. But it's *pau*." Todd used the Hawaiian word for "done" that he'd learned years ago when he and his dad lived on Maui for a while.

"When one season ends, you gotta welcome the next season."

Christy pulled her hand away and said, "I just don't see how you can give in and give up so easily."

"I'm not giving up," Todd said. "I'm acquiescing. There's a difference."

Christy needed to think through his comment before responding. She wasn't sure how she felt about Todd's attitude toward all this. For a glimmer of a moment she remembered the way she felt on Sunday while making meatloaf. That had been a sort of "acquiesce" for her as she considered the change of seasons that was upon them. But now the change had come and she did not feel like accepting it with quiet grace.

Something in her still wanted to fight.

"All I'm saying," Todd said calmly as if he could read the fire in her eyes. "Is that we need to start to dream a new dream."

Christy clenched her teeth. She didn't know if this was one of those things that were inherently different in the way men processed pain and loss over the way women processed the same experiences. Or was this Todd's way of coping? Was he deliberately closing the door on what was behind and only looking toward the future so that it wouldn't hurt so much?

Whatever it was that was happening in his spirit and mind, she wasn't in sync with him at all.

"I've been thinking about a possible new dream for us for a while now. This could be the catalyst we've needed to usher us into it."

"Into what?" Christy asked cautiously. If she wasn't mistaken, there was a light in his eyes that hadn't been there for the last week or so. "What are you thinking?"

A slow grin pressed up the corner of his lips.

"Todd?"

He couldn't possibly have a new dream already, could he? Not a true dream.

With a husky voice, his chin jutted forward, and way too much twinkle dust in his eyes, Todd said the same three words that had struck terror in her heart early in their dating years.

"Papua New Guinea."

nine

If Christy could have screamed in response to Todd's suggestion that they move to Papua New Guinea, she would have let loose with a wild shriek that would have raised the roof. If she could have expressed any sort of shock or objection or even posed a question, she would have.

But she was struck dumb.

What could she say? There were no words in her at that moment to respond to her husband's long embedded desire to serve as a missionary in a remote village in Papua New Guinea. She thought he'd gotten that dream out of his system when she was still in high school and had purposefully released him from their steady relationship. She broke up with him so that he'd be free to go live in a grass hut and sleep in a hammock and eat roasted bugs whenever he wanted.

Was he saying now that since he ended up in Spain instead of the South Seas, the dream was still there? It was more than she could process at the moment.

Christy was so glad that Todd's phone started buzzing

right then. It was his dad calling and that was even better because it was sure to be a long call. It also meant that all discussion about Papua New Guinea could be tabled for the moment. The only decision they needed to make about their future was whether or not she should take the part time research position with Dr. Swanson. Thankfully, she didn't have to decide right away.

Pulling herself together, Christy made her way to the kitchen to see if she could find something to eat. She didn't feel like making dinner and didn't know if or when Todd had eaten.

She settled on a big glass of ice water and a hardboiled egg, which she peeled and ate over the sink with a pinch of reddish colored sea salt that Marti had sent home with her to try.

The egg, even with the fancy salt, had no taste to Christy. She swallowed the rest of the water and retreated to their bedroom. As she passed Todd she could hear him saying, "No, I'm serious, dad. If you need help with anything at all, let me know. I've got time to help out now."

She didn't know if Todd was volunteering to do renovations on his dad's house in Las Palmas or his home in Newport Beach. And at the moment, she didn't want to know.

Christy stretched out on the bed and felt her heart pounding in her ears. She didn't know what to think, what to do, what to pray. Physical and emotional exhaustion pulled her into dreamland by the ankles and she did nothing to resist the convincing tug.

During the next few days Christy's life, her heart and her gut were squeezed like never before. She felt as if someone had punctured a small hole in her soul and slowly and steadily all her hope and joy were leaking out.

When she and Todd called her parents to update them on the big changes, Christy found it difficult to help them understand why Todd had resigned. Todd explained how he had been out of the loop on a lot of what had been happening behind the scenes at church. As a result of not being included in those meetings he hadn't been aware of the major decisions that were being made by the church leadership. It seemed so unfair to Christy but she knew she couldn't say that out loud.

Todd managed to stay consistent and kind in every conversation. He kept telling people that he and Christy were trusting God for what was next for them. She started to wish he'd stop saying that because it wasn't entirely true. Todd might be trusting God, but she wasn't sure she was. Especially if trusting God included a one way ticket to a village full of mud huts and people who wore bones through their noses.

When Christy left for work on Friday morning, Todd said he'd clean up the apartment while she was gone. However, when she arrived home their nest was in even more disarray than when she'd left that morning. Todd was stretched out in the recliner and looked like he had spent the day watching a stack of old surfing DVD's that Christy had never expressed an interest in watching with him. The only slightly helpful domestic thing he'd done that day was call out for pizza.

Christy felt no motivation to straighten things or make anything else to eat. She put on a pair of sweats, helped herself to the last two pieces of pepperoni pizza and talked Todd into watching two of her favorite chick flicks. It was a sad, sorry existence, but it was all either of them could manage on Friday night after the week they'd been through.

On Saturday morning Christy woke at eight o'clock and coaxed herself to go back to sleep. Todd had left early for his breakfast meeting with Jake. She still couldn't believe that Todd had wanted to have this meeting with his replacement, especially only days after the painful, cataclysmic shift in their lives.

Her original plan for the morning was to snap out of her funk and get busy cleaning the apartment while Todd was gone. Now that she was awake, cleaning was the last thing she wanted to do.

She closed her eyes and tried to forget about the boxes from Todd's office that were still stacked up along the living room wall. The kitchen table had turned into a cluttered catch all. The sewing machine was still set up, awaiting her apron project that had not moved since she cut out the fabric and stacked it on one of the chairs. She knew the sink was full of dishes and the dishwasher was full of dishes and the laundry basket was full of dirty clothes. The only thing that was empty was the refrigerator.

And that morning, Christy didn't care. Well, she cared, but not enough to pull out of her slump and turn into a busy bee. Instead, she gave in to the depression induced slumber and didn't wake until she felt Todd's hand gently stroking her cheek.

"Hey." His voice sounded gravely.

Christy opened her eyes and saw Todd peering down on her, looking concerned. She shifted her position and made room for him to sit beside her on the bed.

"You okay?" he asked.

She nodded half-heartedly. "How are you?"

"I'm okay. You want something to eat?"

"No."

Todd's rough hand pressed against her forehead as if checking for a fever. "Can I get you anything?"

"No. What time is it?"

"It's almost noon. I thought you were going to call Katie this morning."

"No." Christy stretched and covered her mouth as a long yawn rolled out. "I'm going to call her tomorrow morning. It worked out well for me to call her last Sunday morning so we set it up for me to call her again tomorrow. I had a feeling you and I wouldn't be going to church this week."

Todd adjusted his position and looked forlorn after Christy's comment.

To change the subject quickly, she said, "Have you been at breakfast this whole time?"

"No. That only lasted about an hour."

"How did it go?" Christy straightened up into a sitting position and faced Todd.

"It was okay. It didn't go the way I thought it would be but it was okay."

Christy waited for him to elaborate.

"Jake's pretty confident that he's got this wired. I offered to help if there was anything I could do but he's thinking it's best for the kids in the youth group if I don't show up at anything and confuse them."

"Confuse them?"

Todd held up a hand before Christy could start taking jabs at his report. "I told Jake we wouldn't interfere. He wants to do this his way. I said I'd give him space."

"Space and a lot of grace," Christy muttered.

Todd reached over and gently tugged on a free-falling strand of her hair.

"It just seems like . . ." Christy didn't know how to complete her sentence.

"I know." Todd squared his broad shoulders and said, "I went over to Greg and Sallie's and talked through a few things."

Christy was surprised that Todd was talking things over with the senior pastor and his wife now that both of them were no longer on staff. She knew that Todd had often tried to get time scheduled with the senior pastor to get advice and direction but it had rarely happened.

"Was this a meeting you had set up ahead of time?"

"No. I drove by and saw him in the yard so I stopped. We had a good talk. A really good talk. He never intended for any of this to go the way it did and I guess I needed to hear that from him."

Christy wished she'd been with Todd so she could have been in on that conversation with the former pastor and his wife. She was grateful that the conversation had been helpful to Todd. It helped her remember that the way everything unfolded at church was not the result of a conspiracy or an evil plot to oust Todd. At least that's the way he saw it. His resignation was his choice as a result of watching a whole series of decisions and their outcomes be played out in a short space of time and with a lot of strongly opinionated people involved. She'd heard him say that enough times but her heart had yet to be convinced. She wanted to be mad at someone for what had happened. Todd seemed resolved to not give space for any anger to take root.

"I also stopped and got some groceries," he said.

"Oh, good. More bean burritos and popsicles." The sarcastic reply flew out of her mouth before she could stop it.

"What do you have against bean burritos and popsicles?"

"Nothing." She tried to sound sweet and not sour, like she felt inside.

"I don't believe you." Todd started to tickle her sides. "You better get used to frozen bean burritos because until I get another job, that's about all that our budget will be able to handle."

She felt surprisingly feisty, in spite of the depression that had anchored her down the last few days. Perhaps it was the extra sleep that bolstered her and prompted her to make light of the sad reality of Todd's comment. Christy reached for Todd's pillow and gave him a good fwap on the shoulder in an effort to get him to stop tickling her.

"I'll tell you what, Todd Spencer. You better enjoy all the

bean burritos in California while you can because if we end up going where you want to live next, we'll be eating twigs and beetle larva."

Todd grinned and quickly swung the pillow, saying, "Does this mean you spent the morning dreaming of our new life in the jungle?"

"Who needs to move to the jungle?" Christy was on her knees on the bed now. She countered with a swing of her pillow and all the sass she could muster as she said, "This apartment has turned into an overgrown jungle! All we need is a few vines to swing on from room to room."

Todd got on his knees and pounded his chest, giving Christy his best imitation of a Tarzan call. She laughed and swung at him with both pillows. She hoped the neighbors couldn't hear their crazy antics. No, actually, she didn't care if anyone could hear them. She was just happy to have her husband back. They needed this moment; this chance to laugh together.

There was so much they didn't have: a plan for the future, money in the bank, answers to lots of questions. But they had this. They had each other. They had many years of friendship and they definitely had love. A deep, constant, crazy-making love for each other that seemed to ever find new ways to leak out of their volatile spirits and connect them with each other in sweet and silly ways.

When Christy got on the call with Katie the next morning, the conversation started with Katie chattering about her wedding plans and Christy was glad for that. She'd rather focus on Katie and Eli's future than start off with a review the past week she and Todd had weathered. Todd had gone to church that morning without her. It seemed to be something he needed to do while at the same time he understood why Christy needed to stay home and talk to Katie.

"I keep thinking about your wedding," Katie said, "I loved

your wedding."

Christy adjusted her position on the bed and moved the laptop to the side so she could stretch out as they talked. Katie was in her bed as well, just as she'd been the week before. Only this time she had answered the call without dental floss in her teeth.

"I loved our wedding, too," Christy said.

"Your wedding was epic. You were the first one to dream up using that grassy area on the upper campus at Rancho Corona and I've heard that it's become a regular wedding spot now."

"I loved the palm trees," Christy said, reliving the memory of the way the soaring palms had rustled their shaggy fronds when she and Todd walked down the aisle as husband and wife. It seemed as if even the palm trees were clapping that day.

"You've always been a palm tree kinda girl," Katie said.

"What about you?"

"I think I'm becoming a tea field kinda girl. Wait until you see the field here at Brockhurst. It's my favorite place to go for a walk with Eli."

"Do you think you guys might have your ceremony in the tea fields then?"

Katie raised her eyebrows and pointed her finger so that it looked as if it might come right through the screen and tap Christy on the nose. "Now there's an idea. I hadn't thought of that. We were talking the other day about a destination wedding."

Christy scrunched up her nose as if it had been tapped. "What kind of destination? You're already in Africa."

"I know, but we were thinking of going to the Serengeti. That's where Eli would like us to get married. In the middle of the Savannah somewhere with elephants and lions and zebras."

Christy laughed.

"No, I'm serious. He's saying we could go on a safari with the wedding guests and then stay in tents beside a river that has a hippo pool and crocodiles." Katie's clear green eyes validated that she was telling the truth.

"And what are Eli's spectacular ideas for your honeymoon?"

"That's it. The tents by the river."

"With the hippos," Christy added.

Katie gave a smirk. "The hippos would stay in the water, not in the tent with us."

"At least you hope they'll stay in the water and not come stampeding through your honeymoon suite in the middle of the night!"

They laughed and made more jokes about the crocodiles being trained to deliver room service and how romantic the mosquito nets look.

"So? What does all this talk of honeymoons mean?" Christy asked. "Have you guys decided on a wedding date yet?"

"No. Not yet. And I'm okay with that. At least for now. There's too much else going on. Plus, like I told you before, everyone who will come to our wedding is right here at the conference center. Except for you and Todd. So it's not as if we need to work around a lot of holidays or family schedules. You tell us when Bryan and Carolyn are getting married and we'll work around their dates."

"Do you think there's any way your parents might be able to come?" Christy asked.

"No. Not at all. My dad's not able to travel. I don't know if I told you this, but when I called and told them Eli and I were engaged the only thing my mom wanted to know was if I was pregnant."

Christy's heart ached all over again for her dearest friend.

Katie's parents had never shown much affection or support for her. They were quite a bit older than Christy's parents and in many ways Katie had pretty much raised herself. She was the only person in her immediate and extended family who had graduated from college. Her parents did surprise her and showed up for her graduation from Rancho Corona. But neither her parents nor her older brothers could understand why she went to a Christian college, let alone why she wanted to go to Africa and do international missions work.

"I'm not," Katie said with a wry upturn of her lips. "Pregnant, that is. Since you were so quiet over there after I just said that, I wondered if you needed a confirmation that Eli and I are being good."

"I'm glad you are, Katie." Christy smiled a knowing little smile as she thought about several of the intimate times she and Todd had recently shared. "It's so worth waiting until you're married. Trust me."

Katie leaned in closer to the screen as if scrutinizing Christy's expression. "See? That's the convincer right there. Every time you tell me that, you get this dreamy look as if being a virgin when you marry gives you some mysterious, extra special happy glitter and little cherubs come out and sprinkle it over you whenever you get to go to bed together."

Christy laughed.

"I want that."

"I want you to have that, too," Christy said. "But you do realize it's not always like that."

"Let me keep believing that it is. You can counsel me through all the hard stuff after we're married. And speaking of hard stuff, what happened this week with Todd and the meeting and his job and everything?"

For the next thirty minutes Christy went over the events of the past week. It felt as if her insides were being squeezed once again. She cried a little and got angry. She bit her lip and concluded with a weary sigh. "All that to say, we don't know what's next."

Katie's compassionate, concerned expression began to turn into a small sunburst. "Chris! What if you guys came here, to Kenya? Forget Todd's obsession with Papua New Guinea. Come to Africa!"

Christy had no words. Inside she was screaming "No!"

ten

*T*odd did a sweet and silly thing on Monday night when Christy got home from work. He had spread a blanket on the living room floor of their still super-cluttered apartment and had set up a picnic for the two of them.

"We can't go have a picnic on the beach tonight," he said. "But we can turn up the heat and pretend."

Christy was tired and irritated that the apartment was still such a mess. She was in a bad mood after a wearying day and did not see the charm in Todd's efforts. It took her an extra measure of patience to sit on the blanket beside him and eat the carrot sticks, and peanut butter and honey sandwiches he'd made for them.

"We need to talk about a couple things," he said.

Christy knew what they needed to discuss. She'd been avoiding the topics all weekend. No way was she ready yet to talk about Papua New Guinea, or Katie's wild idea of them moving to Africa. And she didn't want to have to decide if she should commit herself to the research assistant position for Dr. Swanson. She just wanted to go take a bath, get lost in a book or a light-hearted movie and then sleep at least eight hours because tomorrow morning she had to be back at work where she'd fend off another round of questions from co-workers as well as customers. Everyone from church who was now aware of all the changes was showing up at the bookstore and finding a way to side up to Christy to ask if she and Todd were going to be okay.

Christy appreciated their sentiments. She really did. But it made it difficult to move ahead when she was being continually reminded of their situation every time a familiar face entered the bookstore. Todd was still navigating a few phone calls here and there but for the most part it seemed that all his time off had given him a chance to rest and regroup and start getting logical about what they should do next.

"First thing I wanted to tell you is that I applied for a couple of jobs today," Todd said.

"You did?"

"They're all temporary, part time jobs. Yard work, pool cleaning. But I need to do something. None of them called back but maybe they will tomorrow." He sounded positive and upbeat. For some reason that made Christy frown. She expected him to still be slogging through the mud the way she was.

Todd reached over and gave her knee a squeeze. When she didn't look up or respond, he squeezed it two more times. "Hey. What's going on?"

Christy shook her head as if to say, "nothing". She didn't want to get even more encumbered by talking about her thinned out emotions right now. With her best acting skills rising to the surface she looked over at Todd and told her face to look pleasant.

"Long day," she said. "That's all."

He studied her expression and seemed convinced enough

to introduce one of the major topics that they needed to discuss. "You need to give Dr. Swanson an answer by Wednesday, right?"

Christy nodded. She still had peanut butter on the roof of her mouth. Taking a drink of water she added, "We need the money. I can do the work anywhere. It would be foolish to turn it down, don't you think?"

"I don't know."

A tear bumbled over her lower lid and careened down her cheek, she felt furious with herself.

You are stronger than this! Stop crying. You can do this.

Todd reached for Christy's hand and said, "You don't have to take the position, you know."

"Yes, I do."

"No. You don't. We'll figure out something else. I want you to do what you want to do, what you love to do, what you were created to do."

Christy reached for a napkin and dotted the tears away. She was tired of crying all the time. "I don't think we have that luxury, Todd. I need to do what I need to do. And I can do this. I can do the research job and work at the bookstore at the same time, at least for as long as they keep giving me hours at the bookstore."

He pulled his hand away and said, "Or you could do something else."

"Like what?"

"I don't know."

"Are you trying to say I could do something else like go to Papua New Guinea? Or Africa? Or some other remote corner of the world. Is that what you think we should do?"

Todd shook his head. "No. At least not now. Not until after my dad is married and we've taken that trip to that remote corner of the world. Being there for my dad on his wedding day is a top priority for me."

"I know," Christy said softly.

"Until that happens, I don't feel like we can make any significant decisions to pick up and make a big move or a big life change."

"So what are we supposed to do in the meantime? I mean, what happens when we don't have enough to pay rent?"

Todd let out a slow sigh and repeated the brave words that she had heard him telling everyone else on the phone. "We trust God. We wait. We pray."

They sat in silence. Christy put down the rest of her uneaten sandwich. Todd wrapped up the uneaten carrots and started to pick up the dismal remains of their picnic. Christy joined him and without words they started cleaning up the apartment.

Todd sorted out the items in the boxes from his office and Christy went to work in the kitchen. She did all the dishes, scrubbed the counter tops and the sink, sorted out the mail and the rest of the clutter on the kitchen table while Todd got out the vacuum cleaner and vacuumed the whole apartment.

Christy started a load of laundry and changed the sheets on their bed. Together they folded a stack of dried towels and she did a thorough cleaning of their small bathroom. The whole time, neither of them spoke. They learned early on in their marriage that this was the way both of them got recharged. The first time they worked together quietly like this was a few months into their marriage and the shared mix of serenity and productivity was a nice surprise to Christy. She thought she was the only one who needed pauses in her day in order to reset and stay energized. It was comforting to know that they both needed the uninterrupted quiet to think things through.

Todd was the one who broke the silence when he was preparing to take out the trash. "Do you want me to put the sewing machine someplace or leave it where it is?"

Christy thought a moment. It felt so good to have everything else in the apartment finding its way back to where it belonged. But she liked the idea of working on the aprons again soon.

"You can leave it on the table."

"Okay. Anything else you can see that needs to be done?"

"I don't think so."

"I should have done all this for you earlier today. I got wrapped up in looking for jobs online and the day was gone before I knew it. I was able to send off my resume to four different churches. All of them are within driving distance. I saw postings for positions in Texas and Michigan and a couple in Arizona. For now I'm only applying to churches in our area. After my dad's wedding, if I still don't have a position, are you open to moving to another state?"

Christy realized these were some of the things Todd had been ready to talk about when she came home. He'd held back and now it all came out in one big tumble. With all her heart Christy wished she could summon up an enthusiastic response. But all she could say was, "Can we talk about this later?"

"Sure."

Christy thought Todd looked more tired than he'd looked during the past week. With all the time he had at home she thought he would have been taking naps. That's what she'd want to do if she was able to stay home. It was surprising how exhausted a person could become when they're depressed and stressed.

That night Christy and Todd fell into bed at eight fifteen. Such an early bedtime was unheard of for either of them. They held each other as they fell asleep and didn't awaken until the alarm went off on Christy's phone.

Todd got up with her, even though he didn't have anywhere to go or anything to do that morning. As he made little comments about how he'd spend the day praying and calling about jobs and finishing the laundry, Christy was grateful she had a familiar job to go to, even if her day was going to be sprinkled once again with well-meaning church people who wanted to express their concern. To be in limbo the way they were and to be stuck at home without direction would be pretty awful, she decided.

"I'm going to be praying today, too," Christy said as she peeled the skin off a banana, the only piece of fruit in the house. The banana was riddled with brown, mushy spots, but she ate around them and tossed the rest in the trash.

She leaned against the kitchen counter and said, "I've been thinking about the research position a lot and at this point, Todd, I really think the best thing for me to do is tell Dr. Swanson that I'll go ahead and take it."

"Are you sure?" Todd asked. "Because every time you talk about it I get the feeling that it's not something you really want to do."

"Cleaning pools and mowing lawns is not something you want to do, but you're willing to do it since we need the money."

"I don't mind cleaning pools."

"And I don't mind doing research." She could feel his steeled gaze still on her as she opened the refrigerator and scanned the sparse selection for something she could take to work with her for lunch.

Just then Christy's phone rang. She glanced at the name on the screen and looked over at Todd.

"It's Dr. Swanson."

Todd hesitated before saying, "Are you going to tell her yes, then?"

Christy nodded.

Todd gave her a chin up gesture, indicating she should take the call. He looked resigned to the same conclusion that

Christy had come to in the shower that morning.

"Good morning," Christy answered, hoping she sounded more cheerful than she felt.

"Oh, good. I'm glad I caught you, Christy. I'm afraid I have some unpleasant news."

Unpleasant news? Christy felt her anxiety level shoot up the scale. She didn't move.

"Yesterday I found out that a problem has arisen with the grant I'd been offered. The foundation has put all their funding on hold for two years. This means the research project must also be put on hold for the next two years. I'm very sorry to have to tell you this over the phone but I knew I wouldn't be able to meet with you in my office until next week. Please accept my apologies, Christy. I know it's been difficult for you to decide if this was going to work out for you, but if I'd had any idea at all that the foundation was in a precarious position, I wouldn't have strung you along."

"That's okay." It seemed a moot point to tell Dr. Swanson that she'd just decided to take the position. Christy tried to sound as sympathetic as she felt. "I'm sorry things turned out this way for you. I know how eager you were to work on this project."

"I appreciate your understanding, Christy. And again, I'm so sorry to have to tell you of this turn of events. But please know that I would welcome you to my office any time you might be on campus at Rancho Corona. Just let the department assistant know so she can coordinate your visit with my schedule."

"Thank you. I still feel honored that you thought of me for the position."

"You are a delight to be around, Christy. It would have been my honor to work with you."

Christy hung up and felt like she was anything but a delight to be around.

"What happened?" Todd asked.

"The foundation withdrew the grant. Or postponed it or something. Dr. Swanson won't know for another two years if she'll be considered for it again. The project is off. There's no job."

He came over to Christy, wrapped his arms around her and held her close. Christy nestled her nose into the bend of his neck and let out a heavy sigh.

"I kind of want it now even more. How pathetic is that?"

He kissed the side of her head. "I felt the same way right after I resigned at church. I wanted to get hired back on even more than I wanted to be hired the first time. I guess I still feel that way. So how pathetic is that?"

They held each other quietly for a few more minutes until Christy knew she had to get going or she'd be late to work. Before she could pull away, Todd whispered a prayer in her ear. His voice was husky and when he pulled away, they kissed twice and then a third time with lingering tenderness.

"I've gotta go," Christy whispered.

"I know." He let go of her and seemed to be putting on a brave face. "It's going to be okay. All of it. God is doing something. We just don't know what."

For the next two weeks it seemed that Todd repeated those same lines at least a half a dozen times. Not only to Christy and to himself but also to anyone they talked with. Christy heard Todd say it on the phone to Rick, after Rick had updated them on how he and Nicole were back in a taking-it-slow dating mode and not rushing to make any decisions. Todd encouraged Rick and then started talking about cleaning pools as if he had landed his dream job for a fabulous salary.

That's when Christy realized that Todd's über optimism kept feeling odd to her because it wasn't the way he usually talked about things. He was usually more easy-going and

"whatever" about life. Typically, he was neither super optimistic nor dismally negative. He was steady and thoughtful.

In response to Todd's Mr. Sunshine outlook lately, Christy realized she'd taken on the role of being the dark cloud
that quelled all brightness. It was not their usual roles and it
wasn't good.

The only really good thing that happened during the
month after Todd resigned was a call they got from his dad
on a Monday night in the middle of October. Bryan updated them on all the details of how he had proposed to Carolyn in the Canary Islands. They heard about the beautiful
sapphire ring he gave her next to a fountain and something
about a poem in Spanish that he quoted to Carolyn. Christy
and Todd didn't understand the significance of the Spanish
poem but they could tell that Bryan Spencer was one happy
groom-to-be.

"Have you set a date yet, Dad?" Todd asked.

"We've narrowed it down to April, but don't have the date
confirmed yet. How does April sound to you two? We want
you to stay here as long as you can."

Todd and Christy exchanged glances.

"Are you still there?" Bryan asked.

"We're here," Todd said. "And April sounds great, Dad.
We're really happy for you. We'll come whenever you set the
date so don't worry about trying to coordinate anything with
us. We'll fit into your schedule."

"Thanks, son. Any leads on work yet?"

"I'm cleaning pools and that's going great. No churches
have called me back yet about open positions in the area for
youth pastors. But Christy and I are hopeful there will be
something soon. We know that we're in a season of waiting
right now. It's good. It's making us more patient. We know
God is doing something. We just don't know what."

"Keep that perspective going, Todd. It'll all work out."

"We believe that," Christy added. She hoped that if she kept saying the words that the truth would start growing inside her doubtful heart.

Todd and his dad got into a lengthy discussion about the progress Uncle Bob was making in getting the tenants evicted from Bryan's beach house. Everything there was taking a long time to get settled as well.

"Talk about developing patience," Bryan said. "If the Newport Beach house isn't challenging enough, you wouldn't believe what I'm going through on the house I'm renovating here in Las Palmas."

The conversation meandered through descriptions of building permit delays, unfair pricing on supplies, inspectors who liked to be paid a little extra and problems with the electrical wiring on the old house.

"Enough of that," Bryan said. "We knew it would be a long process when we started."

"Tell us about Tikki and Matt's wedding last weekend." Christy couldn't relate to the building permit problems or the eviction procedures her father-in-law was experiencing in both Las Palmas and Newport Beach. But she could relate to two of her friends from Rancho Corona getting married. She was eager to hear about their wedding since it was held in Las Palmas at a famous chapel.

"The wedding was wonderful. Carolyn and her family certainly know how to celebrate. Tikki was a beautiful bride. I think Matt was stretched quite a bit because of all the cultural differences. But he and Tikki are very happy and it was a beautiful day for them."

Christy smiled, thinking of her old childhood friend, Matt Kingsley, being married. And to a girl from Rancho Corona, no less. Tikki and Matt had both attended Rancho Corona University when Christy and Todd were there and Christy had a few classes with Tikki. When Matt brought

Tikki to Todd and Christy's wedding as his guest, Christy noticed the comfortable connection between the two of them and wondered if they might end up together. She wasn't surprised when she heard that they had.

But no one could have known then that Tikki's mom, Carolyn, had been Bryan's summer love so many years ago. None of them could have predicted that Bryan and Carolyn would reconnect, fall in love, and now be planning their wedding on the eve of Matt and Tikki's wedding. The full circles in Christy and Todd's lives kept expanding and every time they did she saw the ways that God had been working behind the scenes all along.

That small reminder during their call with her father-in-law helped Christy to scoop into her spirit a fresh batch of courage for the unknown future she and Todd were facing. With all her heart she wanted to believe that God was working behind the scenes right now for them, too.

So much was changing. But at the same time, all the fine threads seemed to be connected. It was as if each person, each experience, were the threads that had been carefully selected and braided together long ago. Christy kept that image in mind as they rolled into November. Picturing God's complex tapestry being woven together was more hope-bringing to her than all the well-meaning comments she'd heard from well-meaning people who thought Todd had been treated wrongly.

One evening as they were standing together in the bathroom, brushing their teeth, Christy swished the toothpaste out of her mouth and told Todd about the image of all the treads being woven together in a complex tapestry.

He seemed to be thinking about her words as he finished brushing his teeth. Christy removed her eye makeup with a soft cotton ball and leaned in to wash her face.

Todd stood back, watching, as if all of Christy's girly routines still fascinated him. "I like what you said. About the tapestry. That's a great picture. I think we should be more confident that every single thread is being hand-selected by God in this prolonged season of waiting. He's weaving them together. When the time is right, we'll be able to see the pattern of what He's doing."

Christy smoothed a light lotion over her clean face. The fragrance carried a mix of coconut and mango. She knew Todd loved the way she always smelled when they went to bed. "Like a tropical dream" he once said.

In Todd's funky depression and sporadic jobs as a scruffy pool cleaner and delivery guy for a nursery, he hadn't seen the need to shave for over a week. He ran his hand over the sparse stubble on his chin and fixed his gaze on the shower curtain. "You know, to us, it looks like a colorful mess.

Christy followed his gaze to the multi-colored shower curtain that had thin stripes running vertically. "What looks like a colorful mess? The shower curtain?"

"No, the tapestry image you were talking about. Think of all those threads. All those pieces that God is connecting. It's like we're only able to see the underside with all the cross overs and knots. When the time is right, God will turn the tapestry over and we'll see the design on the top side. Every stitch will be exactly where it needs to be in order to create the purposeful pattern."

He looked so confident at that moment. It was as if he really had something to hold on to on their faith journey into whatever was next for them. Christy was so glad that she had been the one to bring a visual image to Todd. He was always the one who came up with great analogies. She had a feeling he'd be processing this word picture for awhile.

But then it happened.

Todd crashed.

eleven

*T*odd's melt down happened the day before Thanksgiving and it was nothing like Christy had ever seen him go through. For almost of decade she had watched easy-going Todd navigate a sea of challenges and let downs with a calm spirit and a deep sense of trust in the mysterious ways of God and His perfect timing.

That Wednesday night, everything Christy knew about God and about Todd was put to the test.

Christy stayed at work an extra hour that day to help get everything ready for the big sale the day after Thanksgiving. She made a quick stop at the grocery store and entered their apartment a little after seven o'clock with two bags of groceries.

"Need any help?" Todd was focused on the screen of his phone and didn't look up.

"No. I've got it."

"Level nine," he called out, as if she was supposed to be impressed. As long as she'd known Todd he'd never been particularly devoted to any sort of video game. A few weeks ago they'd canceled their cable service in order to cut expenses and he'd started playing a game on his phone. He'd had no work from the pool cleaning business or the yard work company in almost a week so he'd spent a lot of time in the recliner improving his game skills.

Todd joined Christy in the kitchen and gave her a kiss on the cheek. His scruffy, sparse, blond beard was scratchy on her cheek and definitely not her favorite look on him.

"Put me to work," Todd said. "What can I do?"

His choice of words struck her as sad in light of his unemployment status. For several weeks he'd been searching for anyone who would "put him to work". He'd been sending his resume to all the youth pastor positions he could find as well as anything else he thought he might be able to do, since he knew it might take a while to hear back on the church positions.

Last week he'd turned in three applications for jobs; a deliveryman for a pizza place, a part time attendant for an after-school daycare program and the one he was most interested in was as an interior house painter.

Yesterday all three answered him with "no's". The painting business said the position had been filled. The daycare program told him he was over qualified since he had his BA and several years of youth ministry experience. The pizza place said he was under qualified because he'd never worked as a deliveryman before.

She knew he was trying to sound upbeat when she gave him the task of chopping onions and celery and he asked, "Should I wear an apron?" But she could hear in his voice the heaviness that had settled on him since yesterday when he received so many "no's" at once.

"Do you really want to wear an apron?"

"Sure. Pick one for me."

"How about this one?" Christy went for her latest creation made out of the blue and orange printed tablecloth fabric she brought home from work.

"Is this the one you made last night?"

Christy nodded and looped the apron tie over his neck. He tied it behind him and then tucked his hands in the long front pocket. Christy had made the pocket out of half of a linen dish towel that had small palm trees on it. She smiled, seeing her homey handiwork being put to use.

"We'll have to learn how to do the cozy kitchen dance," she said as she finished unloading the groceries. "This is such a small space for two people."

"That all depends on who the two people are." He gave her a grin and pulled out the cutting board so he could set up his work space by the sink. One thing Christy had discovered about Todd after they got married was how he was all about having his designated space. She guessed that was a result of being an only child who was now learning how to share his living area with someone other than his dad or his college apartment mates.

"I found a good recipe for stuffing online but I'm adding sausage and leaving out the mushrooms." She placed a frying pan on the stove and opened the two packages of sausage, dumping them into the pan.

"Your dad will like that," Todd said.

"That's what I thought. He loves sausage. And my brother hates mushrooms. So I'm good."

"Yes, you are." Todd caught her eye and gave her a wink. "You're very good."

Secretly, Christy hoped his wink didn't mean that he was feeling extra amorous again tonight. She was so tired. The last few weeks his romantic interest had been at honeymoon level. It hadn't been quite the same for Christy. He had all this extra time on his hands while she was working all the extra hours she could get. As a result the teeter totter of romantic advances had definitely been tipped in Todd's direction.

"Hey, I heard from my dad today. He and Carolyn finally set a date. April fifth. I let Eli know and he said that he and Katie had been looking at April eighteenth as one of their top choices for their wedding date. So it looks like it's going to work out great. We'll go to my dad's first before the wedding and then maybe stay there a few days after the wedding, before we go on to Kenya."

"Great."

Neither of them seemed able to muster up the kind of enthusiasm they should both be feeling for such a great adventure ahead. It wasn't because of the cost of airfare, since Todd's dad and Katie had both made it clear that their transportations would be covered. And who knows if Marti was serious about wanting to come along and help finance the trip. What made it difficult to get excited about was the uncertainty of their future.

"What about Uncle Bob?" Christy asked. "Did you talk to him today? Did he say what time he and Marti want us to get to their house tomorrow?"

"Marti wants to eat at four o'clock tomorrow but I'd like to try to get there before noon. I want to go over to my dad's place and have a good look at it now that the house is finally vacant."

"It is?"

"Yeah. Finally. Bob said his friend got the police involved with the eviction and it was a mess. The locks were changed today and I told my dad I'd go in tomorrow and take pictures. I also told him I could help with the clean up so he can get it listed soon with a reputable rental agency."

Christy quietly calculated what the gas was going to cost if Todd was going to start making lots of drives to Newport Beach. "How much work do you think the house is going to need?"

"I won't know until we get inside tomorrow. It could take a couple weeks if it's as bad as I think it might be."

Christy bit her lower lip. She knew Todd would willingly volunteer to take on the all the necessary repair projects for his dad since he liked doing that sort of work. What concerned her was how much would such an act of service end up costing them if Todd was making the drive every day and working there instead of at a paying job.

Or what if he decided to stay in Newport Beach the whole time he's working on the house? That would save gas money and at least three or four hours of drive time on the freeway every day. But then I'd be here alone. I can't take time off from work to join him. Not when we're heading into the busiest time of the year at the book store. Todd and I need every penny we can get.

Christy stood frozen in place, thinking through the possibilities of what the month ahead might look like for them. Fear of the future seemed to be creeping in with long, octopus-like arms that threatened to entangle her heart and pull her down.

"Hey." Todd waved a hand to get her attention. "You okay? What are you thinking?"

It took her a moment to think of how to state her question without sounding panicky. "I was just wondering if your dad might pay you for the work."

Todd met her anxious gaze with an equally anxious look. "It's my dad. I'd never ask him for payment."

"I know, but don't you think you could ask him this time? I mean, if there is a lot of work to do, you'd be saving him what he'd be paying someone else. And it could take a couple weeks, like you said. It's not the same as just winterizing the deck for him on a Saturday afternoon."

Todd didn't reply. Christy read his silence as her cue to keep trying to talk sense into him.

"Todd, if you take this on it means you won't be bringing in any income during that time, however long it takes. And that means we won't have enough money to cover our bills in January. We're cleaning out our savings in order to pay rent next week for December and I'm working as many extra hours as I can, but if you don't get paid for another month . . ."

Todd stood only a few feet away, onion in hand, cutting board in place. He hadn't cut into the onion yet so she knew the tears that glistened in the corner of his eyes sprang from deep inside his hurting heart.

"I hate to be the one saying this, but we haven't really looked at the reality of what our situation will be in a few weeks and we need to figure this out. Especially now that we're talking about being gone for several weeks in the spring. I mean, we're trusting God with everything but we have to be realistic, too. I love your dad and I want you to be able to help him all you can, but . . ." Christy stopped herself because you could tell that Todd was trying very hard to hold it all together.

Todd looked away. A sob caught in his throat and came out in a choking cough.

"Oh, Todd." Christy went to him and wrapped her arms around his middle, hiding her face against his trembling chest. That's when she felt him cave. His arms encircled her, his chest pressed against her. She felt a shift in his weight as he leaned on her, depending on her to hold him up.

Christy used the counter to support her back. She knew she couldn't fully support the bulk of his frame. But she didn't have to.

Todd loosened his hold on her and slid down to the floor on his knees. With his head hung and his palms flat on the top of his thighs, he began to sob. Not just cry, but sob.

Christy's hand flew to her mouth as she tried to keep her own sudden sob from leaking out. She had seen Todd cry before and she'd seen him fold into this contrite position before. But she had never heard him gasp and sob in such a painfully, broken-spirit way. The sound reverberated through her bones.

With quick, tender motions, Christy went down beside him. She stretched her arm around his broad shoulders and leaned in, kissing his tears before they streaked down his face. "It's okay," she whispered. "It's okay."

"No, it's not." Todd's raspy words were followed by a shoulder-shaking sob.

"It will be okay, Todd. You'll see. Everything will work out. God is with us. He's forever with us. He is." Christy had been telling herself those same words for weeks but when she spoke them now to Todd they felt real and true. The power of such deep hope that came over her in the midst of this heart-breaking moment surprised her.

"It's going to work out. I know it is."

Todd shook his head. "No. It's messed up. All of it. It's not supposed to be like this. I promised to love and care for you." He drew in a short breath. "I promised to provide for you. And I'm not keeping my promise."

Tears sprung to Christy's eyes. She cuddled in closer. "Yes, you are, Todd. You are. You're keeping your promises to me. We're just going through a really difficult time of transition. But we'll make it."

"I wish I could believe that right now." A deep gut-wrenching moan escaped from his throat. Extracting himself from Christy, Todd pulled himself up and stood at the kitchen counter with both hands gripping the edge as if he thought he'd topple over if he didn't hold on.

Christy didn't know what to do. Were her comforting gestures making him feel claustrophobic? Did he need to be alone so he could cry out all his frustration in a wolf-howling-at-the-moon sort of way? She didn't know the best way to respond to Todd in this moment and it exasperated her terribly.

"I never should have resigned," he said in a low voice. "I should have thought of you, of us. It was foolish of me to make that decision. If I'd stayed on part time, at least we'd have some steady income."

Christy knew that what he was saying was pointless because over the past two months they'd heard all kinds of reports about what was happening at the church. Every time they heard about another change that had been implemented under the new pastor, Todd would say, "I don't think I could have supported that decision." More than once he had said that his leaving was God's timing, even though it was such a disruptive way for it to happen.

And even if Todd had stayed on at the church part time, they wouldn't be able to last long on his salary if it had been cut in half. Plus, Christy knew he would have been working just as many hours if not more.

No, his logic was off. Way off. She didn't know if she should say that or let him continue to vent all the crazy things he was thinking and feeling right now since that was what always helped her most when she fell into downward spirals like this.

His ranting made her think of how God had led the children of Israel out of Egypt and then they complained to Moses and said, "At least back in Egypt we had leeks and onions." But she knew she couldn't say that to him when he was in the midst of such turmoil.

Rising and placing the palm of her hand on the middle of his back, Christy silently prayed that God would reveal the truth to Todd and fill him with hope and peace.

"I just don't know what to do." He drew in a deep breath and reached for a paper towel to wipe his nose and the last of his tears. "I never thought we'd be in this place. I thought I'd stay on where I was at the church for the next twenty years. Or ten years, at least. I loved what I was doing. I loved those kids."

"I know."

"I'm not really good at anything else." He turned to face Christy; his eyes were red and filled with so much sorrow. "All I ever wanted to do was reach out to teens and lead them to Christ because somebody did that for me when I was that age and it changed my life."

"I know. You'll be able to keep doing that, Todd. Something will open up. Maybe you'll hear back from one of the churches where you've been applying."

His jaw flinched. "I've sent my resume out to fourteen churches, Christy. Fourteen! Every morning I check the on-line list of open positions. The only one I heard back from said they wanted a single guy." He slammed the palm of his hand on the counter and sent the onion rolling into the sink. Christy stood back, giving him space.

"I can't even paint walls or deliver pizzas." Todd wadded up the used paper towel and threw it into the trash can with force. "I'm stuck in the water. I need a wave. I need a good wave to get me back to shore, man. I don't want to be stuck here."

He tilted his head back and stretched his head from side to side, relieving the built up tension. "At least if I help my dad with his house for a week or so, I'll feel like I'm doing something."

"Then that's what you should do."

"But I can't ask him to pay me. I just can't."

"Okay. I understand. Or at least, I'm trying to understand. I really am."

"I know you are." Todd reached over and took her by the hand. "It's killing me to put you through all this."

"It's okay," Christy said.

Todd shook his head. "No, it's not. You keep saying that, but it's not okay."

She didn't know what to say. It felt like they were back at the beginning of this whole agonizing conversation. All she could do was pray for peace, deliverance, answers, hope.

Todd let go of her hand and reached for the onion in the sink. Without any more conversation he went to work chopping up the onion.

Christy returned to the stove. She cooked the sausage and added the onions after the sausage was drained. They worked in silence. At first it felt painful to Christy, to be in such a suspended, unresolved position. After a few minutes she felt calmed. God was doing something. She knew it. They couldn't see what it was, but He was at work and when the time was right everything really, truly would be okay. She'd never felt her faith stretched like this before. Her spirit felt strong.

Todd chopped the celery and she thought about the aprons she'd made. Her original intent was to give them as Christmas gifts. But now she had a new idea. A woman brought in a flyer that morning to The Dove's Nest advertising an annual Christmas Craft Fair that she hosted at her home. Christy wondered how much money she'd make if she was able to sell her aprons there. She liked the idea of finishing the last two after they were done in the kitchen. That would make a total of eight aprons she'd managed to get out of the cast off tablecloths. Anything she made would be pure profit. That would help a little.

Her thoughts fluttered here and there on all things aprons and craft fairs, while Todd emptied the dishwasher and started loading the dirty dishes waiting in the sink. When he finished he stepped over to Christy and gave her a hug.

"Thank you," he whispered into her hair.

She drew back and looked up, giving him a look of hope.

"I mean it, Kilikina. Thank you for riding this out with me. I am so chewed up about putting you through all this. It makes me mad that I crashed the way I did."

Christy rested her head against him again and drew in a deep breath. "We're in this together, Todd. Always. You know . . . for better or worse, richer or poorer, sickness and health."

A slight smile surfaced to Todd's lips. "We're right there with the worse and poorer part of marriage, aren't we? Let's pray that neither of us add the sickness part."

"Amen," Christy agreed.

They held each other close, swaying slightly and breathing deeply.

Todd's voice rumbled against the side of her head. "The thing I keep saying to myself is that God doesn't drop his babies on their heads."

Christy pulled back and gave her husband a puzzled look. "What did you just say?"

"God doesn't drop His babies on their heads. It's true. He doesn't. He takes care of His children. I know that. I believe that. And now I'm having a chance to trust Him and start living as if I believe everything I've ever told anyone else when they were going through deep waters."

Christy smiled. This was her Todd. This was the man of conquering faith that she'd married. He had resurfaced from the dark pit into which his spirit had tumbled.

Welcome back, my true love. I'm right here. I'm with you. Forever with you.

"We're in the middle of a test, aren't we?"

"Definitely." Todd agreed. "God is being especially quiet through all this."

"That's because the Teacher is always silent during the test."

Todd chuckled.

She lifted her chin and smiled at him. "All we can do is

keep taking the test. We know the answers. And it's like you said, you've told other people these answers before. I mean, you've taught this class! You can do this. We can do this. We have to just keep taking the test."

Todd's look of affection for her was deep and tender. She leaned in. Her lips met his in a lingering kiss. Her arms looped around his neck and she kissed him again.

That night Christy gladly left the last two unfinished aprons right where they were by the sewing machine and put all her creative efforts into thoroughly loving the man she married.

twelve

*T*he worst thing about emotions, Christy decided, is that you can never trust them. You think you have them under control and then they rebel on you and run wild through your veins.

Between Thanksgiving and Christmas Christy was certain she had experienced every emotion possible. She used to think she was on an emotional roller coaster during high school and college. Ha! Those dips and loop-de-loos were nothing like what she was experiencing now. This season of testing was like being on a roller coaster going backwards. They couldn't even see the terrifying dips before taking the plummets.

It started on Thanksgiving Day when they arrived at Todd's dad's house and put the new key in the changed lock. Todd opened the door and all they saw was chaos. The evicted squatters had not left peacefully. They ruined everything. It felt like they were entering the scene of a violent crime.

The sofa had been shredded with a knife and stuffing

was coming out. Trash and food were scattered everywhere. Two of the walls had big holes punched in them. The recently renovated kitchen was demolished. Cupboards hung by one broken bracket, the granite counter top had huge cracks, the microwave had been pulled out, all the lights were shattered and the floor was filthy.

Christy couldn't even go into the bathrooms or bedrooms. She helped Todd take photos for his dad of the living room, kitchen and front deck. Then she had to go outside for air. The stench in the house was nauseating.

The damage was far more extensive than Todd or his dad had fathomed. It was incredibly difficult for either of them to believe that someone would do this to the house that had been the only home Todd had known since he was in elementary school. He and his dad had put a lot of muscle strength and care into the house over the years. As much as Todd wanted to rent a dumpster and start cleaning up, he had to wait. Uncle Bob had started helping Bryan with further legal proceedings and until those details were settled, the renovation had to be put on hold. An insurance adjuster had to come do an inspection and pictures needed to be taken of the house as it was.

It was exasperating to Todd to not be able to jump in and start making things right.

Over the next few weeks, both Christy and Todd took turns having sudden moments when their emotions took a dive. They would be going along, feeling strong, trusting God, doing great and then one small thing would happen and one of them would take a dip on the backwards roller coaster.

It was exhausting.

Every morning Todd said something about how he was dying to make things right at his dad's house. Every night he prayed for a break-through on his dad's house and on a job for him. Every time he got a call to go clean a pool, Christy tried to cheer him on as if he'd been offered the job of his dreams.

Then when he went another two or three days without any responses to his resume, the inspection on his dad's house, or any calls to do pool cleaning or yard work, he'd pull out his guitar, compose a melancholy song and stop shaving again.

For Christy there were no upturns. Only dips. The first was when she contacted the woman about the Christmas Craft Fair and was told that she was too late to have a table that year. In her imagination she had already sold all eight aprons and was gleefully taking orders for more. But none of her money-making dreams came true.

Katie sent several emails pressing Christy to set up another call time for the two of them but Christy kept putting it off. She wanted to wait until she had some happier updates before they talked. Finally she realized this was where her life was at the moment and Katie of all people would understand whatever popped out of her mouth during their call. If she needed to have yet another good cry, Katie was definitely her safe haven friend to go to.

On the third Sunday in December, Christy got the laptop set up while still in her pajamas and made herself comfy in the recliner. Katie called right on time. She was in the lounge area of the conference center, wearing her Rancho Corona University sweatshirt with the hood over her head.

"Is it cold there?" Christy asked.

"Yes! I need mittens. Send mittens! No kittens. Just mittens!" Katie laughed at her silly rhyme. "Eli started a fire for me here in the lodge. See?" She turned her laptop so Christy could see an open hearth, large stone fireplace with a cracking, amber fire cheering up the room.

"Is Eli there?" Christy felt self-conscious about being on

screen in her pj's even though they were her most modest pair and more like sweats and a baggy top. Every other time she and Katie had talked it had been when Katie was in the privacy of her room.

"He'll be back. He went to go make us a couple of Malindi Chais."

"What is that?"

"Fabulous Kenyan tea with spices. You'll love it. I'll introduce you to Malindi Chai lattes and all the rest of my favorites when you guys come in April. Oh, Chris, you have no idea how excited I am to see you guys in only a few months! This is going to be epic!" Katie scrunched up her nose. "Do people still say epic? All the groups coming from the US are saying it but I'm so out of touch with what's popular anymore that I wouldn't know what's cool and what's not."

Christy's heart felt happy just being in the "presence" of her energetic friend once again. She wished she'd called Katie sooner.

"I still hear it used around here," Christy said.

"Good. So, where's Todd? Is he there? I'm sure Eli is going to want to say hi when he gets back."

"He had a yard job."

"On a Sunday?"

"I know. It's the first time he's worked on a Sunday morning at one of these side jobs. We're all messed up on our days. When he was asked to basically not be around the youth group anymore at church, we floundered on Sundays for a while. Then we visited a church that ran their service on Friday nights."

"So, you go to church on Friday nights now?"

"Sometimes. Last week we visited a local church where Todd had sent one of his resumes."

"How was it?"

"Fine."

"That doesn't sound very enthusiastic."

Christy shrugged.

Just then Eli's face appeared right behind Katie's. He held up a mug to Christy and said, "If you were here I would have made one for you, Christy. Good to see you."

"Good to see you, too." He was wearing a knit cap and twists of his brown hair curled out at the edges. Eli had a thin nose and penetrating eyes. His trademark goatee was back. Christy remembered how Katie had called him "Goatee Boy" when she first met him at Todd and Christy's wedding. There was nothing "boyish" about Eli, especially now as he appeared larger than life, leaning over Katie's shoulder.

"Todd's working," Katie said, turning to look up at Eli.

He kissed her on the nose and Christy felt a smile rising as she watched this sweet interaction between them. The whole time that she had been around Katie and Eli, Katie was extracting herself from her relationship with Rick and trying to figure out why Eli was just always so "there" in her life. Eli had set his affections on Katie the first time he saw her but then patiently waited until Katie was ready to see him for who he was.

It took almost their entire senior year of college. But when Katie finally discovered what a true-hearted God lover Eli was, she fell for him hard and fast. Todd had spent time with Eli in Spain several years ago and had been one of the strongest influences in Eli's choice to go to Rancho Corona University. Christy and Todd were the first to agree with Katie that Eli was a man worth paying attention to.

The only challenge for Katie was that she needed to get on a plane and fly to Kenya in order to spend time with Eli. That wasn't a problem for her since she'd come into some inheritance money and had wanted to go to Africa for some time.

Christy felt as if she was at long last catching a glimpse

of the glad results that happened because Eli was patient and Katie took a risk. Theirs would be a sweet love. She knew it. His kiss on Katie's nose confirmed it.

"If Todd's working on a Sunday morning," Eli said, "Does that mean he was hired on at a new church?"

"No. He's been doing some yard work and that connected him with the owner of a local nursery. The nursery has been giving him delivery jobs. It's not consistent or a lot of hours, but it's work."

Katie and Eli were now cuddled up close on the sofa, sipping their tea. "Tell me about you guys. How are the wedding plans coming along? Is the date still April eighteenth?"

"Yes. April eighteenth. You guys need to book your flight," Katie said. "As soon as you do, tell me and we'll reimburse you. And remember, you agreed to let me cover this so no back talk."

"You might have to fight Aunt Marti for the honor of covering our airfare."

Katie jutted her neck out at the camera and raised her eyebrows. "Aunt Marti?"

Christy timidly nodded. "Sorry, but she and Uncle Bob would like to come to your wedding. That's all she talked about at Thanksgiving." Christy grimaced, expecting an immediate protest and cautiously asked, "How do you feel about that?"

Katie turned to Eli. He shrugged. She took an extraordinarily long sip of her tea, her eyes locked onto her computer camera.

"I take it you'd prefer they didn't come," Christy said. "I understand. Believe me. I completely understand. Don't worry. I'll find a diplomatic way to tell her."

"I didn't say they shouldn't come."

"Do you want them to?"

Katie glanced at Eli again and then back to the camera.

"You know what's weird? Deep down I kinda would love for them to come. I don't have any family coming, as you know, and in an odd way, Bob and Marti are the closest thing I've ever had to an aunt and uncle. I mean everyone needs one crazy relative at their wedding, right? What kind of wedding would it be without Marti there? Does that make any sense at all?"

"Yes, it does. Absolutely."

Katie's expression turned soft and her voice sounded melancholy as she said, "It kinda makes me want to cry a little knowing that Bob and Marti would come all this way to be at our wedding."

Christy grinned. "I know."

"Do you think Bob and Marti will be willing to stay in a tent?" Eli asked.

"A tent?" Christy asked.

Katie nodded enthusiastically. "We're doing a safari wedding, Christy!"

"You are? Really?"

"Yes! We've got it all lined up. You will not believe how cool it's going to be. Game drives in the morning, campfires at night. We'll stay in the Masai Mara region of the Serengeti for three days. The third day will be our wedding day. You guys should plan to arrive around April tenth. Or earlier if you can. That way we'll have four or five days here at Brockhurst before we fly down there."

"Wow, Katie. I thought you were only kidding when you were talking earlier about a destination safari wedding."

"The safari was my idea," Eli said, looking pretty proud of himself. "When Katie agreed, that's when I knew I was definitely marrying the right woman."

"You didn't know till then?" Katie took on a mock shocked expression.

All three of them smiled, knowing the answer to that

question.

Turning her attention back to Christy, Katie said, "Wait till you get here. I'm hoping you and Todd will love it so much that you'll know that this is where God wants you to live for the rest of your lives."

"She's been praying pretty selfishly lately," Eli said. "It's been rough being so far away from you guys."

Christy felt a lump rising in her throat. "I know. We've missed you guys so much. Especially with all that's been going on lately."

"We wish we could be more of a support to you guys in all this, Christy. In a few months you'll be here and that's going to be epic."

Christy grinned at Katie's use of her new word.

"We can't wait to see you guys," Eli's gaze was on Katie and it was intense and filled with hope. The two of them looked so content and at home with each other.

"Before I forget," Katie said, "I'm lost on one minor detail for the wedding and I was hoping you could help me."

"Sure. Anything."

"I need a dress. I went into Nairobi with Eli's mom a few weeks ago. They have all the same sort of bridal shops like we had in California. Well, I don't know if they were the same franchises but they have several stores where you can go in and try on dresses and have them altered for you and everything."

"You didn't find one?"

"No. I didn't even get close to finding something that would work. I don't know if it's my shape or the styles that are popular here but the whole excursion ended poorly."

"Sorry to hear that, Katie. What do you want me to do?"

"I want you to help me find a dress. You and I are close to the same size. I've lost a little weight since coming here so I might even be closer to your size now. I'll send you my measurements."

"Do you have any idea of what you want?"

"Something simple." She turned to Eli. "Close your ears. You're supposed to be surprised."

"That won't be a problem. With you, Katie, I'm always surprised."

Christy and Katie both laughed. It was so true.

"I'll send you some pictures," Katie said. "I've been looking on-line and I have a few ideas. I'm hoping you won't mind going into some of the bridal shops there, trying on the dresses and sending me pictures."

It wasn't exactly the process Christy expected in order to find a dress for Katie. But it made sense. "Okay. I can do that. Would it be okay if I started after Christmas, though? This is a busy time at work."

"Of course. We've got three whole months if you start in January. How hard could it be to pull together a wedding in three months?"

Christy laughed again. She hadn't laughed this much in the last week or two. "As long as you honestly mean it when you say the wedding is going to be simple, three months should be enough. Trust me though, Katie. There are a lot more details to think about than you'd imagine. Do you want me to email you my check off list from our wedding?"

"Yes! Send me anything and everything that you think will help. We'll only have about two hundred people at the reception."

"Two hundred? I thought you said it was going to be a small wedding. What happened to 'simple'?"

"It is small and simple. The actual wedding ceremony on the safari will only have five or six people there. It'll be Eli's parents, you and Todd, Bob and Marti, apparently, and . . ." she turned to Eli. "Who else?"

"Us?"

"Oh, right. Us. We'll be there." Katie laughed.

"So who are all these people coming to the reception?"

"The reception is going to be here at the conference center and it will be held a few days before the wedding. Nothing fancy. Well, maybe a little fancy. Candles, and lots of food, and maybe some decorations. Everybody who works here, is staying here, or who can easily travel here will come to the reception. You can help us with that when you get here."

Christy leaned back and covered her face with her hands. "What?"

Christy faced the camera again. "Katie, that kind of a reception is too big to start working on when I get there. Do you have anyone there who can help you now?"

"Eli's mom. And the cook said he'd make whatever I want to serve that night."

"And me," Eli said.

"Okay. Listen. I'll send you the check off list from our wedding and then you and I can start another list for the reception. We should probably have set times when we call each other over the next few months, just to work out the glitches."

"Sunday nights are by far the most open time for me," Katie said. "But that takes you away from church."

"Not if we keep going to the Friday night services. Let's talk at this time every Sunday starting in January."

"Great. You're the best, Chris."

"I haven't done anything yet."

"But you will and it will be amazing. All of it. Thank you."

"It's my pleasure." For fun, Christy added, "Anything for you, *rafiki*."

Eli's expression lit up. "Hey! You're working on your Swahili. Excellent. You're ready to come to Kenya."

"Not quite yet. Soon."

"Very soon," Katie echoed.

Christy carried with her the rest of the day the beaming expression on Katie's face when they signed off. She couldn't believe how excited she was getting about helping Katie and preparing for the journey in April.

It was the happiest she'd felt in quite some time. Having something to work on that she loved to do was life-giving and fulfilling. Christy understood even more clearly why the past two and a half months had been so painful for Todd. He needed this project of bringing his dad's house back to life. And he needed a job. A good job at a place where he could start teaching again and working with teens.

She closed her eyes and prayed fervently that the Lord would lead Todd to the right path of whatever was next for him. Soon.

thirteen

*T*he best thing that happened to Christy the week before Christmas was when she read an emailed Christmas letter from a friend of hers who was living in Brazil. Christy had met Sierra Jensen in England when they were working together with a mission organization. Sierra was a free-spirited young woman with wild, curly blond hair and a distinct flare for creating her own unique fashion statement.

Even though Sierra was younger than Christy, they hit it off and had remained friends along with Katie when they were all back at Rancho Corona University. What Christy loved most about Sierra was her courage and creativity. More than once Christy had been motivated in the past to take risks and follow her dreams as a result of Sierra's influence. When Sierra accompanied Christy and Aunt Marti on their scouting trip to Switzerland, Christy quietly processed her decision in light of the enthusiasm Sierra showed for the extraordinary international experience that was offered to Christy. If Sierra could have gone to school in Basel and worked at the orphanage, she would have grabbed the opportunity in a flash.

The international opportunity Sierra ended up grabbing was a chance to work in Brazil. Her Christmas letter made it clear that she was still enlivened by the experience, obstacles and all. It was her personal note to Christy at the end of the letter that felt like a real gift to Christy. Sierra wrote:

I think of you often, Christy, and when I do I think of your calm spirit. In every setting I've ever been in with you, you always made me feel welcomed. I try to have that same open spirit with all the young women I work with every day. There's something life-changing about knowing that you are wanted and that you are thought of in sweet and lasting ways. That's how you make me feel, Christy. And now I'm trying to model that here in this place where it would be easier to grow suspicious and guarded, especially because of the cultural differences. For a long time I've wanted to tell you what an influence you've had on my life and how grateful I am for you. I don't know when I'll get to see you again but I'm already looking forward to that day, whenever it may be – here or in eternity.

Those simple, kind words gave Christy a boost of confidence. When she went to work each day she tried to focus on other people and not on the complex challenges she and Todd were working through. That attitude of focusing on others especially helped when their lives began to change even more.

Four days before Christmas Todd received the call that was the start of a cosmic shift in the lives of Christy and Todd as a couple, and as individuals.

The call was from his dad, saying that all the required forms had been filed and cleared and renovation could begin on the house in Newport Beach. Bryan even had some money coming in due to a clause in his homeowner's insurance policy that Uncle Bob had helped him dig out and activate.

"So what does this mean?" Christy asked after Todd hung up.

"It means I can get to work on the repairs as soon as I can get up there." His expression seemed to light up like a Christmas tree.

The comparison seemed ironic to Christy. They had decided to save money and not get a tree that year. And without a tree, Christy didn't feel motivated to pull out her small box of ornaments that were buried in the back of the closet. She put their limited money and time into baking Christmas cookies for friends at work and wrapping up her homemade aprons to give to the special chefs in her life.

"I won't be able to go up there until this afternoon," Todd said, checking his phone. "The nursery set me up with another delivery this morning at ten. It's just a load of stepping stones for a new house in Temecula. I could be done as early as noon."

Christy turned away from where they were standing by the closet and finished dressing for work. She was determined to not let Todd see the fear that was coming over her.

Todd walked over and put his hand on her shoulder. "Will you be okay here? I mean, when you get home from work, will you be okay if I'm not back yet? I might end up staying at my dad's house until pretty late tonight."

Christy reigned in all her anxious tremors and courageously said, "If you don't have any more work scheduled at the nursery for tomorrow, why don't you stay overnight in Newport at Bob and Marti's?"

Todd lowered himself to the edge of the bed and drew Christy down beside him. "Are you sure? Because I can drive back. I don't mind."

"It doesn't make sense to do all that driving. Or to spend all that money on gas. If you're going to start in on this big project, you might as well stay up there. It'll go faster that way."

"That's true. You'll be coming up on Christmas Eve, so that's only a few days that we'll be apart. And if you want me to come home before then, I will."

"Okay."

Todd studied her expression. "Are you really okay staying here, though, for a few nights on your own?"

Christy nodded. She knew she was appearing a lot more confident than she felt. It wasn't that she didn't feel safe at their apartment or that she was afraid to be alone. The biggest issue for her was what would happen to them financially if Todd spent weeks on the renovations and didn't bring in any income during that time?

Over the past few weeks she'd thought about it a lot and tried to think through how all this might roll out. The most logical, economical way for Todd to do this was by staying in Newport Beach. She'd had time to get used to the idea and was settled in her heart that this was the way it needed to be.

Todd took Christy's hand in his and gave her three squeezes, their longtime secret message of I-love-you.

"You are a gift to me, Christy. You know that, right? God gave you to me and you are a gift. An excellent gift." His eyes misted over. "I know this project is difficult in a lot of ways. It's going to be a crazy amount of work. I'll have to call in an electrician, a plumber, and other specialists who can do the stuff I don't know how to do. What I'm hoping is that I can learn from them. I can develop my skills and that will make me more marketable for other jobs like this. So even though we won't have any income while I'm doing the renovations, I'll be getting training and that's going to help in the long run. It's kinda like I'm going to school to learn a trade only I'm learning while helping out my dad at the same time."

Christy hadn't thought of the project that way before. It made sense and somehow calmed her fears a little bit.

"I know these last few months have been gnarly for us."

He gave her a tender look. "But I've felt my faith in God grow. Haven't you?"

Christy nodded. "Yes. Definitely."

"And you and I have had more time together than we had ever since we got married."

"Yes, we have."

He kissed her temple and whispered, "I've loved all our times together. In that way, it's been like an extended second honeymoon."

Christy smiled softly. She had loved all the time they had to be together, too. They had experienced deeper intimacy and far more lingering times together in bed than during their first eighteen months together.

It struck Christy that the intimacy they had enjoyed over the past few months had been exactly what she hoped might happen if she had taken on the research position. That job would have given them more time to be together. As it turned out, she didn't get the job, but she did get what she was hoping for – a deeper closeness with her husband.

Funny how I got what I wanted, but not the way I wanted it.

"You know," Todd said. "All along both of us have kept reminding each other that God's got us. He's holding everything together. He's with us."

"Yes. I know He is."

"We've had to make a lot of cuts and sacrifices, but look at how it's working out. We still have money in the bank. Not much, but we're not in debt."

"Not yet," Christy said quietly.

"I know we don't have enough to pay our rent in January. But I have some money still coming in and you'll have another paycheck before then. It'll be just enough."

Christy wanted to believe that.

"These are manna days," Todd said. "You know how God provided manna for the children of Israel when they were in the wilderness? It was just enough for each day. They couldn't gather extra and store it up because it would spoil. He gave them only what they needed, when they needed it. I feel like that's what He's been doing with us. He's been providing us with just enough, right when we need it."

Christy knew Todd was right. She didn't quite share his optimism yet, but she'd seen how everything had been working out for them. They did have just enough. God was providing.

Todd shifted his position and held her hand a little tighter. "I still don't know what God is doing but do you remember that verse I told you that I was focusing on about a month and a half ago?"

"The one in Psalms 27?"

"Yes, that's the one."

"It's come back to me many times." Christy had underlined it in her Bible, written it on a card that she affixed to the refrigerator with a magnet and, after reading it dozens of times, she now had it memorized. She recited it to Todd. "'Wait for the LORD; be strong and take heart and wait for the Lord.'"

Todd nodded. "Trust, wait. Every time I've prayed about us and about what to do next, the word that kept coming to me was 'wait.'"

Christy knew that. They'd talked about this before. Several times. She knew they were in a season of waiting. Part of her did not want to have this conversation again simply because there were no answers.

She started to get up and said, "It's like we talked about a few weeks ago. 'The teacher is always silent during the test.' It definitely feels like we're being tested and God is definitely being silent through it all."

Todd reached for her arm and motioned for her to sit back down.

"I think all that is about to change."

"What do you mean?" She sat beside him and tried to read what was going on by looking into his eyes. In the morning light that filled their bedroom, Todd's eyes had taken on a shade of blue that reminded Christy of the ocean water in Hawaii. They'd gone swimming at dawn in those warm, clear, turquoise blue waters on their honeymoon and Christy knew she would never forget the experience or the shade of pure blue of the Pacific waters surrounding Hawaii. Oh, how she wished she could be transported to that paradise right now and dive into those healing waters!

"I think God is about to do a new thing for us. I don't know what, but as I was praying last night it seemed like he was nudging me to get ready."

"Get ready for what?"

Todd shrugged. "I don't know. It's still a mystery." His eyes glimmered with optimism.

They sat in silence for a moment. Christy's skepticism kicked in and she asked, "Doesn't it seem odd to you that out of all the churches you sent your application to, none of them called you in for an interview?"

"Yeah. It is odd and it bothered me. You know that. But now I think we're going to be leaving this area and doing life and ministry somewhere else. I don't know where, yet."

Christy's throat tightened as the name of Todd's longtime dream location came to the forefront of her mind. She knew she had to say it out loud.

"Papua New Guinea?"

He shook his head. "No. I still don't think we're supposed to go there. I can't say why I don't think so, I mean aside from all the jokes you like to make about not wanting to eat bugs and live in a hut."

"I know. I'm such a demanding wife."

Todd grinned.

"Any ideas of where we are supposed to be living if it's not here?"

"Not yet. All I know is that when I woke up this morning I felt the same way as when I was praying last night. Something is about to change and we need to be ready."

"Not to be a faith wimp here or anything, because I do know that God nudges you like this and tells you what He wants you to do. I've seen Him prompt you that way for years. I wish I heard from him that way, but I usually don't. So, I have to ask . . . how are we supposed to get ready if we don't know what we're getting ready for?"

Todd shrugged again. It wasn't the despondent, resigned sort of shrug she'd seen so often over the past few months when he came up short on answers. This time the light in his eyes keep glowing. Hope was springing up.

"All I know, or I should say all I sense, is that before long we'll be living somewhere else. I don't know where, but there aren't a lot of streams for us to drink from here right now. And there aren't any open meadows here where I can do the work of a shepherd and that's what I know I was created to do."

Christy liked Todd's analogy of how he was created to do the work of a shepherd. She would agree with that. She would also agree that the springs and meadows of the area where they lived were drying up for them.

What Christy liked even more was that Todd was expressing his heart the way he used to before all the kafuffle happened at the church and he was no longer up in front of students every week, teaching them and sharing insights like this. She could see how this season of refining was bringing Todd back to the core of who he was and what he knew to be true about himself and about God. For Todd, the deeper understanding always came to him in analogies. She hoped he was writing all these insights down in the journal where he logged the ideas for new songs.

"I haven't thought about all this the way you have with the imagery of being a shepherd and how the streams have dried up. For me, it's more like a hot air balloon."

Todd seemed humored, as well as intrigued, with her analogy.

"It's like we've been tied to this area because of college and work, church and friends. All those connectors have been ropes holding us here. For good reasons. This has been a good place for us to start our lives together."

"I agree."

"But now we don't have as many ropes anchoring us here."

"That's true."

"It seems like the only thing keeping us here is my job. That's the final rope that has us tethered to this area."

"Maybe that's enough to keep us anchored here for another year or less. Once God releases that last rope, we'll float off to a new meadow." He gave her a shoulder bump and added, "You like the way I combined our two images there? A hot air balloon floating off to a new meadow?"

"Yes. I noticed." Smiling at her husband and reaching over to brush back his long hair from his forehead, Christy said, "I notice everything about you, Todd. And I know that you are a gift to me, too. A handsome, wonderful, God-blessed gift."

He drew in her words as if they were honey to his weary soul. Leaning close, he pressed his forehead to hers.

Christy closed her eyes and sat quieted in their moment of tender intimacy. "I love you," she whispered.

"I love you," Todd echoed. He continued the thought in a prayer, welcoming the Holy Spirit into their moment of unity. He concluded by praying, "We love you, Lord. With all our hearts. We are Yours; mind, body and soul. Use us, both of us, together, to bring honor and glory to You. Use us to further Your kingdom here on earth. We quiet our hearts before you and willingly wait on You."

The intense depth of their intimate moment in sacred communion lingered over Christy as she drove to work. She could still feel the closeness of Todd, the lingering scent of his slightly minty shaving lotion and the sweetness of God's presence as they'd prayed together.

Christy entered the bookstore, ready to give it her all that day with a steady heart.

Rosalyn waved to Christy when she entered and motioned for her to follow her over to the café side of the building. Christy followed Rosalyn to an empty booth.

"Have a seat, Christy. Would you like something to drink?"

"No, thanks." Christy noticed a stack of papers on Rosalyn's side of the booth next to her opened laptop. She guessed Rosalyn was getting everything in order for the clearance sale the last week of December, followed by January inventory week.

"So, I've been trying to figure out a few things." Rosalyn looked frazzled.

"Do you need some help? I can stay longer tonight if you need me to."

"No." Rosalyn said quickly. "No. I don't need you to work any extra hours. In fact, I kept you on too many extra hours this month as it is." She looked at Christy with a painful tightening in her expression. "Listen. There's no easy way to say this. I have to cut back. Our numbers are way down. I have to let someone go."

Christy held her breath. Someone?

"I have to let you go, Christy. I'm so, so sorry. I wish it didn't have to be this way. I've put it off, hoping things would pick up this month. If there was any way at all that I could keep you, I would. You know that, right?"

Christy nodded mechanically.

"You have been a joy to work with. You really have. I hate losing you. I wanted things to work out here, especially with Todd being unemployed, and I know how hard it is to get a new position when you're in ministry."

Christy could hardly move.

"I honestly tried everything I could think of to keep you on, Christy. I want you to believe that. When you told me how much time you need to take off next spring for your friends' wedding, I thought I might be able to keep you on at least until then. The thing is, we haven't been busy enough to warrant keeping you on even for these last few days before Christmas. It's . . . well, it's not good."

Christy felt her throat tightening as she pressed to speak the words that would prompt Rosalyn to say what she seemed unable to say. "When is my last day?"

"Well, I've been trying to figure that out. You'll have some extra pay coming to you in a severance. I hate to do this, especially right before Christmas. It's been difficult, you know. But I think, well . . ."

In the midst of this horrible moment of being let go, Christy felt sympathy for Rosalyn. She was a scattered sort of woman and that fragmented personality had overflowed in her managerial skills. Christy thought of Sierra's kind words about Christy's gracious spirit and she decided that she wanted to end this agony for both of them.

"Do you want me to leave before the end of the month?"

Rosalyn didn't reply. Her lips were parted but no words came out. She seemed to be waiting for Christy to speak again.

"Sooner than the end of this month?"

Rosalyn's head bobbed slightly. "It's the sales numbers that are prompting this Christy. You know that, right? The pay period ended yesterday. It would make it easier for me to not include you for just one day during the next pay period.

You understand, don't you?"

"Are you saying that yesterday was my last day? You'd like me to not even work today?"

Rosalyn's chin dipped. "It would be best," she said in a small voice.

Christy felt her chest tighten.

"I knew I should have talked this over with you last Friday but you brought in cookies for everyone and with Todd still unemployed, I couldn't bring myself to do this to you. It's tearing me up, Christy. I'm so sorry."

Christy numbly reached across the table and gave Rosalyn's hand a quick squeeze. "I'll go get my things out of the back."

"All right. Thank you, Christy. Thank you for understanding."

With her head pounding and her eyes welling with tears, Christy slipped into the back room, collected her few belongings and slipped out the side door without saying anything to anyone.

She drove straight to their apartment and closed the door, locking it behind her. Her heart pounded as wildly as if she'd been chased all the way home.

With her back to the door she stood frozen in place and started crying. Her tears flowed quickly but she made very little noise. After the sweet time she and Todd shared that morning, her heart seemed supernaturally prepared with enough padding to take this latest blow. The shock was overwhelming but not devastating. She'd known for several months that her dismissal was a possibility but she thought the conversation would come after the New Year.

But, then, she also thought Todd would have a new job by now.

Reaching into her purse for her phone, she called Todd. Gratefully, he answered on the second ring.

"Todd?"

"Hey. What's up?"

"Todd, the last rope was just cut."

"What?"

"On our hot air balloon. That last rope holding us here was released."

"What are saying, Christy?"

"I just got fired." As soon as she said the words a rush of tears came gushing out.

"Where are you?" Todd asked.

"I'm . . . I'm home . . ." She choked on the words, feeling like this echoing apartment was anything but a "home" at this moment.

"I'll be right there," Todd said.

"What about the delivery for the nursery?"

"They called me right before you did and said that the people cancelled their order so they didn't have any work for me today. I already turned the car around. I'm halfway home. Do you want me to bring you anything?"

"No."

"Okay. Just take a deep breath. I'll be there in five minutes."

Christy hung up and went to the recliner. She closed her eyes and leaned back. Her whole body felt oddly light. She'd never been in a hot air balloon, but this was how she always thought it would feel. To be caught up in a rush of movement that felt airy and floaty and strangely calm as if she had no control over where she was going or what would happen next.

And she didn't.

fourteen

$\mathcal{T}$odd came home with a hot drink for Christy in a to-go cup. Even though she'd told him on the phone that he didn't have to bring her anything, he went to her favorite drive through coffee place and brought home her favorite soothing beverage of late – an English Breakfast tea latte.

"Tell me what happened."

Christy repeated the conversation she'd had with Rosalyn and when she finished she took a sip and found that the latte was comforting. Just what she needed to calm her stomach. Todd's presence and his steady words were what she needed to calm her heart.

Christy knew that with all that they had faced in the last few months and now with this latest shock, she should be hysterical.

She wasn't.

Neither was Todd. They were calm. It really did feel as if the two of them were clustered together in a small basket and were floating off somewhere, attached to a hot air balloon.

At first it helped to say nothing and simply be together in silence. The silence quickly turned into a resonating reminder of the emptiness of their lives at the moment and Christy felt a wave of despair sweep over her. Todd closed his eyes and prayed for them. He ended with a brave, "May Your kingdom come and Your will be done in our lives. Amen"

Christy drained the last sip of tea. In barely a whisper she asked, "Now what?"

"Do you want to come to Newport Beach with me?"

"When?"

"We don't have to go right away. We could stay home today and get an early start in the morning."

"What will we do here all day?"

"Talk, if you want. Or we could watch one of your tissues-instead-of-popcorn DVD's."

As sweet as it was that Todd was willing sit around and watch chick flicks with her, that's not what she wanted to do. She didn't want to wallow. For weeks they had been in limbo. It was time for action. Decisions. Forward movement.

"What if we sold one of our cars and moved in with Bob and Marti?" Christy felt as if the words were forming in her mind at the exact moment they were tumbling out of her mouth.

"Whoa!" Todd gave her an incredulous look. "Where did that come from?"

"I don't know. I'm just tossing out ideas here. I don't want to wallow anymore. It makes sense, don't you think? We could sell whichever car would bring in the most money, we could move in with Bob and Marti and you'd be right there to work on your dad's house. I can find temporary work somewhere in Newport Beach for a few months. I know Bob and Marti wouldn't mind if we stayed with them. It would give us a chance to recalibrate. Think of how much money we'd save if we moved out of this apartment. Especially now that our rent went up this month."

Todd rubbed the side of his jaw and seemed to be taking in the suggestion.

"Todd, think about it. Neither of us can take on any sort of permanent jobs anywhere because of your dad's wedding and Katie and Eli's wedding. Who would hire either of us knowing that we'd be taking a chunk of time off in three months? And you haven't had anything open up in this area in the last three months after applying all over the place. Plus, you're going to be tied up working on your dad's place for who knows how long. It doesn't make sense for us to keep the apartment and for me to stay here alone while you're in Newport Beach."

Todd moved from rubbing his jaw to rubbing the back of his neck. "You have a point."

Christy got out of the chair and walked into the kitchen to throw away her paper cup. "You said it this morning when you said that you sensed that our time here was coming to a close."

Christy reentered the living room and stood before him with her hands on her hips in an old cheerleader pose she learned in high school. She felt like a cheerleader at the moment. Something hopeful and encouraging was bubbling up inside her in spite of the fact that less than an hour ago she'd been laid off.

"How much of a coincidence is it that all the restrictions or whatever you were waiting for on your dad's place have been lifted the same day that I lose my job? The final cord on our hot air balloon has been cut."

The troubled lines in Todd's forehead began to disappear. "You're right."

Christy playfully cupped her hand behind her ear and said, "What was that you said? Lemme hear it one more time."

"You're right, Christy. I have no trouble saying that as

many times as you want to hear it. You're absolutely right. I think the waiting time is over for us and what you're suggesting makes sense. That is, if your aunt and uncle are open to the idea."

"You know they will be."

"And you know that your aunt will drive us a little crazy."

"Yes, I know." Christy sat beside Todd on their uncomfortable couch. Todd had made it using his old orange surfboard, "Naranja" as the seat and the cushioned backrest of the back bench seat of his demolished VW van, "Gus the Bus". Katie had dubbed the one-of-a-kind sofa, "Narangus" and everyone who came to their apartment thought it was awesome. But it was terribly uncomfortable.

"It could work." Todd stretched his legs out and said, "You are suddenly a well-spring of ideas. Do you have more insights into what the future holds for the Spencer clan?"

"No. My insights end there. Let's just get through the next few months, take the big trip to Africa and then hit reset on our lives and careers."

"Okay. Let's do it." Todd jumped up and then he stopped and sat back down. "Let's pray first."

"Of course."

"And then let's give your aunt and uncle a call and pay a visit to the apartment manager's office."

"Okay."

Before Todd started praying for them he looked at Christy a little more closely and said, "Are you sure you're alright with all this? You don't need more time to process what happened with your job? You're not in shock or anything are you?"

"No. I have no regrets. I really don't. I worked hard when I was there. I liked it but you know it wasn't my dream job. I think I've been ready to move on for a while but I didn't let myself think that because we needed the money. If we sell one of the cars and can avoid paying rent for a few months we should be okay. Don't you think?"

"Yeah. It definitely sounds doable. What do you want, Lord?" Todd rolled right into an open prayer asking God for direction, confirmation, wisdom and peace.

Over the next hour, God gave them exactly what they asked for. They both felt an unexplainable peace about the plan that unfolded in their conversation. Uncle Bob said, "Yes, of course. When will you move in?" Then Todd went to the rental office and received the biggest surprise of all. He returned with his eyes wide.

"What did they say?" Christy asked. She'd finished the laundry and everything they owned was miraculously clean at the same time.

"You won't believe this. Remember how our rental agreement was up for renewal last month? When I went in and renewed it, I thought I was renewing for six months but I must have accidently checked the box for month to month. That's why our rent went up this month."

"So what does that mean now if we want to move out?"

"It means we can move out the end of this month and not have to pay any penalties for an early termination of our agreement."

"Sounds like a God thing to me." Christy always thought of Katie when she said that phrase since Katie was the first person she'd ever heard say, "It's a God thing".

"There's more," Todd said. "They have a waiting list right now so they'll credit us back for each day if we move out before the end of the month."

"Are you kidding?"

Todd's grin was wide and his eyes were lit up. "How long do you think it will take us to pack up?"

Christy looked around their sparsely furnished apartment. "Where will we put everything?"

"In my dad's garage. I could probably borrow a truck from the nursery. What do you think?"

Christy tilted her head back and started laughing with the sheer joy of having direction for their future.

Todd ran his fingers through his hair. "I feel like we were stuck in the mud for months and now suddenly everything is happening so fast. This is crazy cool. Do you want to see if we could move out by tomorrow? I know that's asking a lot but if you and I get at it right now, we could have everything boxed up and ready to pack out of here in the morning, don't you think?"

Todd waited, his eyebrows elevated, his head tilted, waiting for Christy's response.

The challenge was too enlivening to pass up. "Let's do it!" She said. "Let's try, and see if it comes together. What should we do first?"

"I'll go pick up some packing boxes. You can start putting clothes in our suitcases."

"Okay. And I'll call my aunt and uncle and see if we could come as soon as tonight."

"I'll get the paperwork going at the office and be back with the boxes." Todd spontaneously strode over to Christy and planted a vigorous smacker of a kiss on her lips. "You're the best, you know that, don't you?"

Christy beamed.

Over the next four hours they worked like overly caffeinated elves on the night before Christmas Eve. Christy used large trash bags for the clothes that didn't fit in their suitcases and saved the boxes for kitchen items. She did a lot of sorting and tossing of anything that was broken, such as her broken shoes that had triggered her melt down earlier in the fall. The memory of that moment seemed as if it had happened years ago and not just months ago.

Todd came back to the apartment with an update on how

they needed to have the apartment cleaned by noon tomorrow. "We're committed to clearing this place out," he said, waving the signed papers in the air. "No turning back now, baby. We are outta here."

"What about the truck."

"Good news on that, too. I can borrow it at no charge as long as I bring it back with the gas tank full and have it at the nursery by ten tomorrow morning. I'm going over there now to pick it up, unless you need me here."

"No. Go. I'm good here." She stopped and twisted her hair up into a tight bun at the base of her neck. "Wait. Todd?"

"Yeah?" He stood by the open door, letting in the cool air of the December morning into their apartment. "Tell me we're not absolutely insane for doing this."

He grinned. "We might be just a little insane."

"Only a little, though, right?"

He stepped back inside and said, "When I was walking back from the office just now I was thinking about the children of Israel again. Remember how they waited to be delivered out of slavery in Egypt and Moses kept asking Pharaoh to let them go? Pharaoh kept saying 'no' and God kept sending plagues. Then at just the right time, Pharaoh said, 'Go. Get outta here.' They left in the middle of the night without even taking time to let their bread rise so it could be baked."

Christy knew the account of Moses and the children of Israel leaving Egypt but she didn't remember any details about leaving in the middle of the night or not baking their bread. In the last few weeks Todd had been digging into studying his Bible more than ever. It didn't surprise her that he had all the details of the exodus at the tip of his tongue.

"The thing is, the Bible says that they left on the exact day they were supposed to leave. It was 430 years to the day. It says that. To the day. God's timing. His perfect timing."

"And His mysterious ways," Christy added.

"Yes. Definitely. His mysterious ways," Todd repeated. He pulled his car keys out of his pocket. "Call me if you need anything. I'll be back with the truck."

Christy returned to her packing and had the phone on speaker so she could make some calls as she worked. The first call was to her mom. After she explained the events and decisions of the last few hours her mom said, "I can hardly believe everything you're telling me."

"I know. It sounds ridiculous but it feels so right."

"Do you kids need help? I could send David up to lend a hand. Today is the first day of Christmas break for him."

Christy knew her sixteen year old brother had just gotten his driver's license, but it seemed a bit trusting of her mom to turn over the car keys to him and let him drive over an hour to Todd and Christy's apartment by himself and then another couple of hours, depending on traffic, to Bob and Marti's.

"I think we're okay without having David come. We have a truck we're borrowing. David might want to stay at Bob and Marti's with us after Christmas, though. I'm sure Todd could use his help on all the renovations at his dad's house."

"How do you think your aunt would feel about the added company?"

"She won't mind. Well, I guess I should say, Uncle Bob won't mind. He loves having us there. Plus, I think David scored some major points with Aunt Marti at Thanksgiving when he offered to do the dishes. Uncle Bob said he did a good job."

"He's certainly getting lots of experience at the restaurant where he's working."

"Ask David if he wants to stay and help us, if he's not working at the restaurant, that is. I'll handle things with Marti. And Mom? Don't worry about Todd and me. We both are really excited about this. We know that it's the right timing and everything."

"I believe you, honey. It's a lot to take in."

"I know. Tell Dad for us, okay? And tell him to not worry. We'll see you guys in a few days up at Bob and Marti's."

"See you then. Oh, and Christy, I hope you remembered that it's only one gift from each person this year. We meant it when we said we wanted to make this a simple Christmas."

Christy almost laughed. "Don't worry. It will definitely be only one present per person from us this year. I did make cookies, though, and I'm bringing those. But we won't count those as a present."

"Did you make those Christmas gooey bars your dad loves?"

"I did. They were a favorite with everyone at work, too." It surprised Christy that she could so easily mention "everyone at work" and not a pinch of remorse came over her. She did want to go back and say a proper good-bye to everyone. But in her heart she felt no regret, no sense of agony over how Rosalyn had handled the layoff. It was time for her to leave The Ark. She left, as Todd had said, on the exact, right day. She believed that.

Todd returned and the two of them kicked into their silent chore-doing mode. They didn't stop to eat or rest or talk. They kept working as a team until everything, including their bed had been triumphantly loaded into the truck that Christy thought smelled a bit earthy from all the plants that were usually hauled in it.

At seven thirty that night Christy and Todd were in the cab of the truck, side by side, rolling down the freeway toward Newport Beach. A bag of what remained of eight tacos rode along on the seat beside them. Both of them were exhausted.

"We're really doing this." Todd reached for his soft drink cup and took a loud, long, last slurp.

"Yes, we are."

"Do you know what Moses said in his prayer?"

"You really have been camped out in the book of Exodus lately, haven't you?"

"This is actually from Psalm 90. I just read it yesterday. In the first verse Moses says, 'Lord, you have been our dwelling place throughout all generations.' Isn't that good?"

Christy waited for the analogy that apparently illumined him but escaped her at the moment.

"God is our dwelling place. Not an apartment, not a certain town. Not a particular spot on the globe; whether it's Newport Beach or Papua New Guinea. Our home is in God, with God. Wherever He leads us, that's home for us. He is with us."

Todd's words settled on Christy like a warm blanket. With her belly full of tacos and her heart full of hope, she leaned her weary head against the closed window and floated off on a dream cloud. She felt as if she were safely tucked into the hot air balloon that their life had become. Wherever they landed, God would already be there. He was preparing a place for them. He always had been and always would be their dwelling place.

fifteen

*T*odd's dad's house was a dismal sight when they arrived at nine fifteen that night. Things looked even worse in the dark than they had when Christy first had a limited look around. Thankfully the garage was fairly empty. Bob was there waiting for them and had brought a broom to sweep out the garage, an emergency lantern and a thermos of coffee.

Christy hugged him tight and thanked him for being there for them.

"It's my pleasure." Uncle Bob was always the gentleman. Always willing to help others.

Holding up the lantern, Bob said, "I had a feeling the electricity would still be turned off. You'll need to give them a call first thing in the morning, Todd. Did you get the final copy of the power of attorney papers from Bryan?"

"Yeah. I haven't printed them out yet, but I received them."

"Then you should have everything you need to make decisions on his behalf. Do you kids need some coffee?" Bob held up the thermos.

"You thought of everything," Christy said.

"I'll take some." Todd poured the steaming java into the lid of the thermos and the rich fragrance of Bob's gourmet Italian roast coffee wafted Christy's direction.

"I'll have a sip or two."

"Do you want to have another look inside?" Bob asked. "It would be good to make sure the new key works."

The three of them walked around to the front deck with Bob holding the lantern and Todd cradling the thermos under his arm while Christy held the cup and stopped to take a soothing sip. The key worked. The air that escaped the house smelled horrible and they decided to not go in yet, but to leave the door open and let the deadly odors escape and be replaced by the fresh sea air.

Both Christy and Todd were wearing their old Rancho Corona University sweatshirts, a twinsie move that she hadn't noticed until they returned to the garage and started unpacking the truck. They definitely had a lot less energy with the unloading than they had with the packing of everything earlier in the day.

Bob had anticipated their bone weariness and called upon two younger guys from his men's group at church to come and help them. They arrived about five minutes into the unloading process and worked like soldiers, getting everything stacked into the garage in a short amount of time.

Christy leaned against a stack of boxes and said, "We never could have done this without you guys. Thanks so much."

"No problem. Let us know if you need any help when you start the renovations, Todd. This is a great location. Sweet little house. It's a crime what happened to it."

"I agree. Thanks for the offer to help. I'll let you know how things go." He reached out and shook hands with both of them before they left. Turning to Christy he said, "I guess we can lock up, go get some sleep and then hit the road nice and early to get the truck back in the morning."

"You forgot to add take a shower to the to-do list."

"That's a given," he said.

Marti was already in bed when Christy and Todd arrived at their house and Christy was grateful for that small reprieve. Marti would have lots of questions and suggestions and opinions. Christy had run out of all her charm and patience about an hour ago and knew she wasn't up to a late night girl chat time with her aunt. It felt great to take a hot shower and crawl into bed with Todd in the upstairs guest room. Sleep came upon them both with instant persuasion and carried them beyond dreamland to the place where not a single thought has energy to stir until an annoying wake up alarm breaks into the bliss.

Marti wasn't up when Christy and Todd quietly made their exit at six the next morning. Bob was awake, though. He'd put together some breakfast bagels and his own special Christmas blend of peppermint mocha lattes for both Christy and Todd, complete with a tiny candy cane on top of the travel mugs.

"We'll be back this evening," Christy said.

"Call if you need anything," Bob said. "I'm going to head over to the house in about an hour and use the extra key you gave me to get in and open things up. It should be pretty well aired out by the time you're ready to get in there and start working."

Christy gave her uncle a kiss on the cheek. "Where would we be without you?"

"In a much less jolly state of existence," Bob quipped.

"So true," Todd said. He headed out the front door and called over his shoulder, "Later."

"Later," Uncle Bob replied.

Christy had woken up with a headache. Surprisingly, Uncle Bob's magic peppermint mocha elixir helped subdue it a little on their drive back to Murrietta Hot Springs. The headache, along with a tense shoulder ache, came back soon after she'd finished cleaning the bathroom of their vacant apartment while Todd cleaned the kitchen floor.

The apartment manager came by to remind them that a carpet cleaner that would be arriving at noon.

"We're almost done," Christy said. "Should we turn in the keys to you now, in case the carpet cleaner arrives after we're gone?"

"Sure. I can take them now. I still need to do a walkthrough."

Todd chimed in from the kitchen and said, "Kitchen is ready for inspection."

The walkthrough took only a few minutes. Christy made sure to point out every quirk that had already been that way when they moved in. The manager was satisfied and told them to stop by the office for their refund.

"Will do," Todd said.

He and Christy stood for a moment in the open doorway of the apartment after the manager left and took one last look at what had been their first dwelling place as a married couple. Christy slipped her arm around Todd's waist and he put his arm around her shoulders.

"Remember when we first moved in?" She leaned her head on his shoulder. "I think Katie bought us this welcome mat. Or maybe she bought us the potted flowers we had by the front door when we were first married and I bought the welcome mat. I don't remember."

Todd turned around and picked up the battered mat, giving it a shake to get all the dirt off. "Then we need to take this with us."

Christy followed him down the apartment complex walkway one last time. She knew she'd be taking all the memories with her for the rest of her life. This had been a sweet little haven for them where they had shared many happy times.

They were almost to the rental office when Todd picked up his phone. From the way he was responding to whoever it was that had called, Christy pieced together that someone they knew wanted to come by the apartment that evening to see them. She wondered how many more awkward calls the two of them would answer in an effort to explain their sudden exodus.

"I could meet you at The Dove's Nest in about twenty minutes," Todd said. "Would that work? Okay. Great. We'll see you there."

"Who was that?"

"Mr. Stanley. From church."

Christy felt a little nervous. Mr. Stanley was one of the most vocal parents in the group that tried to persuade Todd to put up a fight to stay at the church. She hadn't heard anything about any of the families in that group since a week or so after Todd resigned.

"He's going to meet us at The Dove's Nest."

"Did he say why?"

"No, he didn't." Todd turned to Christy before they entered the apartment rental office. "I figured I could meet with him while you are saying goodbye to your friends at The Ark. It seemed logical for him to meet us there instead of here at the empty apartment."

"Makes sense. I don't think we'll be there very long, will we?"

"No. Just in and out. We'll drive both cars over there and then leave from there for Newport Beach."

Todd's prediction of being "in and out" at The Dove's Nest and The Ark turned into an hour and a half of sweet, difficult, tearful and encouraging conversations. Christy appreciated the chance to have one last round of goodbyes and hugs. The closure felt good not only for her, but it also seemed to help Rosalyn, who was still apologizing for having to let Christy go.

Mr. Stanley had already come and gone by the time Christy left The Ark side of the connecting building and met Todd. He was waiting in a booth by the fireplace at The Dove's Nest. Christy settled in across from Todd and saw that he had ordered a turkey sandwich for her.

"I already ate," he said. "Couldn't wait."

"Thanks for ordering this for me."

"I knew you liked the turkey sandwiches here."

"It's the cranberries they add to it that makes it so good. It's like having Thanksgiving leftovers."

Todd leaned back in the booth and looked around. "I've been trying to figure something out. Is this where I proposed to you?"

Christy was about to take a bite of her sandwich. She put it down and gave Todd an oh-brother look. "You don't remember where you proposed to me?"

"I know it was here at The Dove's Nest, by the fire. I was trying to remember if it was here in this booth or if we were sitting at one of the tables?"

"We were at a table. That one over there. We had lot of people with us that night. Remember how excited we all were to be together in this brand new café?"

Todd nodded.

Christy glanced at the bronze plaque inset on the side of the fireplace that read *Is any pleasure on earth as great as a circle of Christian friends by a fire? C.S. Lewis*

She began to reminisce about how Katie had brought a bag of stale candy hearts that were imprinted with two word phrases. The gathering of Rancho Corona students at the table with them started a game of lining up silly sentences while Todd meticulously dug through and found three hearts that said, "Marry me, Marry me, Marry me". He lined them up in front of Christy. Not until she read the invitation all three times did she realize what was happening.

"All I remember about that night," Todd said, "Was that you were so beautiful. I looked over at you and I knew I didn't want to wait another day, another minute to propose to you."

Christy reached across the table and laced her fingers through Todd's. "Did you ever imagine when you proposed to me that night that our married life would turn out like this?"

"No. Not at all. I hoped it would be good, but I didn't know it would turn out this awesome, as Doug would say."

Christy's idea of "turn out like this" had been referring to how difficult the last few months had been and how unpredictable and somewhat chaotic their life seemed at the moment. Todd, however, had taken his usual eternal-perspective position and was focused on all the good things about being married.

She knew he was no longer in the muddy swamp of frustration and despair. They were moving on to something wide open, wild and wonderful.

They just didn't know exactly what that was going to be.

Christy noticed a large, red envelope on the table next to Todd and asked about it.

"It's a Christmas card from the Stanley's," Todd said.

"Is that why he wanted to meet you? To hand deliver a Christmas card?" Christy thought that seemed a little odd.

"No. He said he wanted to thank me for encouraging them to stay on at the church and not pick up and leave when I did."

"Are they still there?"

"Yes. He's on the Elder Board now and feels like the church is in a good position to move forward and be a strong outreach to the community."

"Did he say how Jake was doing and how things were going with the youth group?"

"Jake resigned."

"What? You're kidding! Already?"

"He said he wasn't cut out for the position."

"Who do they have now?"

"No one yet."

Christy leaned back and let go of Todd's hand. With slow and even words she said, "Are you thinking that maybe you should go back there? Or at least reapply to go back on staff, part time or full time?"

Todd paused only a moment before saying, "No. It was a good season while we were there. I don't feel compelled to go back. Not at all."

Christy felt a little surprised at his answer but mostly relieved.

"Now, if you had asked me that a few days ago," Todd said. "My answer might have been yes. And the reason I would have said yes would have been in order to have a sure thing to go back to."

"You're certain that you don't want to go back?" Christy asked.

He let out a slow steady breath through his nostrils and nodded confidently. "I'm sure that I'm not supposed to go back there. God will send the right person. It's not me this time. You and I are on to some new adventures."

Christy had lots of time to think about what adventures might be ahead for the two of them as she drove by herself back to Newport Beach. Todd was driving in the slow lane most of the way so that she could follow closely behind him. She set a goal of looking at the online lists every day for a job in Newport Beach starting the day after Christmas. It was fun to think about the sort of job she might be able to find. The possibilities ahead were an enlivening mystery.

Todd went to his dad's house first instead of going to Bob

and Marti's. Christy parked next to him across the narrow street in front of the house. She saw a big dumpster parked in front of the house.

"Did you order the dumpster?" She asked Todd when they were both out of the cars.

"Yeah, I called for it yesterday when I found out I was able to get into the house. I didn't expect them to deliver it so soon. I'm going to have a look inside. Do you want to go on over to Bob and Marti's?"

Christy was really feeling the effects of the past two days and decided to pass on another chance to enter the war zone.

"I'll be over there in twenty minutes or so," Todd said.

Christy entered Bob and Marti's and followed Bob back to where he was watching a football game.

"Is Aunt Marti here?"

"No. She's out shopping and she's meeting a friend for dinner tonight so you might not see her until tomorrow."

Christy jokingly said, "If I didn't know better I'd think she was trying to avoid us."

Bob turned off the sound on the game and said, "I should tell you something."

Christy lowered herself to the comfy sofa and waited.

"Your aunt is having a difficult time with this arrangement. With you kids being here, I mean. She'll adjust. She always does. I wanted to let you know so that you wouldn't be caught in the cross fire if she says something."

Christy felt her stomach clench. "Did she not want us to come and stay with your guys?"

"Let's just say she would have been more comfortable with the set up if it had been her idea. Now, I know you're going to want to apologize and I won't have you apologizing for anything."

"I feel bad. I should have . . ."

Uncle Bob held up his hand to silence her. "Nope. I mean

it. None of that. You and I both know that your aunt likes to have things a certain way and this time it was too quick for her to make the kind of preparations she would have wanted to make."

"What kind of preparations?"

"She's been wanting to renovate the upstairs guest room bath."

"The bathroom is fine just the way it is."

"It's something she's talked about for months. As you know, she had the guest room expanded and renovated last year when we did our bedroom but she didn't have the guest bath done then. It's been on her to do list ever since. I think she can wait a few more weeks or months. Like I told you on the phone, Christy. *Mi casa es su casa.* You and Todd are welcome here anytime for as long as you want to stay."

Christy bit her lower lip. She knew how particular her aunt was about plans and arrangements.

Why didn't I call Marti instead of Bob and slant the conversation in such a way that she would have been the one extending the invitation? I know better. I wish I'd thought this through.

"Chris-teee," Uncle Bob said with a warning tone. "Wherever you're going in that pretty little head of yours right now, you need to turn around and come back. She'll be fine about all this. You know she will. All we have to do is give her a day or two and she'll be telling people this was all her idea to begin with. You'll see."

Christy wished she could be as confident as her uncle. The worst part was that she and Todd had no place else to go. She was beginning to feel a like Mary and Joseph. It was only two days before Christmas Eve and now it looked like there might be no room for them at the inn.

sixteen

$\mathcal{A}$t sixty-thirty a.m. on Christmas Eve, Christy and Todd had a horrible argument.

What made it even more frustrating was that it started when they were in Bob and Marti's guest room and had to keep their voices hushed so that Bob and Marti wouldn't hear them.

Todd had set his alarm to get up at daybreak in order to get back over to his dad's house. He had spent the past two full days there, working twelve hours both days, hauling anything that was trashed out to the dumpster including damaged carpet that he ripped out single-handedly.

Christy had helped for hours, breaking fingernails, acquiring an assortment of bruises from carrying furniture and tearing the side of her favorite pair of jeans. It was difficult, demolition work and the house still smelled awful. Todd had told Christy a number of times to take a break and go back to Bob and Marti's but she would rather stay with Todd than chance a toxic encounter with her aunt.

The two times she had seen Marti, her aunt was breezing out the door wearing her fixed, fake hostess expression. Marti said nothing negative to Christy. She just made it clear that she was busy and had too much to do before Christmas to stop for even a moment.

Christy decided to not tell Todd about what Uncle Bob had confided in her. She didn't want to add to his stress and quietly hoped that Marti would come around to wanting them to be with them so that a confrontation of any sort could be avoided.

The knowledge that they were not welcomed had been building up inside Christy to the boiling point. She was exhausted and had never been a morning person the way Todd was. So when his alarm went off she let out a moan and said, "Can't you give it a rest for a few hours? Let's sleep some more."

"You go ahead and sleep," Todd said. "I want to get an early start."

"You don't have to try to finish the whole house in a week."

"It's going to take a month, Christy. At least. Not a week."

"I know. I'm just saying, it's Christmas Eve tonight."

"I know." His voice carried an edge of irritation. "That's why I'm getting an early start."

Todd got out of bed and got dressed in his work clothes.

Christy leaned on her elbow and said, "Did you see the note Aunt Marti left for us?"

"No."

"She wrote out the schedule for tonight. Dinner is at five o'clock because Bob has talked her into going to Christmas Eve service with us at seven."

"Okay."

"She also wrote that she wants you to play your mandolin for us after dinner like you did the first Christmas after we met."

Todd stood by the side of the bed with his hands on his hips. "Why is she writing all this in notes? Why didn't she ask me?"

Christy knew the real reason her aunt was avoiding conversation with them but she said, "She likes to be organized. And we've hardly been around." Christy had no idea why she was defending her aunt that way. She could tell that Todd was irritated and she didn't want to strike any matches to the tinder that had been gathering inside of her, either.

"Could you tell her for me that I won't be able to play my mandolin this year? I can play something on my guitar if she wants, but not the mandolin."

"Why not the mandolin?"

Todd stood his ground and thrust his hands into the back pockets of his dirty and torn jeans. "I took my mandolin to the pawn shop last month."

Christy sat up and stared at him. "You did? Why?"

"We needed money for the electric bill. I hadn't played it in a long time. I did what I needed to do to get some money."

"Todd, we could have sold the sewing machine instead."

"You like the sewing machine."

"You liked your mandolin. We have to get it back. What pawn shop did you take it to?"

"We don't have to get it back, Christy. Not now. Not until we have some money in the bank."

"We will have money in the bank as soon as we sell one of the cars."

"We can't sell the cars."

"Why not? I thought that was part of the plan."

"Which one are we going to sell? The Volvo that your aunt and uncle helped us buy? Or Katie's Subaru, that she gave to us? Either way, we're going to be cheapening a gift that was given to us."

"Why would you say that? Katie wouldn't mind. Neither

would my aunt or uncle. They would understand."

Todd gave Christy a stern look. "Would they? We thought your aunt wouldn't mind us staying here but she does."

Christy lowered her eyes. "Did she say something to you?"

"No. And that's the point. I've been in the same room with her three times now and every time it's clear that she does not want us here."

"It's not that she doesn't want us, it's that it would have been better if it had been her idea. That's what Uncle Bob told me."

Now Todd looked hurt. "When did he tell you that?"

"A few days ago."

"And you didn't fill me in on that helpful bit of information?"

"I didn't want you to feel the way you're feeling right now."

"Christy, it's not your responsibility to decide how I'm supposed to feel. We're a team. I tell you what's going on. You need to tell me what's going on. The only way we're going to make it through this transition is if you honor me enough to give me important information like this. I don't want to spend Christmas with your family and have your aunt shooting daggers at us the whole time."

"You know how she is."

"Christy," He raised his voice and then caught himself and lowered it back to the tense whispering level they'd been using. "You don't need to make excuses for her. I know that's how things have been in your family all your life but it's not healthy. It's not okay for stuff to go unsaid and for people to have to walk around on egg shells. In our family, we get things out in the open and talk it through. That's how you and I work as a family. You can't switch communication systems just because we're staying here, for however long that might be. Talk to your aunt this morning. Get things settled.

If she wants us out of here, we'll go."

"Where will we go?"

With a flustered look he grabbed his sweatshirt and said, "I'm working on that. As soon as my dad's house is livable, I'll ask him if we can stay there. Or, you'll have to ask your parents if we can move in with them in Escondido for a while."

"They don't have room for us."

"Then I'm out of ideas. All I know is that I'm going over to work on my dad's house. I'll be back here in time for dinner at five o'clock and I'll let your aunt know that I won't be playing the mandolin for her. Got that? I'll tell her. You don't have to. I will."

"Todd . . ."

He headed for the door. With his back to her in a terse whisper he said, "I can't talk about this anymore. I've gotta go."

She was surprised at how quietly he closed the guest room door. But then the whole argument had felt surreal with their lowered voices and the intense comments delivered with more facial expressions and body language than vocal volume.

Christy flopped back in bed and pulled the covers over her head. She was too angry to cry. She wished he'd come back so they could finish talking. What was it he said about how the two of them talked things through as a family? Why didn't he stay and talk things through now?

And why did he pawn his mandolin? Why didn't he tell me he was going to do that? He's mad because I didn't tell him about Aunt Marti being in a snit. Well, I'm mad because he didn't talk with me about giving up his mandolin before he did it. Grrrr!

Christy knew there was no way she was going to manage to get any more sleep now. She threw back the covers and tromped into the bathroom to take a shower. She'd taken a shower last night but taking another shower seemed the only way to process everything right now. The steaming water from the shower head soon matched her steaming thoughts.

She took to her usual mental jogging trail and started going through the paces of how they'd gotten to this point.

Did I press too much for us to do this? To drop everything, leave our apartment and come stay here?

No. Staying at our apartment wasn't an option financially unless we would have gotten a credit card and taken out an advance on it. But Todd is adamant that we don't go into debt and only use a credit card if we can pay it off every month. We couldn't have paid rent unless we sold one of our cars.

And why doesn't he want to sell one of the cars? I know they were both gifted to us, but I don't agree with his logic. We should feel free to sell one if we need to. And we need to.

Unless I find a job. I could start working the day after Christmas. That would help.

Christy had been looking every day at the jobs posted on various websites for that area and so far she hadn't found anything she could do except clean houses. Todd said he'd rather have her help cleaning his dad's house than for her to be cleaning someone else's house.

But at least I'd get paid to clean someone else's house.

That thought prompted another round of thoughts on the mental jogging trail of how Todd shouldn't be doing all this work for his dad for free since they needed money so badly right now. She wanted to tell him that he should get a job three days a week and then work at his dad's three days a week just to bring in some income.

But then, it would take so much longer on the house and I know he'd be over there working on it every day as soon as he got off work.

Christy got out of the shower and tried to decide if she should put on her torn jeans and go over to help Todd, or if she should put on something nicer and wait for her aunt to get up.

She decided to put on something nice and stay at Bob and Marti's that morning so that she could hopefully have a talk with her aunt. It seemed she would be of more help to Todd if she smoothed things over here rather than go swing a hammer there. Todd probably needed the time by himself to think, as well.

Of course, we wouldn't be in such a strained place right now if Marti would have managed to be a little more gracious about our staying here. If she were more welcoming, we wouldn't be in this predicament.

Christy stopped herself right there. She realized how ridiculous it was to be mad at someone for not being more hospitable and welcoming in their own home. Christy and Todd were the ones who were invading Bob and Marti's space and presuming upon their graciousness. She realized how self-centered she was being for harboring hurt and anger at her aunt simply because Marti had been presumed upon at a busy time and wasn't able to express feelings of happiness over having them there.

Christy's thoughts got off the mental jogging trail and in her heart she went to the verse she had started praying whenever she felt like her spirit needed another shower. The verse was from Psalm 51:10.

Create in me a clean heart, O God, and renew a right spirit within me.

Christy first read those powerful words on a decorative wall plaque they sold at The Ark. More than once she had repeated the verse as a simple prayer during times at work when she knew that her attitude was way off. This morning was definitely one of those times. As soon as she opened her eyes, Christy felt better. Her thoughts weren't going round and round the same track. God had cleansed her heart and was renewing a right spirit within her.

She hoped Todd was experiencing the same heart changing thoughts. She hated that he'd left when things were still
unsettled between them. His directive had been for her to
talk to Marti and she knew that's what she needed to do before going over to help Todd.

Spending a few extra minutes in the bathroom, Christy
put on a little make up, knowing that her aunt would notice.
She put on a nice sweater and a clean, but slightly crumpled,
pair of pants. At least she wasn't wearing her frayed jeans.
Her aunt would notice that, too.

Christy's plan seemed well-positioned for success when
she went downstairs and found that both Bob and Marti
were up and working together in the kitchen. Marti was lining up serving bowls on the kitchen table and Bob was making scrambled eggs.

"Morning, Bright Eyes," Uncle Bob said. "Are you and
your man interested in some breakfast?"

"Todd went over to the house already."

"What about you?"

"No, thanks."

Marti turned around and with an overly bright expression she said, "I don't suppose you'd like to try one of my kale
and strawberry matcha breakfast shakes?"

Christy swallowed. She knew this could be a turning
point moment in her relationship with her aunt. For nearly
a decade Aunt Marti had tried everything she could to persuade Christy to join her on one of her diets or health food
kicks. It was one area where Christy had always held back
and refused to try her aunt's concoctions. She knew that if
she conceded this morning and supported her aunt's idea of
a tasty breakfast, it could change Marti's disposition in an
instant.

Christy swallowed again and avoided looking over at her

uncle. She knew he would be stunned as the answer tripped over her lips and shot their way to her aunt's waiting ears.

With all the gumption she could muster, Christy said, "Sure."

Marti was double-stunned. For a moment she stood with her lips parted and her eyes unblinking. When she found her voice, Marti said, "Wonderful. You'll love it. I use only the purest matcha. It's 100 percent and better for you than just green tea as a drink."

Christy kept swallowing. She didn't know if her body was trying to grease the runway so that the breakfast shake would slide down faster or if she was already trying to tell her body to take in fluids and keep them down.

Marti bustled about getting the shake ready for Christy. She chattered excitedly the whole time as if she were on an infomercial and trying to sell this great new, healthy product to millions of viewers and not just to Christy.

"The kale is fresh, of course, and I use strawberries I bought last summer and froze myself in glass containers because you know you don't ever want to use plastic these days for anything."

When Christy did glance over at Uncle Bob, he pointed his spatula to the pan of left over scrambled eggs and gave her a wink as if to say, "These will be waiting for you."

Marti didn't use the blender on the counter. Instead, she pulled out a larger, more complex looking food processor from one of the cupboards and went to work, dropping in the dark green, leafy kale first before adding the frozen strawberries, crushed ice, water and a scoop of some kind of mysterious green powder. With a push of a button, the machine began to whirl the ingredients together into a strange shade of green that Christy didn't think she had ever seen before.

With efficient movements, Marti poured the drink into a tall glass and handed it to Christy with a look of great satisfaction. Lowering her chin and narrowing her eyes, Marti fixed her gaze on Christy and said, "Now drink it. All of it."

Christy moistened her lips, swallowed again and put the glass to her mouth.

seventeen

The first sip of Aunt Marti's organic breakfast beverage went down quickly. To Christy's great surprise, it tasted good. Not great, good. Kind of like a cold version of the tea latte Todd had brought to her earlier that week only more earthy and green tasting.

"It's nice," she said honestly.

Marti pulled her shoulders back and glanced at Bob. With a sweet air of satisfaction she said, "I told you. This is the best one I've ever come up with."

Turning back to Christy she said, "Do you notice how there are no strawberry seeds at all? They are completely blended into the drink. You won't have any tiny bits in your teeth or any clumps of kale at the bottom of the glass. And it's so good for you. You have no idea."

Christy took another long drink. She actually liked it. She couldn't believe it, but it was true. She had crossed over to Aunt Marti's side of the breakfast war. And now she knew there was no going back to indulging in Uncle Bob's great waffles or sharing donuts with him after one of his Saturday morning runs to the donut shop whenever Marti and her super-sonic blend-o machine were standing by to meet all of Christy's breakfast nutrition needs.

"Thanks, Aunt Marti," Christy said with a sincere warmth in her voice. "Thank you for convincing me to try this. I really do like it."

"I knew you would."

"And thank you, too, for putting up with me and Todd and the way we imposed ourselves on you guys. We didn't know where else to go or what else to do." She hoped she wasn't sounding too helpless and pathetic with her choice of words. It was true, though. They didn't have a plan B, but what Christy had wanted to focus on was her appreciation of her aunt and uncle's graciousness in the midst of a busy time. Not her neediness.

"Well, of course, Christy, darling. You are always welcome here. You know that."

For the second time, Christy refrained from glancing at her uncle since it would be too difficult for them to hide one of their shared, knowing glances from Marti.

"Todd and I appreciate your hospitality more than we could ever say. This is a difficult transition time for us."

"It certainly is."

Christy went on, in hopes of getting everything out in the open. "I'd like to be able to talk with you both about how you feel about us staying here and how long you think we might be able to stay. And I'd like Todd to be in on that conversation. Do you think the four of us could sit down sometime and talk about what's best for you guys?"

Uncle Bob stepped over to where Christy stood by the kitchen counter and said, "You both are welcome here as long as you want. Isn't that right, Martha?"

She studied Bob's expression before saying, "Yes. Of

course. But Christy does have a point. We never had a chance to discuss the specifics of their stay. I like her idea of the four of us sitting down and having that conversation soon. Not today, of course. And certainly not tomorrow. Let's talk the day after Christmas when everyone else has gone home."

Christy started to nod her agreement. Then she remembered how she had invited her brother to stay on after Christmas. "Actually, I . . ." she grimaced.

"What's wrong? Did you change your opinion of the drink? It can give you bit of a backlash if you drink it too quickly. All you need to do is drink a lot of water. Bob? Would you be so kind as to get Christy a large glass of water?"

"No, I'm fine. I don't need any water. What I was going to say was that I think I may have overstepped my place again."

"What did you do, Christy?" Aunt Marti's stern look was beginning to cast a shadow over her earlier gracious expression.

"I asked my mom to see if David wanted to stay here after Christmas so that he could help Todd."

Marti froze in place.

"The more the merrier," Bob said. "David is welcome to stay as long as he wants. Don't you agree, Martha?"

Christy could almost see the snuffed-out flaming emotions that smoked from Marti's nostrils as she exhaled. With a controlled glance at Christy and then back to Bob she said in a semi-calm voice, "It looks like we'll need more food around here. You don't mind seeing to that, do you, dear?"

"Not a problem." Bob's relieved look made it clear that all was well at the moment.

"Finish your breakfast drink, Christy, dear. I could use your help with setting the table for this evening. And I have a mound of gifts that still need to be wrapped. Todd won't mind if I borrow you for a few hours, will he?"

"No. He won't mind." After Christy being the one to say

that other people "wouldn't mind" for the past few days, this time she really was sure that Todd wouldn't mind if she helped Marti. Just to be certain, she sent him a text.

He replied with "GOOD. GOT A TEXT FROM DOUG. THEY ARE HERE AT TRACY'S PARENTS. I SAID WE'D GET TOGETHER WITH THEM AFTER CHRISTMAS. OK WITH YOU?"

"YES! OF COURSE. IT WILL BE SO GOOD TO SEE THEM."

A surge of hope rose in Christy as she thought about how great it would be for Todd to have time with Doug. She was excited to see Tracy, too, and their little boy, Daniel. Christy hadn't seen Daniel in months. She tried to imagine what he was like now that he was eighteen months old.

Doug and Tracy lived in a little house about an hour south of Newport Beach in a coastal town called Carlsbad. The longtime friends had made all kinds of statements before Christy and Todd got married about how they'd still get together regularly, even though it would mean lots of time on the freeway and in traffic. Those intentions hadn't been realistic in the face of jobs and ministry and the fact that Doug and Tracy had a wee one who still pretty much set the schedule for them. Christy was grateful that Doug and Todd had connected and set up some time for them to be together.

As Christy followed Marti into the large, open space that encompassed the living room and dining room, she noticed for the first time that the dining room table had been moved from where Marti usually had it. The extensions were already in place in the long table. The custom shaped table pad was in place and the gold tablecloth waited over the back of two of the luxuriously upholstered chairs.

"You can start with the tablecloth," Marti instructed. "The china and silverware are in the china cabinet. We'll need seven places set so make sure you space them in an aesthetically pleasing way since we don't have an even number of guests."

"Will do."

"As soon as you finish, come upstairs to my bedroom and we'll get the gifts wrapped."

Christy couldn't remember ever being invited into Bob and Marti's bedroom to wrap gifts. But then the downstairs guestroom would soon be occupied by her parents and the "den", as Uncle Bob still liked to call it, was where David would stay on the large sofa that faced the even larger flat screen television.

Marti's renovated master bedroom had a commanding view of the ocean and an extended patio that was directly above the outside patio area. It was Marti's private hideaway and not usually open to spectators or used as Santa's workshop.

"I'll be up to help you soon." Without thinking, Christy added, "You do remember that this is supposed to be a simple Christmas this year. We agreed on only giving each other one gift."

With her jaw set, Marti said, "Christy, darling, it's Christmas. The whole reason for the season is giving gifts to each other, is it not? If I choose to give more than one gift to a person in our family, it's only because I am living out the spirit of Christmas. I will not have anyone dictate to me rules about how I can give gifts." She turned and tromped up the stairs.

Christy thought about her aunt's comment as she set the table with the beautiful, fine china plates and gold plated silverware. She loved the feel and the creamy shade of the china plates. She noticed the reflection of the glimmering Christmas tree lights on the crystal stemware. Cheerful Christmas music played in the background and the fragrance of the tall evergreen tree by the window filled the room.

It was moments like this when she didn't judge her aunt for her expensive taste and her passion for details when it came to decorating. Marti loved creating art and Christmas was her chance to pull out all her favorite colors and scents and sounds and turn her home into a gallery of yuletide beauty.

Deep down, Christy knew she had a good dose of her aunt in her when it came to creating beauty in her surroundings. It was a trait that Christy's mom didn't have. Christy valued the blended elegance of the space she was helping to amplify as she set the table. She thought about how she should enjoy all this while she could because she couldn't imagine ever owning the sorts of things her aunt owned. Nor could she ever imagine living in a house like this on the beach.

Outside it was still foggy; a luscious, feathery sort of fog that would undoubtedly burn off by noon. The weather, the decorations, ornaments, lights and heady scent of the evergreen tree all infused Christy with the feeling that it really was Christmas. Until that moment, she hadn't caught up with the fact that this was the night they would celebrate the birth of the Savior.

Marti's impression of the meaning of Christmas might center on giving presents but for Christy, the true focus was on the one gift God gave on that first Christmas Eve so long ago. She wished she could find a way to express the truth to Aunt Marti that Jesus was the reason for the season. She thought about how it had taken Uncle Bob awhile before he came to believe that he needed a Savior. Would Marti ever reach that same place in her heart and bend her knee to the King of Kings?

It seems that Aunt Marti has always had such a difficult time accepting the truth that everyone has sinned and needs the forgiveness that Christ alone has provided. Since she's able to buy whatever she wants, I don't think she can process the thought that salvation is a gift and there's nothing you can do to earn it or pay for it.

Christy thought about how Katie had said long ago that it would have to be a total God-thing for Marti to ever surrender her life to the Lord. Christy had edged her way around the topic with her aunt several times over the years. Even though Marti seemed open at various times, she always came back to the line that she had her own beliefs. Once she'd told Christy that if she ever tried to push her opinions or beliefs Marti would reject her for life.

Christy paused and looked out the window at the world immersed in white, vaporous fog.

I'd rather have her reject me for life than reject You for eternity, Father. Please draw her to You. Show her Your unending love for her.

The same thought returned to Christy that evening as they gathered at the elegant table and enjoyed the meal that Marti's caterer had prepared for them and placed on the table in all of Marti's serving dishes. Marti didn't need to give the appearance of the meal coming from their kitchen. It was just them and they all knew the dinner had been catered.

These are my people. My family. I want all of them to be together one day in heaven. I wish Marti would give her life to you, Lord. That's all I want for Christmas this year. Honest.

Christy's father sat at one end of the table, his large, farmer hands tearing a dinner roll in half and generously dressing up each half with fresh, dairy butter, his contribution to the meal. Her mother sat next to him and across from Christy. She had a pleasant expression on her face the way she always did around her over-shadowing sister. Christy often marveled that her homespun, gray-haired mother who was round in face and frame had come from the same family tree as sleek, stylish, petite Marti.

The two sisters had never been "friends" according to Christy's mom but they had always placed high value on being related. Their Midwest upbringing instilled in both sisters a high value on family and home. The older Christy got, the more she appreciated her mother's calm, steady ways. If Christy had grown up with a sister who was so opposite from her, she's not sure she would have been as persistent to preserve the relationship as her mother had been with Marti.

Todd had arrived at ten minutes to five o'clock and had come to the table in clean clothes but with his hair still wet from the shower and smelling of cocoa butter body wash, which Marti kept stocked in all her bathrooms. He didn't have much to say. It was evident that he was exhausted. Christy noticed a new bruise on the back of his right hand. If it was sore, it didn't slow Todd down from digging in and eating more than any of them.

Uncle Bob sat at the other end of the table with Marti on his right, next to Todd. She made comments on how good it was to all be together again and how delighted she was to have them around her table. Her comments sounded sincere enough and Bob's genuine affirmations with a hearty toast and a few jokes helped cover up any hidden messages of "imposing relatives" that Marti might be harboring.

Christy found herself spending most of the meal gazing across the table at her brother, David. His was the place that had been set in such a way as to balance out the space across from Marti and Christy. At sixteen, David was turning into an impressive young man. Since Christy didn't see him that often now that she and Todd were married, it surprised her how much he'd seemed to have changed and grown even since Thanksgiving.

The biggest change with David was that he'd used his hard earned money from his job at the pizza place to shed the glasses he'd worn since he was five and buy contact lenses. David had always resembled Christy's dad with his large build and reddish tints in his auburn hair. Without the similar glasses he was now taking on his own distinct look.

And look how cute he is. When did my brother get so adorable?

Most of her life Christy had viewed David as her pesky little brother. The nearly eight year spread between them meant that Christy did a lot of babysitting when he was a toddler. It also meant that she was off to college and married before he became interesting enough to carry on a complete conversation.

David was in the prime spot at the table to direct the conversation. And direct, he did. He had funny stories to tell about crazy things that happened at the pizza parlor and interesting facts about some of the new movies that were out in theaters that Christmas.

At one point Christy wanted to interrupt him and say, "Excuse me, but who are you and what did you do with my annoying little brother?" She wondered if the simple act of him coming out from behind those glasses had given him this added boost of confidence. What she admired the most was the way he openly expressed a deep respect for God and a polite respect for the rest of the adults at the table.

"By the way, Todd," David said. "I was able to get two days off from work so I can help out any way you can use me at your dad's house."

Todd gave him a thumbs up since his mouth was stuffed with mashed potatoes.

"My, my," Marti commented, leaning over to look past Christy. "I'm glad someone is enjoying the dinner to the fullest extent."

Todd swallowed and said, "It's delicious, Marti. All of it."

The rest of them joined in with their praise. Marti gave one of her regal waves of her hand as she lowered her chin and received their accolades. "As soon as our guest minstrel is able to take a break from enjoying his Christmas Eve feast, I would like to invite Todd to play my favorite Christmas carol for us on his mandolin."

Todd turned to Christy and saw the uh-oh look in his tired eyes. She knew that he'd forgotten to tell Marti that he wouldn't be able to accommodate her Christmas wish. His last words that morning when he'd left their room on the tail of their whispered argument was that he would let Marti know that he wouldn't be playing the mandolin for them. She was glad she remembered that. Otherwise Christy would have thought that she'd forgotten to follow through on that significant communication piece.

"I'll have to ask for your pardon this time around," Todd said.

"Did you fail to tell him, Christy? I distinctly remember writing the specifics on the note I left for you yesterday."

Christy leaned back. In every way she felt as if she was stuck in between the two of them.

"She told me," Todd said. "I forgot all about it. My apologies."

"Oh, Todd. I'm so disappointed. I was looking forward to your serenading us. Are you sure you couldn't go get your mandolin and come back? We'll wait."

Todd kept his gaze steady as he calmly said, "Not tonight."

"Why not? We have time. You can run over to the house while Bob gets dessert ready for us. I'm assuming your mandolin is in the garage with the rest of your belongings."

"No. It's not in the garage." Todd didn't offer an explanation.

Christy wanted to spill the story so badly. She wanted her life to turn into a teary Christmas special right then and there. She could see it all. First, she would reveal to her family that her selfless husband had hocked his mandolin in order to pay their electric bill. Then she would scamper over to the Christmas tree where she had tied a big, red bow around Todd's ransomed mandolin and hidden it behind the many boxes she'd wrapped for Marti.

In Christy's dream world, she saw herself bringing the mandolin to Todd and with all the love in her heart she would tell him how she had gotten his beloved instrument back. While he thought she was helping Marti wrap gifts, she had actually driven back to Murrietta Hot Springs, found the pawn shop and found the mandolin. In order to buy the mandolin back, she had tried to trade it for the sewing machine, only to be told that the old machine wouldn't bring in enough money.

To make up the difference she had cut off her long hair, sold it and bought back the mandolin. Then zipping effortlessly through horrendous holiday traffic, she had made it in time to calmly take her place at the dinner table without anyone noticing her short, short hair.

This would be the final tearful scene when she presented Todd with his beloved mandolin and he kissed her under the mistletoe while simultaneously playing a soulful rendition of Greensleeves in order to fulfill Aunt Marti's Christmas wish.

But this was not a dreamy, sweet Christmas movie. This was real life. And in Christy's real life she still had her hair and her sewing machine, but her husband did not have his mandolin.

Worst of all, there was nothing Christy or any of them could do to when Aunt Marti rose from the table a few minutes later and offered regrets for being unable to accompany them to the Christmas Eve service.

"This is the tragedy of being a sufferer of migraines," Marti said before bidding them farewell with the back of her hand pressed against her forehead in over-the-top melodramatic fashion. "One never knows when they will be stricken."

With a swish of her gorgeous, long, flowing holiday skirt, Marti made her exit and headed for the stairs. Christy knew her aunt would be sequestered in her hideaway bedroom for the rest of the night.

"Dude," David said under his breath and raising his eyebrows at Marti's dramatic departure.

"David," his dad said firmly.

"Norman," Christy's mother said softly as she reached over and touched his arm.

"Mom . . ." Christy began.

"Christy," Todd whispered.

Uncle Bob started laughing. It was such a jolly, belly laugh it seemed he was trying to do an imitation of Santa Claus. They all exchanged looks around the table and realized how crazy their family dynamic was.

"Bob," Todd said with a jovial nod.

"Todd," Bob retorted, still chuckling.

With an elbow nudge, Todd kept the silly game going as if any of them had the ability to control or direct the others by speaking their name with just the right inflection. "Christy," he said.

"Mom," Christy repeated, smiling across the table at her mother this time.

"Norman!" Christy's mom said it in such a funny, eyelash batting way that they all burst out laughing again.

Then as the final word their family's odd interactions at a Christmas gathering, David gave a long drawn out, "Duuuude."

eighteen

$\mathscr{C}$hristy's mom quietly took on the role of holiday hostess after Marti made her departure from the dinner table. She suggested they save dessert until after the candlelight service and get to church early enough to find parking as well as room to all sit together.

Christy made a quick scramble upstairs to get a sweater. She paused before going down to join the others and stepped with quiet paces over to Bob and Marti's bedroom door. Christy wanted to believe she could tap on the door and be permitted access to Marti's hideaway since she'd been allowed in earlier that day to wrap gifts.

She stood by the closed door and tried to decide what she would say if Marti let her in. It was important to Christy that her aunt came to the candlelight service. How else was her heart going to get softened and be receptive to the true meaning of Christmas?

From the other side of the door Christy caught the sound of a moan followed by the distinct and disturbing sound of her aunt vomiting.

She really is sick. All these years I thought she was faking it when she said she had a migraine. I wonder if there's anything I can do for her.

Hurrying downstairs, Christy sided up to Uncle Bob and said, "I could hear Marti getting sick. Do you think she'll be okay if we leave her?"

Bob nodded. "She'll let me know if she needs me. This is something she's struggled with for a long time. She definitely prefers to be left alone."

"Does she need anything?"

"No. She has medication. It takes a while to kick in. I bet she'll be tip top in the morning."

However, Marti was not tip top the next morning when the rest of them gathered around the Christmas tree, ready to open presents.

"Should we wait and see if she's feeling better later in the day?" Christy asked. "I know how much she enjoys this part of us being together at Christmas."

"No, she wanted us to go ahead without her," Bob said. "She'll find her way down if she's feeling up to it. Her main concern was that she didn't ruin the day for everyone else."

Christy caught her brother rolling his eyes at Uncle Bob's statement and she wanted to slug him. There were many times when Christy was the one rolling her eyes at what she thought was Marti's attempt to draw attention to herself or turn a perfectly normal moment into a dramatic scene. Christy had never entirely considered the possibility that Marti was truly suffering from a legitimate malady.

She refrained from scolding David. It seemed better to try to talk with him privately later. Otherwise Christy would be the one turning what was supposed to be a happy, fun, family time into a grand scene.

And then I would be the "Aunt Marti" this Christmas

morning. One Aunt Marti in this family is enough.

As everyone got settled in on the comfy leather sofas, Christy took in the beauty of the Christmas tree, shimmering with tiny white lights and silver ornaments. One of Aunt Marti's hobbies was to select a theme for her tree each year and buy all new ornaments related to the theme. This year her theme had been "Silver Bells" and each bough was adorned with a single, silver bell tied to the end of it so that whenever anyone brushed up against the tree one or more of the silver bells gave a shiver and sent out a merry chime.

Out the front windows the early morning sunlight cautiously inched its way through the lacey December mist and cast a muted glow on the wide stretch of ivory sand. The ocean had taken on its own silver bell tint as a strong winter wind kicked up the waves and slathered the shore with whisked up, whitened foam.

It wasn't the winter white of snow dusted trees and mountain peaks depicted on Christmas cards. What Christy was gazing at was Newport Beach winter white and to her it was more beautiful than any view she'd taken in of the Alps while she was going to school in Switzerland.

She felt enlivened by all the beauty surrounding her, including the beauty of being with her family.

Christy's mom was the first one to open a gift and the one she chose was Christy's handmade apron. Her *oohs* and *ahhs* were far above what Christy remembered her mom usually attributing to any of Christy's handmade gifts over the year. She passed it around so everyone could have a closer look.

"I love it, Christy. You are so clever. I never would have thought to make a pocket out of a dish towel. The size is just right. It's so sweet. Thank you, honey."

"I'm glad you like it, Mom." Christy felt more grown up and accomplished than she ever had at a Christmas gathering with her family. Over the years she'd attempted to make all kinds of gifts and most of them caused her embarrassment when they were opened. Especially the year she went a little crazy with puff paint on white tee shirts. This year she felt like she'd finally achieved the goal she'd always aimed for but always missed.

Her dad opened his gift from Christy and Todd next. Christy had adjusted her apron pattern to an extra-large, daddy-o size and had been creative with the fabric. His was made out of a muslin paint tarp that Todd brought home from one of his side jobs a few weeks ago. Christy had washed the tarp and laid out the pattern on part of the tarp that had the most interesting splatterings of paint colors. She trimmed it with black piping that she found in the 99 cent bin at the fabric store.

Her dad liked his apron, too. At least he acted like he did. He even put it on and demonstrated how he was able to tie it around his round middle.

"I thought you might wear it when you barbecue," Christy said. She honestly couldn't remember the last time her dad had barbecued, but it was a thoughtful possibility.

"By any chance is there a gift there for me from Christy?" Uncle Bob asked.

"Yes. And I bet you will never guess what it is." Christy picked his gift from under the tree and took it over to him.

"I'm hoping it's a barbecue apron." He tore off the wrapping and expressed appreciation and delight that was equal to what Christy's parents expressed.

While Christy was making Bob's apron, which was similar to her dad's, she wondered if a barbecue apron might bring unpleasant memories back to her uncle. Several years ago Uncle Bob had tried to get his old gas grill to light and it burst into flames. He was severely burned and still had scars on the side of his jaw and ear, although they were now barely noticeable after several skin grafts and plastic surgery.

"You did good, Christy," Uncle Bob said. "These are top notch."

"I'm glad you like them."

Todd stroked Christy's stocking covered foot with his bare foot. She looked over at him and received his wink and grin. It was one of those glimmering moments when she realized *I am married. This is my life. These are my people. I am loved.*

The sweet glow of those anchoring thoughts settled on her spirit and Christy felt as if she'd just received a little gift from God in the midst of all the chaos of the past week and the uncertainty of the last few months. She may not have a job or a home or any inkling of what the future held, but she had this; a loving husband, two steady, caring parents, a brother who was turning into a fun person to be around and a generous aunt and uncle who had made their beautiful home the family gathering place.

For the moment, this was her favorite gift of all.

David, who had been patiently waiting to get to open one of his gifts, said, "I can't decide if I should get it over with and open my gift from Christy or start with something from Aunt Marti."

"Don't worry, David. I didn't make an apron for you."

"But I did," Todd teased. "I thought you could use a carpenter's apron when you helped me over at the house."

David's thick eyebrows folded in a scowl.

Todd laughed. "I'm only messin' with ya, man. Go ahead. Open your gift from us."

David's gift from Christy and Todd was one of Todd's old skateboards that he'd renovated with new trucks and some cool stickers to cover the worst dings.

"This is the one you taught me on, isn't it?"

Todd nodded.

"This one has always been my favorite. They don't make

'em like this anymore."

"I know." Todd was still playing footsie with Christy. "I have mine in the car so we can get some time in the driveway this afternoon."

"Awesome," David said.

Christy couldn't stop grinning. David was turning into a Doug-in-the-making. All he had to do was start giving everybody great bear hugs and he would definitely be the next Doug.

For many years her family's tradition was to put out a lot of nibble food and lounge around in their pajamas on Christmas morning. The last few years her dad had especially liked saving Christy's gooey bars for the gift opening time. She had added a plate of them to the finger foods on the coffee table and watched as her dad reached for another one.

"These are my favorite, Christy," he said before taking a bite.

"I know."

Christy's mom was more interested in the plate that held the small chunks of cheese. Wisconsin dairy farm roots ran deep in her parents. And the older she got, the prouder she was of her upbringing. One year her aunt and uncle had received several gift assortments of "Cheeses from Around the World" and Bob had made a joke of offering cheese to them every time they turned around. Ever since then, a variety of cheese had been added to their Christmas morning nibble-fest. Christy knew it was another one of their silly, sweet traditions that would carry on for many years.

The gift opening continued for another hour and a half. Marti's gifts for each of them were thoughtful and expensive and mostly of the electronic or apparel variety. As grateful as Christy was for all the lavish gifts, her favorite present was the gift Todd gave her. It was a handmade sewing basket complete with a pin cushion, needles, two dozen spools of thread in every primary color, a good pair of scissors and a tape measure that rewound itself into the shell of a pink snail.

"I love this, Todd! Thank you so much. My grandma used to have a sewing kit like this."

"I know. You mentioned it, oh, a hundred times over the last few months."

Christy looked over at her mom. "Look. How cute is this. Did you know about this?"

Her mom nodded.

"She was my accomplice," Todd said while Christy's mom grinned proudly.

"Do you recognize the snail measuring tape?" her mom asked.

"Yes. That's why I said my grandmother used to have one like this."

"That actually is your grandmothers. She sent it for you when I asked and she's so pleased that it's yours now."

Christy got a little teary. She loved her grandma and wished she could have come from Wisconsin to spend Christmas with them. Christy had lots of enchanting memories of spending childhood Christmases with her grandparents when she was growing up on the farm in Wisconsin. When Christy was in high school and her family moved to southern California, she thought it was the best thing that ever could have happened to her and to her family.

Now that she was older, she missed so many of the Midwest values and traditions she'd taken for granted when she was growing up. Her brother was eight when they moved and didn't have half the memories Christy had of their cousins, Grandma's cookies, and her Grandpa's rumbling voice as he read the account of the first Christmas from the Bible in Luke chapter two.

Every Christmas Eve service at their small church was highlighted by two things in Christy's memory; sitting up straight on wooden pews and holding a candle, waiting in the darkened chapel for her grandmother to light the wick, and her grandfather's reading of Luke chapter two. She decided that she'd ask her dad if he could start reading it every Christmas Eve starting next year. Christy always liked the thought of sharing the golden, candlelit moment of Christmas on Christmas Eve and celebrating the gift God gave us when He gave us His Son on Christmas morning by giving gifts to the ones she loved.

As the others were sorting out the final gifts that waited to be opened, Christy cuddled up next to Todd and whispered, "When we have children, I hope we'll live close enough to my parents so that they'll always have grandpa and grandma memories of their Christmases."

Todd kissed her on the side of her head and said, "You are a blessed woman, Kilikina. I never had a Christmas with any grandparents."

Christy looked up at him. There were so many things about her life that she'd taken for granted and had never considered how different it must have been for Todd during his childhood. He and his dad had been everything to each other – mother, father, sister, brother and every other relative.

In that tender moment beside the Christmas tree, Christy understood more clearly why Todd needed to do the renovations on his dad's house without any payment. His father's wedding was the top priority in the coming year. Todd and Bryan had been all the family the two of them had for every birthday and holiday. This was Todd's way of giving a deeply thoughtful gift to his dad. This was his only way of holding on to and continuing his family traditions and memories – Todd needed to save the house he'd grown up in as a way of showing his dad how much he honored and loved him.

Christy made a promise to herself that she would not complain again about Todd putting all this effort into the renovations or not bringing in any income. He had to do this. She had to find a job. That was how she would be able to free Todd up so that he could have the luxury of giving this great gift to his father.

As soon as the gift giving time was over and the wrapping paper was all cleaned up, Christy started looking online for a job. The first potential position she found was at a grocery store bakery. It wasn't her dream job but the grocery store was located less than a mile from Bob and Marti's. She figured that if they did end up selling one of their cars, she could still walk to work.

She sat quietly at the kitchen counter and filled out the application without telling anyone what she was doing. Her dad was taking a nap in the den with the television on. Todd and David had taken their skateboards out to the street and her mom was loading the dishwasher while Uncle Bob returned from taking out a trash bag stuffed with crumpled gift wrap.

Christy had just pressed "send" when Marti came downstairs without make-up, which Christy thought might be a first. Marti had on a cute, designer resort wear outfit with a zip up jacket.

"Merry Christmas," Marti said with a faint wobble in her voice.

"How are you feeling?"

"Better. Thank you, Christina. How is everyone doing down here?"

"It's good to see you back in the land of the living," Uncle Bob said. "What can I fix for you? A double dose of your 'migraine hang-over remedy.'"

"Yes, please. I would be so grateful."

Uncle Bob went to work, preparing the blended concoction with some frozen spinach, frozen blueberries and several scoops from canisters of healthy looking protein and energy powders along with some sort of tiny seeds which he sprinkled in. He added lots of crushed ice and left the mixture to whirl in the high powered blender. The result was a thick shake that had a purplish, gray tinge.

"Would it be an inconvenience for you to make me a cup of jasmine tea, as well?" Marti asked, taking a seat beside Christy at the kitchen counter. Christy clicked out of the job application file and returned to the screensaver image. It seemed best to avoid anything that might initiate a conversation with Marti about anything that would entice her to offer her opinion.

"Coming right up. Anyone else want a cup of tea? Coffee?"

"Jasmine tea sounds good," Christy said.

"I guess I'll join in, too," Christy's mom said.

"But you drink coffee," Marti said.

"I'll try some jasmine tea."

"You won't like it."

"Maybe I will." Christy's mom closed the door on the dishwasher and took a seat on the kitchen counter stool on the other side of Christy. Christy felt like she was the jam in a cynical-sister-sandwich as the three of them sipped their tea and Marti tried her best to convince Christy's mother why she shouldn't like it. Christy's mother calmly assured Marti that she did like it and that was that.

"Well, good," Marti said at last. "Now I know what to get you for Christmas next year."

Christy used her cup of tea as more of a hand warmer than a drink as she drew in the fragrant steam. She was glad no one was asking for her opinion on the tea or anything else at the moment. In years past, Christy had never been especially sympathetic or attentive during Marti's re-entry sessions when she seemed to be given a wider berth to try to navigate her bullish self back into the harbor where everyone else was calmly anchored.

This time Christy felt a new sympathy for her aunt, even though she didn't think she needed to be so snippy. In an effort to realign the triangle she'd been caught in, Christy said, "You didn't get to open your gifts yet, Aunt Marti. Would you like to open them now?"

"No. I'd prefer to wait until later this evening."

Todd and David entered through the back door that led to the garage. They were red faced and Christy guessed they both had a few new bruises somewhere. It had been weeks, maybe months since Todd had gotten out on his skateboard. She could tell that the skate session had been good for both of them.

The guys went right to the refrigerator for something to drink and stood across the counter from the three women, guzzling the bottles of cold water. Todd grabbed a paper towel and wiped his forehead.

"Interested in a walk on the beach?" Todd's gaze was on Christy. He looked happier and more alive than she'd seen him in quite some time.

Before Christy could answer with a heartfelt, "Sure", Aunt Marti said, "I'm not quite up to it. But don't let me stop the rest of you."

Todd came around to the side of the counter where Christy was seated between her mom and her aunt and leaning close to her he said, "That invitation was only meant for you, Mrs. Spencer."

Forever With You

nineteen

$\mathcal{M}$r. and Mrs. Spencer planted their bare feet in the cool sand and walked hand in hand down to the shore. The clouds had cleared and the morning fog had lifted. It was great weather for a long beach walk.

They fell into a leisurely pace, swinging their hands and exchanging three squeezes, their secret code for "I-love-you". Neither of them spoke. Christy thought the contented communion was too sweet to spoil with words. *When you are so blessed to be able to spend Christmas Day strolling down your favorite beach with your favorite person in the whole world, why would you clutter the moment with words?*

Todd, however, had a different idea. He clearly had something on his mind because he stopped walking halfway to the pier and said, "Let's sit."

The sand had not yet warmed up and the chill penetrated Christy's jeans as soon as she sat down. She was soon warmed, though, when Todd sat as close as he could and wrapped both his arms around her. He buried his nose in her hair and whispered, "I love you. I love this beach. I love being here with you."

Christy smiled. She turned her head and kissed his neck. Her cool lips tingled at the warmth of his skin and the taste of salt.

"I have something special for you." Todd pulled back and presented both his hands to her in downward facing fists, playfully indicating that her gift was in one of his closed hands.

Christy looked into his eyes and silently expressed, "You shouldn't have."

"Go ahead. Pick one."

She covered his left hand with her palm. He turned his hand over and opened his fingers revealing an empty hand.

She pointed to his right hand.

Todd uncurled his fist and revealed two delicate pearl earrings. The luster of the creamy pearls seemed to glow in the thin, winter sunlight.

"They're beautiful."

"They're for you." Todd took her right hand in his and turned her palm up. He placed the earrings in her hand and said, "They remind me of us. A perfect pair. And since pearls are formed in a tight, dark place, basically as a result of irritation, I can relate. Don't you think that's what's been happening with us? All the difficulty and pain of the past few months is creating something in us and in our marriage that is of great value."

Christy lifted her chin and whispered, "Thank you so much, Todd". She barely finished her short sentence before his lips found hers and they shared a lingering kiss charged with tender affection.

She drew back and gave him an inquisitive look. Todd grinned. "You want to know where I got 'em, right?"

"Well, they look expensive and . . ."

Todd pressed his finger to her lips, gently silencing her. "It's a great story. You're gonna love this. When I took my mandolin into the pawn shop the owner was putting jewelry in the front case. I saw the earrings and started thinking about how they're formed inside an oyster and, well . . . I like analogies."

Christy grinned. "Yes, I know."

Todd planted a kiss on the side of her head. "The manager recognized me from last summer when he dropped off his stepson at church for volleyball. Do you remember a freshman guy named Zach?"

Christy shook her head.

"You were there that night and you found out it was his birthday. So you convinced him to come back on Sunday and you made peanut butter cookies for him. Those ones with the chocolate candy in the middle."

"Oh, yes. I remember him. He was so surprised when I gave him the cookies."

"Apparently they were his favorite kind."

"I didn't know that."

"You made his birthday. He didn't stop talking about it. His dad remembered what you did. When he figured out that I was looking at the earrings as a gift for you and realized that I obviously didn't have any money because I was pawning my mandolin, he told me to take them. No charge. He said it was his way of saying thanks for being so nice to his son."

Christy gazed at the pearls in her hand. She hardly knew what to say.

"Go ahead," Todd said. "Put 'em on."

Christy bit her lower lip.

"What? What's wrong?"

"These are pierced earrings. I don't have pierced ears."

Todd pulled back her hair and looked at her earlobe as if he'd never seen it before. "But I've seen you wear earrings before."

"I've always worn ones that clip on."

"Can you make these into clip-ons? Or better yet, can't you get your ears pierced? Don't you just stick a needle through and then put in the earring?"

Christy gave Todd a bemused look. "Yes, something like that." Sometimes she really wished he'd grown up with a sister so that she didn't have to be the one to educate him on things like this. He was always amazed and slightly in awe when she explained to him how her female body worked or any of her beauty routines.

Christy carefully slid the earrings into the front pocket of her jeans. "I'll figure out something. Thank you. I love them."

"Thank you for loving kids like Zach. I was like him when I was his age. A little love and kindness goes a long way. You are generous and so caring, Christy. You have no idea how much you affect other people's lives with your thoughtful ways."

Christy could feel her face beginning to get rosy at Todd's comment. He pulled back and looked at her.

"Are you blushing?"

Christy looked down. "It seems so small and kind of trivial in the whole, big view of life."

"Hey." Todd lifted her chin with his rough fingers. "Nothing in God's kingdom is trivial or small when it's done in love. That's what makes what you do such a gift, Kilikina. You love to create the gifts but you also love the people you're creating the gifts for."

She agreed. It was true.

"Even if you barely know the people, you love doing things for them and those small things help them feel God's love for them."

She'd never thought of it that way before but deep inside her spirit was resonating with everything Todd was saying.

"I don't know why we never gave it a name before, but I

think I know what your spiritual gift is."

Christy raised her eyebrows, waiting to hear what he would say next. For many years when others were talking about how they had the gift of teaching or faith or service, Christy always shrunk back. She never admitted it to anyone but she'd come to the conclusion that she didn't have a particular spiritual gift. And that always made her feel embarrassed.

Todd's expression was fixed on her when he said, "It's hospitality. That's your gift, Chris. You are energized by expressing God's love for people through making them feel as if they are always at home whenever they are around you."

Christy's eyes began to mist over. That was the same conclusion she'd come to several months ago. Hearing Todd affirm it was a huge boost for her.

"Yep. You definitely have the gift of hospitality," Todd repeated, looking out at the ocean. "That's interesting."

"Why is it interesting?"

"Because I saw a bit of it when we were in Amsterdam. Do you remember how you wanted to just get married then and there and work at that hospitality house?"

Christy had forgotten about that

"Maybe that's why I wasn't catching the vision for the research assistant job," Todd said. "It didn't seem like something you had wanted to do all your life."

"It was like I told you. I wanted to have better hours so I could be with you more."

"And here we are," Todd said with a grin. "Nothin' but lots and lots of hours together during the past few months and on into the weeks ahead."

"I know." Christy looped her arm through Todd's and leaned her head on his shoulder. "I got what I wished for. Minus the having a job part of it."

Todd rested the side of his head on hers. She could feel

his voice rumble as he prayed for them, for their future, for jobs, for new ministry opportunities, for a dwelling place that didn't involve Marti's approval or disapproval and then he prayed that God would give them children.

Christy extracted herself from their short stack of head to head coziness and looked at Todd as he said, "Amen."

"Are you asking God to give us a baby now?"

"No."

"But you just said . . ."

"I can't wait to have kids," Todd said. "You know that. But I can wait until its God's timing. We have a couple things going on right now that wouldn't make this the best time to start a family."

"Oh, you mean like both of us being unemployed, homeless and down to our last pennies?"

"Yeah." Todd grinned. "Like that."

Christy gestured toward the vast ocean. "But this is the crazy part. Look at us. It's Christmas Day and we're sitting on our favorite beach, with our bellies full. I have pearls in my pocket and dinner will be waiting for us back at Bob and Marti's. God is taking good care of us."

"Yes, He is." Todd stood up. "And that's what gives me faith to start praying for our kids and get them all pre-prayed up now. Why wait until they're born?"

Christy smiled and took Todd's hand as he offered her help in getting up.

For another half an hour they walked barefoot through the cold, damp sand at the shoreline with their arms closely linked around each other's waist. They discussed baby names, job possibilities, dwelling place options and how difficult, and at the same time exciting, it was to follow Jesus with such complete trust and abandonment.

"You know how I've been reading up a lot on Moses the past few months?" Todd asked. "There's one part that really got to me. It's in Exodus chapter twenty. Moses was about to go up Mount Sinai and the mountain was covered with thick, dark clouds. It says that all the people drew back, but Moses stepped into the deep darkness because God was there."

Christy wasn't sure where Todd was going with this.

"I love that line; that Moses stepped into the deep darkness because God was there. It's the mystery part of following God. I feel like that's what we're doing now. Instead of pulling back in fear, we're stepping into the deep darkness of the unknown future. Into the oyster, sorta. And the reason we're doing it is because we know God is already there and more than anything, we want to be with Him."

Christy loved hearing Todd get excited about a nugget that he had mined from reading God's Word. In years past he would mull over the verse or phrase he'd come upon for a few weeks and then end up writing a song about whatever intimate glimpse into God's goodness that he'd discovered. She hoped he would write a song about this new mysterious truth.

They had made their way back to Bob and Marti's house where as soon as they entered, they felt the brusque kiss of the warmth of the house on their windblown faces. Christy and Todd joined the rest of the family in the den where they were watching one of Aunt Marti's favorite Christmas movies. She seemed to be feeling much better and everyone was in a good mood.

Christy forgot about Todd's Moses comments until the next morning. She was alone in the living room waiting for Todd to come downstairs so they could go meet Doug and Tracy for coffee when Todd's words from yesterday afternoon came back over her.

Moses stepped into the deep darkness because God was there.

Christy lingered in the living room watching the rolling

fog as it moved toward the ocean on this sunless December morning. She pulled her sweater close and couldn't help but wonder where she and Todd might be spending Christmas next year. Would they live close enough to her family to be able to be with them? What if they had a baby by next Christmas? The timing wouldn't be ideal. They'd established that during their talk on the beach yesterday. But it wasn't impossible.

Wasn't that what the angel Gabriel said when he told Mary that even though she was a virgin she was going to have a son and name Him Jesus? "Nothing is impossible with God." Nothing.

Christy let those thoughts rest on her until she was comfortable enough to carry them with her. She didn't want to be afraid in this deep darkness. She wanted her faith to grow. She wanted to trust God in new ways. She'd been saying that for the past few months and in many ways she could see that she had grown and was trusting God with more confidence than ever before. It was a good feeling. A good Christmas, twinkle lights and the fragrance of evergreen sort of feeling.

Todd strode into the living room wearing his navy blue hoodie and a pair of shorts. "Ready to go?"

"Yes. I'm ready."

"It's official. The north swell is heading our way."

Christy caught the look of excitement on Todd's freshly shaven face. She knew he had started checking the surf reports last night before they went to bed and awoke with surfing on his mind. The first thing he said was that he'd wax up one of his dad's old surfboards. He knew of at least two boards that had been securely stored in a hidden shelf in the rafters of the garage. They had managed to stay hidden from the disrespectful former occupants of the house and when Todd discovered them a few days ago he was pretty happy they were untouched.

"The waves are supposed to be five to six feet by tomorrow afternoon and up to twelve feet in two days if the swell continues."

"Cool." Christy said.

"After we meet with Doug and Trace this morning I wanna get to work on the house because at this time tomorrow the waves should be kicking up."

"Sounds good."

They were about to walk out the door when Aunt Marti called to them from the top of the stairs. "Before you leave, may I have a moment?"

Christy and Todd waited by the front door as she made a majestic descent down the stairs wearing a long, luxurious robe and matching pink slippers.

Christy wasn't sure if they should brace themselves for a scolding or a blessing. It was hard to tell what was coming based on the fixed expression on Marti's face.

Marti took the last two steps leisurely. "I've had time to give quite a bit of thought to the arrangements."

"Oh, I forgot," Christy said. "I'm sorry. I'll check them for dead leaves and clean them up when we get home."

Marti looked appalled. "Whatever are you talking about, Christina?"

"The flower arrangements. On Christmas Eve you asked me to keep an eye on the arrangements the florist delivered and check for any wilted leaves. I forgot to check them yesterday."

Marti rubbed her forehead as if she were coming down with another migraine and the sole source of her agony was with Christy.

"I'm referring to the arrangements regarding your stay here."

"Oh."

Todd muffled a chuckle.

Marti seemed undeterred by their comments. "I've decided that two weeks should be sufficient."

"Sufficient?"

"Yes. Sufficient time for us to be imposed upon this way."

"We didn't mean to impose," Todd said firmly.

Marti's thin lips curved up in a terse smile that sent a shiver down Christy's spine. Without words, Marti seemed to be saying, "Oh, but you did."

What she said out loud was, "Surely you can see how we love hosting you and David for the holidays. However, I have workmen coming on January fourth to start in on the upstairs guest bathroom. It won't be convenient for you to be occupying the guest room after the third so you'll need to make other arrangements."

"But, we . . ." Christy had to catch a quick breath.

Todd finished her sentence with more grace than she ever could have mustered. "We are very grateful for your hospitality."

With a wave of her hand Marti said, "You don't need to thank us, Todd. We're family."

We're family?

Every muscle in Christy's body felt the blow of Marti's ironic words on the tail of their blunt eviction.

Todd quickly took Christy's hand in his and held it tightly as if he were applying pressure to the soul wound that had just punctured her. He opened the front door and led her out into the cold, dark mist of the early morning.

She got in the car without saying anything and numbly stared out the window all the way to the café. The words Todd had told her during their walk yesterday kept rolling over her.

Moses stepped into the deep darkness because God was there.

twenty

*A*dorable little Daniel threw his toy truck across the floor for the fourth time and Tracy leaned over to pick it up.

For old times' sake the two couples had selected Hansen's Parlor as their place to meet for coffee. It used to be an old fashioned looking ice cream parlor and Tracy had worked there as a waitress in high school. Christy and Todd had made a lot of memories at Hansen's Parlor back when he always ordered the mango shake with an extra pineapple wedge on the side.

Hansen's had undergone a major renovation. They now served meals as well as ice cream and had an extensive list of specialty coffees and other beverages, including new and improved mango smoothies. The interior décor had changed to a shabby chic, beach style with white washed walls, aqua blue and orange distressed tables and lots of starfish and nautilus shells adorning the walls in glass covered window boxes. The only thing that hadn't changed was the name.

Daniel threw the truck once again and then arched his

back and let out a piercing wail.

"He's so tired," Tracy said, reaching over and relieving Christy of her auntie duties moments before the kicking started again. Tracy gave Doug a strained look and handed Daniel over to him.

Six foot tall, walking teddy bear of a dad, Doug, scooped up the bundle of flailing toddler and said, "Let's go outside, buddy boy. You and me. Come on. No need to holler. Say bye-bye to Uncle Todd and Auntie Christy."

Doug tried to flap Daniel's arm for him in a cute little wave but Daniel would have none of it. He wailed at a decibel Christy didn't think she'd ever heard before.

As soon as Doug and Daniel were out the door, Tracy let out a sigh of relief. "I'm sorry, you guys. I think he's getting his eighteen month molars because as I'm sure you noticed, he's constantly drooling. We should have left him with my mom this morning."

Petite, blond Tracy, with her heart-shaped face and soft voice, had very little left in her face of her young girl look. As a teen, she always was mistaken for being younger than she was. She definitely looked more mature now. Her figure was as petite as ever but she looked broader in the shoulders, which wasn't a surprise after carrying around their little ball of energy.

"You don't ever have to apologize," Christy said. "We love Daniel. And we love you guys. It's been way too long since we've been able to get together."

"I know." Tracy took a long sip of her vanilla latte that had cooled since she ordered it twenty minutes ago. "I can't believe everything you were just telling us. And now Marti is saying you have to be out of their guest room by next week. Will you be able to move over to Todd's dad's house by then?"

Christy looked to Todd for the answer.

"I don't think the place will be livable by then," he said.

"You know you can always come and stay with us down in Carlsbad." Tracy kept her eyes on the front window as if she were ready to be on back up baby duty at any moment. "Our place is tiny, as you know, but you'd be welcome with open arms."

"Thanks, Trace," Todd said. "That means a lot."

Tracy's expression lit up. "Actually, I just had an idea. Do you remember the bungalow my parents own on Balboa Peninsula? They've had it since I was in elementary school and rent it out every summer. It's off season now and unless they have someone in there, it usually sits empty from January until Easter vacation."

Christy and Todd exchanged hopeful glances. "Do you know how much the rent would be?" Christy asked.

"No, but I can ask them, if you'd like."

"Yes," Todd said. "Definitely. Ask them for us."

"It's really small and I think there's a guy living there right now who just got a job at my Dad's company."

"What kind of job?" Todd asked.

"Insurance salesman. I don't know if you knew that's what my dad is doing now. He's the manager of an insurance office in Corona del Mar."

"Do you think he might have any more openings for an unemployed youth pastor?" The way Todd said it made Tracy frown sympathetically.

"I can ask him. It's tragic, though, the way you were practically forced to resign."

"It was my choice."

"But still, the way it went down sounds shady to me. That church had no idea what a gift they had when you were there. I know that the times when Doug was helping you out, back when you first started, he always said that you were doing the job of two pastors. Not to mention all the extra things you volunteered to do, like worship and missions trips."

"When you're doing what you love to do it doesn't feel like work." Todd said it like he meant it.

"And you loved those teens," Tracy said. "I know you did."

"We both did." Todd gave Christy a look of determination and courage and she felt her heart swell with admiration for him. She knew he could easily tip and go to a low place as a result of talking through all this with Doug and Tracy.

"It just seems so unfair," Tracy said. "I wish we could have been there to help you fight your way through the whole mess."

"Fair or unfair," Todd said. "It's done. Christy and I both know that season is over. And the thing is, I love what I'm doing now with the renovations at my dad's place. Of course, there's no income from that, but I know it's what I need to be doing right now."

"Doug and I were just talking last week about how difficult it is to get a job these days, let alone a job you enjoy, even if you have a degree." Tracy pushed aside her emptied latte cup and brushed the crumbs from her carrot and raisin muffin off the edge of the table and into a paper napkin, which she crumpled up and tucked into the cup.

"Yes, we know a little about that," Christy said quietly.

Todd twirled the paper wrapper from the straw, twisting it into a knot. "All I know is that we have to trust God more than ever."

Tracy reached across the small round table where they sat in the corner and gave both Todd and Christy's arms a squeeze. "I just hate the way everything turned out for you."

Christy didn't want their time with Tracy to turn into a pity party. The first part of their time together had focused on all the God things that were happening in their lives. Neither she nor Todd had sounded pathetic about their predicament then. She didn't want to start sounding dismal now.

"The best part is that we've definitely grown closer together through all this." Todd looked at Christy with an affectionate smile and a romantic wink.

"And we know it's going to work out." Christy added, hoping she sounded confident and convincing the way Todd did whenever he spoke those words. "We don't know how, but we do know that God is doing something new in our lives."

"Remember when we were in high school," Tracy said. "And how we were told all the time to follow our dreams and pursue our passions?"

Christy nodded.

"I'm wondering now how to do that, realistically. You know what I'm saying? It's not as easy as we thought it was going to be when we were starry eyed and seventeen. The whole reason Doug and I moved to Carlsbad was because we thought we were following our dreams. We had this vision of being on our own and starting our life together in a little cottage by the sea."

"That's a good dream," Christy said.

"Yes. It was a good dream. But Doug and I are realizing that to make a marriage and family work you have to be practical and face the facts. We have to make decisions based on what's best for everyone, not just what will help us follow our individual dreams."

Tracy looked out the front window again and then checked the screen on her phone as if she were instinctively checking on Doug and Daniel.

"I'll tell you something that I know Doug would have told you if he were still in here. He and I are praying about moving back up here, to Newport Beach."

"You are?" Christy immediately liked the idea of Doug and Tracy being in Newport Beach again.

"We talked about it a lot yesterday with both sets of parents. We don't like the fact that Daniel is missing out on time with his grandparents. We have great parents. Not everyone can say that. We like being with them and we like their influence and involvement in Daniel's life. We were the ones who chased the dream and chose to put all the miles between us. Now Doug and I spend way too much time on the freeway every week and that's definitely not how we want to live."

Tracy turned to look out the front window again. "When you think of it, pray with us about moving up here, okay?"

"You can count on it," Todd said.

"Thanks, Todd. We wouldn't be able to make the move until the spring because of Doug's job, but we want to really soak the possibility in prayer."

Christy recognized the grateful look on Tracy's face. Anyone who was a friend of Todd's for very long knew that if Todd said he'd pray for you, you could count on it.

"I'll ask my parents about the Balboa bungalow," Tracy said. "And did you finish what you were saying about your dad's house, Todd? How long before it's ready to rent out again?"

Todd gave an abbreviated run down of how things were progressing. Christy was surprised to hear him say that he had workmen coming in that afternoon to fix the plumbing in the master bathroom and repair the kitchen sink. That was a promising update she hadn't heard. Originally Todd said he wouldn't be able to get any help until the first week of January.

Tracy looked down at her phone as it vibrated. "It's Doug." She took the call and told him, "Okay. I'll be right out."

With an apologetic look she said, "Sorry, you guys. Doug drove Daniel around the block and he fell asleep. We're going to try to get him down for a nap at my mom's." Tracy looped her large purse over her shoulder and said, "I know Doug's going to come over to the house to help you guys later this morning. I don't think I'll be able to make it but we want to spend as much time with you as we can. We'll be going back and forth to Carlsbad all week, but we plan to be here as much as we can since you guys are here."

Christy and Todd followed Tracy out to the car and gave her a hug. They waved to Doug and saw Daniel sleeping like a little angel in his car seat. Walking hand in hand to their car a block away, Christy hoped she'd always remember the closeness she and Todd experienced lately. From the brief glimpse they saw today of how life had changed for Doug and Tracy once they had a baby, Christy knew it would be that way for them, too, if and when God blessed them with a child. This was a season of sweet communion for her and Todd.

A nostalgic thought tugged her lips upward in a secret grin as she remembered an earlier season like this when she and Todd had officially become "boyfriend and girlfriend". The same feelings of togetherness had covered her during that season when she and Todd had painted a bookshelf that she bought at a garage sale here in Newport Beach. Those feelings of being knit together at the heart were a limited, early version of what she felt now. However, the sentiment was the same.

This is a time to cherish.

When they arrived at Bob and Marti's, the first thing Christy did was ask Uncle Bob if she could borrow one of his hats since painting was on the list for that day. She remembered how playful Todd had been when they painted the bookshelf years ago and she had no desire to end up with lots of paint splatters in her hair.

Uncle Bob presented her with a frayed baseball cap that he wore when he golfed. "Keep it," he said. "Your aunt keeps me well stocked in those designer caps. It will give her an unreasonable amount of joy to know that my inventory is depleted because it means she'll have an excuse to go shopping."

Christy adjusted the cap and pulled her hair through the small opening in the back, using the cap as her ponytail holder. She looked at Uncle Bob as if he were her mirror.

"You could not be any more beguiling. You know that, don't you?"

Todd walked into the kitchen wearing his work clothes and grinned. "There's the woman of my dreams."

Christy had no idea why both Todd and Bob were so complimentary of her in a baseball cap. Whatever the reason, she'd take it and be thankful. Her little heart was hungry and grateful for all the encouragement it could get. As much as she loved their time with Tracy and Doug, Christy felt stirred up inside over all the injustice of the way Todd had left the church. If he still had his position, even if it was difficult or part time, at least he'd have a job.

Christy made herself let go of those thoughts. They had work to do. As soon as she, David, and Todd arrived at the foul smelling house, Todd started in, giving Christy direction on what needed to happen in the kitchen. Every cupboard needed to be cleaned out. All food needed to be thrown out, all the dishes needed to be run through the sanitary cycle in the new dishwasher that had been replaced last week. Todd would then come in with a mixture of bleach and hot water and do a final cleansing.

Christy put on a pair of kitchen gloves and opened all the windows in the kitchen to help with the rancid odor that permeated the kitchen area. On her forage into the first of the cupboards under the kitchen island, as she was pulling out opened boxes of cereal and boxes of crackers, she found the source of the horrid odor. It was a bag of potatoes that had gone rotten. Never in her life had she smelled something so awful.

She immediately threw the bag of rotten potatoes into the trash bin along with the rest of the food and tied the top of the bag.

"What is that smell?" David asked coming in from the

living room.

"Rotten potatoes. Here, could you carry this out to the dumpster?"

"Only if you have a gas mask for me."

"Hold your breath." She handed over the bag, trying to not gag.

To his credit, David did the unpleasant job of getting rid of the trash without complaining. Christy stood at the opened window and drew in several deep breaths of fresh air before returning to the cupboard. She extracted the rest of the items in record time and took out the trash herself the next time around. Once all the cupboards were empty, Christy ran the dishwasher and started wiping down the countertops.

Bob arrived with more cleaning supplies. He had Christy leave while he sanitized the cupboards with his sprayer and mix of bleach and hot water. They left the kitchen to air out and put all the efforts of the afternoon into the big job for the day, which was painting the whole living room. Doug arrived just as the last tarp was put in place.

Most of the furniture had been removed, which made Christy sad. One of the chairs that was destroyed had been Todd's dad's favorite as long as Todd could remember. It was a Scandinavian-style relaxing chair with a high back and rounded arms made of wood. The fabric on the seat and back was tufted and the chair came with a matching tufted foot rest. In all her visits to this house over the years, that chair had been the landmark that made this "Todd's dad's house".

The space around Christy now felt vastly changed. It didn't feel like "Todd's dad's house". It was a blank canvas. When they finished the renovations, it would be something different. Something better. Something new.

Christy reached for one of the paint rollers. In many ways, she felt like her life was going through the same renovation process. She hoped her heart would come out of all the changes improved. She wanted the emerging season of their lives to be as cheerful as the warm "Tuscan Sunday" shade of deep yellow that she was now rolling on the wall.

With great hope, Christy allowed herself to dream a little dream that seemed impossible. She pictured herself living with Todd in the little Balboa bungalow and meeting up with Doug and Tracy at sunset for marshmallow roasts around a fire pit. She and Todd would both have jobs – good, decent jobs that they loved and they would find out they were pregnant at just the right time.

It was a good dream, just like Doug and Tracy's dream of their cottage by the sea in Carlsbad had been a good dream. But what did Tracy say about marriage and family being about making decisions based on what's best for everyone?

Christy felt the pinch as the needle of reality pierced her thoughts and her dream deflated. She and Todd were committed to a life of serving others. They knew that before they were even engaged. How could she graciously be hospitable if they lived in a five hundred square foot space? How important would it be to live close to her parents once they had children?

And why did she think she and Todd could live in Newport Beach? It was too expensive to live here. Her dream was presumptuous and unrealistic. She rolled it away as she rolled the paint on the walls.

Yes, it was time for a new season and a new dream. But not such a big, dreamy dream. She and Todd were in a low and humbled place. They needed to take what they could get and be grateful. It wouldn't have been like this if the leaders at the church hadn't made the decisions they made and forced Todd into his choice to resign.

The more Christy thought about it, the more obvious it was that the church leaders were responsible for them being in the impoverished predicament them were in now. After all the weeks of thinking, praying, processing and believing the best of their unexpected situation, for the first time Christy felt angry. Very angry.

Tracy's efforts to sympathize with them that morning had brought up all the feelings of how unfair this was for Todd and how awfully it had affected both of them. Christy imagined what it would be like to go to those church leaders and tell them exactly what they had done and how damaging it had been. She wanted them to know how hurt and angry she was at them.

But she knew she could never do that. It would make things worse. The whole mess was over. She needed to move on the way Todd was.

Christy wadded up her anger and tucked it into the back corner of her mind and closed the door. She wasn't ready to throw it out quite yet. But she definitely didn't want anyone, especially Todd, to know it was there.

twenty-one

*C*hristy stood in the shower, stretching her neck and letting the warm, pulsing water minister to her sore muscles. Over the last five days she and Todd had made heroic progress on the house. David put all his brawn into helping them the first few days and together they worked crazy, long hours each day. All the painting had stretched and pulled her poor body until she felt like a pretzel.

With additional help from Doug, Uncle Bob and a welcome parade of trained workmen, the renovation had leaped ahead of schedule. Every room except for the upstairs master bedroom was cleared, cleaned and repainted. Every broken faucet, cracked tile and damaged cupboard had been repaired.

The results were worthy of many smiles.

Late last night Christy and Todd had taken the time to step back, draw in a deep breath and admire their handiwork of the fresh, clean downstairs. She felt as if they had been competing on a television show where houses in need of a new life were being renovated in a short time and she and Todd were about to break the record.

Todd's words last night had been, "My dad is going to be so stoked. He wanted to do a lot of these renovations a long time ago. I wouldn't be surprised if he and Carolyn decide to move back here after they're married. At least for a while. He always loved this house."

"You love it too, don't you?"

"Always have."

Christy remembered Todd's words as she turned off the shower and reached for one of Marti's expensive, fluffy bath towels. When they first entered the house it felt like it was on life support. Now it was able to breathe again. The rescue efforts had been a great success.

Todd had scheduled a call to his dad in order to be able to give him the updates and show him all the changes. But Todd ended up cancelling the early morning call because the long promised winter waves, that had delayed their arrival, finally showed up late last night. Todd and Doug had gone out on dawn patrol before the sun rose that morning and Christy was certain they were going to surf until they dropped. An extended surf session was a reward well-earned after all the long hours at the house.

Since the guys were going surfing, Christy and Tracy made plans to go to coffee and leave Daniel with Tracy's mom. The winter waves had brought with them a chilly rain storm and last night Christy had dug through some of their boxes in the garage until she found a favorite old sweater that she hadn't worn in years. It was a sweater she had gotten before going to England with Doug and Tracy back when they were in college. Christy practically lived in this one warm sweater on that chilly trip. She thought it was a fun full circle to be able to wear it this morning when she was going to be with Tracy again.

Christy was dressed and about to slip out of the house when Aunt Marti called to her from the living room. "Do you have a moment, Christy dear?"

Over the past few days Christy had only seen Marti in passing. Christy hoped Tracy would have a final answer that morning on whether or not they could rent her parent's bungalow. If they could, and if they were able to manage what Doug had said would be "next to nothing" rent, then Christy and Todd would be able to comply with Marti's January fourth eviction notice and they could move out of Bob and Marti's without any more humiliating discussions.

Christy stepped into the living room and braced herself for whatever it was that her aunt might want to talk about this morning.

"Are you on your way over to Bryan's house again?" Marti was a picture of coziness. She was seated beside the lit up Christmas tree by the wide front windows, wearing her thick robe and plush, pink slippers once again. She seemed to be lingering in the afterglow of her beautifully decorated room now that she had her space all to herself.

"No, not yet. I'm meeting Tracy for coffee in a few minutes."

"Such a flurry of comings and goings around here this week! I barely saw David while he was here."

"I know. We kept him busy at the house. He was a big help. So was Uncle Bob. We couldn't have done it without them. The house is almost done. We're way ahead of schedule."

"So I've heard."

Christy pulled out her phone to check the time. "I need to get going."

"Yes, so you said. I merely wanted to tell you that I have my travel agent working on finding flights. I need to know what your plans are so that Robert and I can coordinate our flights with yours."

"Flights for what?"

"The weddings, of course. Bryan's and then Katie's. It's going to be quite a long journey. Do you have your flights booked yet?"

"No. We haven't had any time to work on our plans yet."

"But the weddings are only three months away."

"Yes, they are."

"Well, when do you think you might know what your plans are?"

"I don't know."

"In that case, I'll have my travel agent go ahead and make the arrangements for all four of us."

"That's okay. You don't need to book any flights for Todd and me. We'll work on it ourselves, Aunt Marti."

Her aunt eyed her with a flash of irritation over having her suggestion rejected. "I must say, you are certainly enjoying the opportunity to exert your newfound independence, aren't you?"

"My newfound independence?"

"Now that you're living off of someone else's money, I've noticed that you've become more assertive. You're making your own decisions. I've always found that to be an admirable trait for a young woman. And as we both know, Christina, decision making has never been your area of shining strength."

Christy reined back her immediate emotional reaction and said, "What do you mean by 'living off someone else's money'?"

"Isn't Bryan financing you and Todd now that he's come in to such a lucrative estate in the Canary Islands?"

"No. My father-in-law isn't financing us."

"Then he must be paying Todd handsomely for all the work."

"No. Todd volunteered to do the renovation. Bryan's buying the paint and carpet and everything, but Todd is not getting paid for the labor."

Marti looked stunned. "I thought you'd been given a nice sum from Bryan."

"No."

"Then what is your source of income?" Her eyes widened. "You and Todd aren't collecting unemployment, are you?"

"No." Christy felt her jaw clench.

"Well, then, I'm assuming his severance package from the church was substantial enough to carry you all these months."

"Todd didn't receive a severance package. We had a little bit in savings. That's what we've been using until we find new jobs." Christy wished she was not revealing all this to her aunt, especially right now. She tried to pull back and not say any more, but Marti's questions came at her like a swarm of bees and she felt like all she could do was swat at them and get out of there as quickly as possible.

"You're planning to get a job? How can you do that? You'll only be able to work for three months."

"I know."

"Who would hire you for three months?"

Christy kept her lips sealed about the results of the phone interview she had yesterday with the bakery at the grocery store. As soon as she told the manager that she'd need time off in April, the interview ended. Clearly, the answer was "nobody would hire us" but she didn't want to say that out loud.

Marti carefully scrutinized Christy. Her voice came out small and terse. "Christy, why didn't you tell me all of this? Your financial situation and your job situation are a disaster! I had no idea you had no income. I thought you quit your job because you'd received a large amount from Bryan."

"No. I didn't quit. I was laid off."

Marti's hand was at her throat. "Christina! Why would you keep all this significant information from me? This is devastating. How do you and Todd plan to get by?"

Christy fought to keep her emotions under control. "We'll keep looking for jobs and we think we've found a place to go to when we move out on January third. We'll find out today."

"What are you talking about? You're not going anywhere! You must stay here. I'll delay the guest room renovations. You and Todd can stay here as long as you need. Christy, I am flabbergasted." Marti paused and made a sour face. "I hate that word. I can't believe that was the word I chose to use."

Christy glanced at her phone again. "Thanks for the offer to stay longer but I don't think that will be necessary. I really need to get going."

"You can't leave now, Christina. We're in the middle of an urgent conversation. I still can't believe you didn't tell me all this."

"We're okay, Aunt Marti. Really. We can talk about it more tonight, if you'd like."

Marti shook her head. "I don't understand how you can possibly think you're okay when you are penniless, unemployed and homeless. I'm worried now that you two are delusional as well."

Christy hurried out the front door. She was immediately met by a gust of wind and a splattering of raindrops. Dipping her head, Christy pulled her sweater close and made a dash to her car, glad to be out of the swarm of stinging questions. She wished she'd told her aunt that she and Todd were depending on God for all the details of their future. He was their dwelling place. They weren't delusional. They knew that their Heavenly Father was forever with them.

As Christy repeated those thoughts on her way to the café she realized how audacious they sounded. Her heart felt wobbly. All she needed was just one piece of good news right now. That would certainly boost her confidence in God's provisions for them. To go home with a lead on a job for either of them or a confirmation on the bungalow would be all Christy needed to confirm to her aunt and to herself that God was taking care of them.

The place where Tracy had suggested they meet was called "Julie Ann's Cafe" and it was the perfect spot for a morning like this. In the summer the manager opened the huge sliding doors in the back and utilized their large garden space for outdoor dining. This morning the sliding doors where shut, the round patio tables were stacked and covered with tarps.

Inside the small café the tables were limited. Christy counted eight tables and she saw Tracy at the one by the fireplace. Two crossed logs flickered behind the ornate iron fireplace screen. Local greenery lined the mantle where a scattering of red berry decorations wove between a half a dozen mason jars. Each jar held a glowing candle.

"Tracy, this place is enchanting. I've never been here." Christy took the seat across from her friend and tried to smooth down her wild hair. "I hope you haven't been waiting long."

"No, I just got here. I'm glad there was an open table."

Tracy looked at Christy more closely and smiled. "Is that the same sweater I think it is?"

Christy rolled back her shoulders. "You remembered."

"Of course I remembered. I love that sweater. And I love all the memories connected with it."

"I wonder if I wore this sweater the day that you and I got a ride into town with Mrs. Bates. Remember? We wanted to go somewhere to talk so we hitched a ride from Carnforth Hall to that little tea shop." Christy looked around. "It was a bit like this place, wasn't it?"

Tracy nodded. "Do you remember our conversation that day?"

"I'll never forget it." What Christy remembered most clearly was the gentle way that Tracy had shared how much she loved Doug and had silently loved him for years. Tracy's patient love for the man who was now her husband had been tempered in the process by years of waiting for him to be drawn to her the way she had long been drawn to him. Her patience had provided a strong foundation for the love and life they now shared.

"I'll never forget your poem," Christy said. "The one you quoted to me that day about the garden of your heart."

Tracy smiled. "You know, that afternoon at the tea shop was the day you and I promised we'd be in each other's weddings."

"Yes, it was. And we were. I love that we were able to keep those promises."

"Me, too. But I have to tell you, Christy, I wish I'd done a better job of keeping in touch the last year or so. I regret that I didn't do more to keep our friendship green and growing."

"The way I see it, it doesn't matter how long it's been since we've seen each other. The minute we get together again we pick up where we left off. I love that about our friendship, Tracy."

"I know what you mean. I love that, too. But I still wish I'd done a better job of keeping in touch. You and Todd have been through so much the past few months and we didn't even know what was happening. I feel bad that we weren't in closer communication."

"Don't feel bad, Tracy. We weren't talking with a lot of people this fall. It was the way we coped with everything, I guess. Like we said the other day, it made us closer."

Their waiter appeared and announced, "We have spinach quiche today and waffles with bananas and maple syrup."

Christy gave Tracy a surprised looked. She'd never been to a café that had no menus and only offered what the chef decided to whip up in the small kitchen that morning.

"Small place, small menu," the waiter said, as if he'd seen the same look of surprise many times. "Which would you like? Or you can have both. Or you could order one of each and share. A lot of our regulars do that."

Tracy ordered the quiche and a vanilla latte. Christy ordered English Breakfast tea and nothing to eat. Since they hadn't been given menus she hoped the tea wouldn't cost more than what she had in her wallet at the moment.

"Change my latte to a tea, too." Tracy grinned at Christy. "Just like when we were in England."

Their tea was served in mugs as large as soup bowls and both of them laughed.

"Not exactly like the way they served tea in England," Tracy said. "This is bigger than the birdbath in our backyard."

Christy added milk from a pitcher that was shaped like a bird. The milk poured from the bird's open beak into Christy's "birdbath" mug and that got them laughing again. The first sip was warm and cheering and hid all but their eyes when they lifted the cups to their lips to take a drink.

The quiche was presented, steaming and larger than the doily lined salad sized plate it was served on. "Could you bring us another fork?" Tracy asked the waiter. "You have to help me with this, Christy. It's too much for one person."

"I'm picking up a theme here," Christy said. "Tiny café but enormous servings."

"I know." Tracy started giggling again. "Don't you feel like a Hobbit?" They both laughed and dug in to the quiche.

"You have no idea how much I have needed this girlfriend time." Tracy pointed at the quiche. "And this is delicious, by the way."

"Yes, it is." Christy tried to slow down and not eat so quickly.

"Do you get out like this a lot with friends from Rancho?"

"No. Hardly ever." Christy thought about how limited her socializing time with girlfriends had been over the past six months and she missed Katie and all their spontaneous fun times more than ever.

"Me, either," Tracy frowned. "We need times like this. I really hope Doug and I can move up here and that you guys can stay. I'm so bummed that the bungalow isn't available right now for you and Todd."

Christy froze. "What did you just say?"

"We need times like this."

"No, about the bungalow."

Tracy's brown eyes grew large. Her fingers went to her lips. "I thought Doug told you."

Christy shook her head. The room around her seemed to shrink even smaller. And so did all her hopes and confidence.

twenty-two

"Doug was supposed to tell Todd this morning," Tracy said. "But I just realized you haven't seen Todd since the guys went surfing so he wouldn't have had a chance to tell you."

Christy sat quietly, her appetite was gone.

"Oh, Christy. I'm so sorry to break it to you this way. My parents were waiting to hear back from the guy who is staying there. We found out last night that he decided to use his option to keep the bungalow until May. If my parents hadn't already signed the agreement with him last fall, they said they would have loved to have given the place to you and Todd for just the cost of the utilities."

Christy felt sick to her stomach. To live on Balboa Peninsula for just the cost of utilities was unheard of. It was a dream that would never be theirs. She tried to not let her expression reflect her deep disappointment.

"I should have realized that Todd wouldn't have had a chance to tell you yet. I'm so sorry."

"It's okay, Tracy. I knew it was a dream. Besides, my aunt

relented and she said we can stay at their place. It'll be fine. We only need a bed until April. Then we have the two weddings we'll be going to and we'll be gone almost a month."

Tracy looked concerned. "I know I keep saying it, but I wish you guys weren't going through all this."

"Me, too." Christy picked up her fork and poked at the remains of the quiche. "I wish the leaders at the church would have seen the value in Todd's ministry there, like you said the other day. He gave so much to those students. It was so unfair the way things were handled."

Tracy's empathetic spirit unfurled and she started agreeing with everything Christy said. For the next ten minutes Christy opened up the hidden closet where she'd wadded up her anger several days ago. She pulled it out and put everything on the table. Tracy nodded and scrunched up her eyes and took 1n everything Christy was saying with equal indignation.

All of a sudden Christy stopped her tirade. Everything inside her and in the space between her and Tracy seemed to have turned sour. All the rottenness she had been harboring was put out in the open in this charming, perfectly enchanting café where twenty minutes earlier they had been giggling like two Hobbit wives at home in the Shire. She knew this was not how she wanted to spend her time with Tracy.

In a small voice Christy said, "I'm sorry."

"Sorry? No, you don't have to apologize. This was really difficult for you."

"Yes, but I got angry about it and I just now realized that I hid that anger in a bad place. It's turned rotten." Christy immediately thought of the rancid potatoes and how her father-in-law's entire house had stunk so horribly because of those hidden, rotten potatoes. She did not want to pollute her whole life and her dearest relationships by holding on to that anger and carrying it into her conversations.

"Trace, I don't want to give space to anger and bitterness. So many God things have happened as a result of all this. I know that we're right where we're supposed to be, even though it looks so precarious. I don't want anger to sit inside me and poison me like that. Even if other people are unfair, God is always faithful. I believe that."

"I do, too," Tracy said in a calmed voice. "He works all things together for His good. I know He does."

Lowering her eyelids, Christy whispered a prayer of forgiveness in front of Tracy. She looked up and let out a relieved breath. "Okay. Now what were we talking about before I went all rotten potato on us?"

Tracy reached over and gave Christy's hand a squeeze. "Thank you."

"For what?"

"For being the best version of you that you can be. I need more examples of how to do that," Tracy said. "Doug has told me more than once that I cheer people on in the wrong way. I didn't understand what he meant but now I think I do. I get this sense of indignation whenever I see injustice and without realizing it, I think I help people get more fired up about how they were wronged. I really want to learn how to sympathize and empathize in the right way without helping them get all 'rotten potato' as you just said."

Christy lifted her birdbath of a mug and swished the last bit of cooled tea around in a small circle before swallowing the final swig. She couldn't disagree with Tracy's assessment of her misdirected empathy. It had been Tracy's comments about the unfairness of Todd's situation that got Christy thinking about how she had the right to be angry.

"Maybe we can help each other figure out how to be the best version of ourselves," Christy suggested.

For the next half an hour the two humbled friends talked about how they could encourage each other in the days ahead. They agreed that texting Bible verses to each other seemed to be a good place for them to start. They also decided to spend as much time together as they could since neither of them was certain about where they'd be living by this time next year.

"Forget this time next year," Christy said in response to Tracy's comment. "How about this time next month! Or even this time next week."

"Oh! I have a verse for that." Tracy pulled out her phone and scrolled through until she found what she was looking for. "Here it is. I'll text this to you. It's in Deuteronomy 33:27. 'The eternal God is your dwelling place, and underneath are the everlasting arms.' I love the 'everlasting arms' part. He'll catch us even if everything falls apart."

"That's what He seems to be doing. Todd has another verse he likes about God being our dwelling place. He'll like this one, too."

Tracy tapped a few keys on her phone and sent the verse to Christy. A warm smile grew on Christy's lips.

"What?" Tracy looked at her suspiciously. "What are you thinking right now?"

"I was just remembering how you did this for me years ago. Do you remember when you sent me a verse about how the Lord goes before us and how He never leaves us so we shouldn't be afraid?"

"No. When did I send you that one? Last year?"

"No, it was when I was a sophomore in high school."

Tracy looked astonished. "How can you possibly remember that?"

"Because I read it when I was about to be arrested and it gave me so much courage."

"Did you say, 'arrested'?"

"Yes. For shoplifting in Palm Springs. But it wasn't me. It was my friend who put the stuff in my purse. I can't believe I never told you this story."

"I think I remember parts of that story. It was so long ago. But I didn't know about the verse."

"You wrote it to me in a letter and I had it with me and I read it at just the right time."

Tracy grinned. "Talk about us knowing each other long enough to remember when we weren't exactly focused on becoming the best versions of ourselves."

"But we were. At least you were, back then. And you were encouraging me to do the same. I love this idea of texting verses to each other."

When they went their separate ways, Christy and Tracy had a plan. They decided to have a New Year's Eve party at Bryan's house. The carpet wouldn't be installed until the following week so they decided they could spread blankets on the cement floor and have an indoor picnic while the winter storm raged outside. Then they would implement the second part of their plan – a house blessing.

Todd loved the idea of the indoor picnic. When he asked what Christy meant by a "house blessing" she just smiled and said, "You'll see. Just trust me. It's an idea Tracy and I came up with."

He was standing in the kitchen at Bob and Marti's house, breaking into a box of crackers and dipping them into a nearly empty jar of peanut butter. Even though he was tired after the extended surf session that morning, he told Christy he was determined to finish painting the upstairs master bedroom at his dad's house.

Christy said she'd change and help him paint but before she could go upstairs to the guest bedroom, Marti entered the kitchen.

"Did Christy tell you that she and I talked this morning and I insist that you stay here as long as you need?"

Todd nodded, his mouth full of crackers.

Marti looked at Christy and added, "Even if your other housing arrangements are in place, Robert and I insist that you cancel them and stay here."

Avoiding the painful topic of the bungalow not being available to them, Christy thanked her aunt as sincerely as she could and said, "It's only for a few months. And you know that we're happy to help out here any way we can."

Marti flicked her wrist in the air and said, "No need. This puts an end to the discussion. Now, what are your plans for tomorrow evening? It's New Years' Eve, you know."

Marti's countenance perked up when she heard about the indoor picnic with Doug and Tracy. She insisted that she and Bob provide all the food and then offered to "stop by" in order to make sure the two couples had everything they needed.

"Don't stop by," Todd said.

Christy cringed. Even though she'd been thinking the same thing, she wished Todd hadn't been so blunt. This would not be a good way for them to start round two as the troublesome houseguests.

Todd took a swig of milk to wash down the last sticky cracker and added, "We don't want you to just stop by. We want you and Bob to come be part of the party and the house blessing."

"The what?"

Todd glanced at Christy and looked as if he realized he probably should have run the idea of inviting Bob and Marti past her first.

"The house blessing. You'll see what that means when you come tomorrow," Christy said.

Todd looked relieved that Christy had extended the invitation. "Bring a blanket or beach chair. We're low on furniture, as you know."

The next day, around five o'clock, Christy started preparing Bryan's house for the indoor picnic and blessing party. The upstairs master bedroom was finished. All the paint tarps had been removed and all the renovation trash and tools had been cleaned up. The house was empty and fresh and clean. Outside, the blustery storm continued to kick up a breeze and dot the windows with rain drops.

Todd had kept the heat off while they'd been working on the house since part of the purifying process had included giving the house lots of fresh air baths while they worked. A tinge of bleach fragrance fluttered in the air as a result of the deep cleaning Todd had done after the carpet and pad had been removed throughout the house. Not a dot of mold or mildew stood a chance in any corner of the house after Todd completed his rounds. Christy was thrilled that the house now wore nothing but the crisp scent of fresh air every time they entered.

Christy turned the heater on and could hear the humming sound of the warm air as it began to enter through the cleaned vents. She went to work lining the window sills with an assortment of flickering, battery operated candles that Uncle Bob had pulled out of a box in his garage earlier that afternoon. She hoped it would give an added feeling of warmth to the cavernous space.

Todd came in the front door wearing his navy Rancho Corona University hoodie and carrying a couple of beach towels that he dropped by the entrance.

"Do you think we could start the fireplace?" Christy asked.

"Sure. It was cleaned out by the guy who came and inspected it." Todd went over to where the gas fireplace was inset into the wall. It was a funky little fireplace and designed more for decoration than for warmth. Todd said he and his dad had used it only a dozen or so times but the renters had messed with it and it turned into one of the costly repairs.

"We might as well enjoy it," Todd said as he turned it on. The row of equally high bluish flames came alive and licked at the fake log.

"I like it," Christy said. "It's kitchy cozy."

Todd laughed. "Whatever that's supposed to mean."

"It's like Narangus," Christy said. "Part of an era gone by. Not exactly comfortable, but it's sweet and makes you smile whenever you look at it because of all the memories."

Todd's expression lit up. "Hey, did I tell you the carpet guy is coming tomorrow?"

"Tomorrow? On New Year's Day?"

"Yeah. The guy is a friend of my dad's. He said he wanted to get it done on his day off because his schedule is jammed up next week. He's giving my dad a great price."

"That's wonderful. The house is going to be completely done, then."

"I know. I told my dad today and he was just about as amazed as you and I have been at how fast it all came together."

"You talked to your dad today?"

"Yeah. When you went back to Bob and Marti's to take a shower I gave him a call and woke him up. He didn't mind, though, because we were able to do a video call. I walked him through the house. He got pretty choked up. He's super grateful."

Christy could tell that Todd was extremely pleased with the work he'd done and the fact that his dad was so appreciative. She would have loved to have been with Todd when he did the video walk through but it was probably good that Todd was able to make it into a father and son thing.

"Is your dad ready to list it for rent?"

"I asked him about that and he said he had to clear some paperwork of some sort. He said he'd let me know what he needed me to do for him as soon as he could. By the way, I like the candles. Nice touch."

"Thanks."

"Hey, did I tell you that Rick and Nicole are coming to-night?"

"No. When did that happen?"

"I called him yesterday. He just got a new job in Irvine and is moving up to this area next week."

Christy was surprised at that piece of information. "What about the business he started with his brother? Is Rick done with renovating restaurants?"

"Apparently he is. He told me yesterday that he wants to go back into management. He was happiest back when he was the manager at The Dove's Nest. He sold his half of the business to his brother and took a job doing some sort of restaurant training."

"And what's Nicole doing? Where's she living?"

Todd brushed past Christy and gave her elbow a squeeze. "I have no idea. But I'm sure you'll be able to ask her when they get here."

Todd went out to the garage and was making a lot of noise so Christy went out to see what was going on.

"Could you give me a hand?" Todd had moved the boxes stacked on top of Narangus and was about to move the beast.

"What are you doing?"

"Putting Narangus by the fireplace." He looked at her with an expression of eternal devotion. Christy couldn't be sure if the devotion was to her or to his beloved surfboard sofa. "Come on. How can we host a kitchy . . . what did you call it? Kitchy cozy party without Narangus? Think of all the years this pal has been with us; in parts and as he is now."

"He?"

"Yeah. He. Narangus is one of my Forever Friends, as you call them. I am officially inviting him to the party."

Christy didn't even try to protest. She and Todd muscled

Narangus through the kitchen door and placed their old pal in front of the fake fireplace. They sat on the surfboard seat, side by side and gazed at the fire.

Before they had a chance to get into a serious cuddle position the doorbell rang. "Come in," Todd called out. "It's open."

A guy they'd never seen before opened the door and stepped into the vacant space.

"Whoa." He looked around, clearly not expecting what he saw.

Todd got up and went over to him. "Hey. How's it goin'?"

"I thought there might be a party here tonight. Sorry. Wrong house."

"Yeah. This space has been reclaimed."

The guy made a quick exit just as Bob and Marti arrived. Christy and Todd joined them in carrying into the kitchen way more food than they needed for their small gathering.

"I didn't ask if you have any serving platters," Marti said to Christy.

"We have some dinner plates in the cupboard to the right of the sink. Those should work." She started organizing the food on the kitchen counter. Uncle Bob returned with a box full of various beverages and two bags of ice. Christy found a large salad bowl and filled it with ice and the bottled drinks.

Marti set off on her own walk through inspection of the house. Christy had just finished putting out the large wedge of macadamia nut encrusted brie next to a plate of creatively stacked crackers when Marti returned to the kitchen.

"Incredible. That's all I can say. This is a complete trans-formation. I'm amazed."

"Todd and all the guys did a great job, didn't they?"

A bright expression came over Marti. "Maybe I should hire him to do the renovations on the upstairs guest bathroom."

"I'm sure he'd be glad to help do whatever he can."

"Why didn't I think of this before? Todd?" Marti bustled into the living room as Christy did the final arranging of the food on the counter.

She heard the front door open and the jolly sound of Doug's big voice filling the house. "Hey! Look who's here! Bob and Marti!"

Christy entered the living room area just in time to see Doug envelope petite Marti in one of his signature "Doug-hugs". It seemed the embrace left her speechless.

Their next guests arrived a moment later and this time Todd was the one to make them feel especially welcomed.

"Rick! Hey, good to see you, man. Nicole, how are ya? Glad you guys could come."

Another round of hugs was followed by Doug saying, "I heard a rumor that you had food at this party."

"Yes, we do. Thanks to my aunt and uncle." Christy gave them a nod of appreciation and led everyone into the kitchen. As the others went around the kitchen island filling their plates, Christy drew aside to talk with Nicole.

Nicole wore her dark hair pulled back in a loose braid and had on a beautiful white sweater and fashionable jeans. She was a stunning young woman in a classic sort of way.

"I'm glad you and Rick were able to come," Christy said.

"Thanks for inviting us. Did Rick tell you about his new job in Irvine?"

"Todd told me. It sounds like a big change for him after all the restaurant renovations."

Nicole's dark eyes softened. "It's a good change. What Rick and Josh had going was so ambitious. It wasn't what Rick wanted to do, but he got on board in a big way and was driven to make the business a success. I thought the schedule and the expectations were going to kill him. It was way too intense and it changed him. The pressure nearly destroyed our relationship. Maybe he already told you guys all this."

"We knew that you'd called off the engagement," Christy said. She was surprised at Nicole's openness and grateful to be welcomed in this way. Rick and Todd had spent some time on the phone over the past few weeks but Christy still felt like she was just getting to know Nicole.

"I'm guessing he also told you that we're dating now and trying to take it one step at a time."

Christy nodded.

"It's probably the most backwards way of doing things but we both know now that this is what's best for our relationship. We're getting to know each other without being frenzied business partners with his brother. That was not a good triangle for us. The wedding had turned into one more deadline and there was no heart to any of it."

"I'm glad things are working out for you guys now," Christy said. "It must have been a difficult and brave step for you to end the engagement."

Nicole nodded. "It's hard to explain to people, but for us it was the right thing to do. I'm really happy for Rick with his new position in Irvine. He'll be doing what he loves and he'll have regular hours."

"What about you? Where are you living now?"

"I'm sharing an apartment in Costa Mesa with some girl-friends from Rancho Corona. I've been working at South Coast Plaza for the past month. I'm hoping they keep me on after the holidays."

"My aunt will be interested to hear that. She shops at South Coast Plaza all the time. What store are you at?"

"Gerard's. Have you heard of it? It's an interior design store."

"I'm sure Aunt Marti has heard of it. If she's not already a loyal customer, I'm sure she will be once she hears that you're working there."

"Good. Tell her to come in and buy something from me

this week." Nicole laughed at her pointed suggestion, but Christy took the request seriously.

"She'll do it. Believe me, she would love to singlehandedly become the reason why you keep your job. Once we tell her I'm sure she'll be in this week."

"I hope you come with her," Nicole said. "And maybe you and I can meet for coffee sometime."

"That would be great." Christy could understand why Katie and Nicole had become such fast friends when they were both Resident Assistants in the dorm last year at Rancho Corona University. Nicole seemed like the kind of person who could fit into any group of friends with ease and comfortably adapt to any situation. It was easy to see how Nicole could have entered Rick's life last spring, been swept up in his demanding business and gone as far as she could in the fast-paced relationship before blowing the whistle the way she did and asking to slow things down.

Giving Nicole's arm a friendly squeeze, Christy leaned in and in a low voice said, "You just might be the best thing that ever happened to Rick Doyle."

Nicole glowed. "I hope so. I love seeing how everything turned out for Katie and Eli, and I have a few dreams that everything will turn out the same for Rick and I eventually."

"Speaking of Katie," Christy suddenly remembered her promise to her wedding dress-less best friend. "Do you think you might be able to help me find Katie a wedding dress?"

Nicole's eyes lit up. "I'd love to. How fun!"

The two of them made shopping plans and figured out how they could get Katie in on the shopping experience on a video call.

Tracy slid up next to Christy and with a look of eager delight she said, "What do you think? Are we ready to get this house blessing started?"

"Absolutely."

twenty-three

"*O*kay, everyone!" Tracy waved her hands in the air to get their attention and get the small crowd to gather in the living room. "Christy and I came up with an idea and we need your help. We want to write God's blessings on the foundation of this renovated home before the carpets go in."

She held up a handful of permanent markers. "Let me tell you how this works. It's going to be . . ."

"Awesome," Doug finished for her.

Everyone laughed. Everyone, except for Marti.

"What we're going to do," Tracy said, "Is write verses on the cement floor in all the rooms. I have a Bible with me if you need help in looking up your favorite verse."

Rick took the lead and reached for one of the permanent markers. "Does it matter where we start?"

"No. Anywhere on the cement is fine. Do you have a verse already?"

Rick cast an affectionate glance at Nicole and said, "First Corinthians 13. Love is patient."

"It sure is," Doug said. "Here. I'll take one of those."

"Great." Tracy said. "Who else needs a marker?"

Everyone went to work except for Marti who stood by the door, holding her marker and rounding her shoulders back as if she had been called upon to stand back and supervise the event.

Christy watched as Todd went over to where Marti was standing and unabashedly got down on his knees by the door. He closed his eyes a moment, as if in prayer.

Marti stepped back and Christy went over to join Todd. She knelt down beside him and when he looked up Todd leaned over and gave her a kiss. "You know what I'm going to write, don't you?"

"No. I don't. It seems like there have been a lot to draw from these past few months."

"I think you'll recognize this one." Todd didn't reveal his verse. Instead he stretched out his arm and started writing. "How about if I write it and then you go over the letters and make them nice and thick. This verse needs to be the establishing verse for this house for another fifty years."

Christy looked around. The rest of their friends had scattered around the house, calling out to each other.

Nicole's voice echoed from the master bedroom upstairs, "Does anyone know where the verse is that has the line about 'I hold you in my heart'?"

"Phil. 1:7," Christy called back.

Todd looked up at her and when their eyes met, they shared a deep-hearted smile.

"Phil?" Nicole called back.

"Philippians," Christy replied.

"Oh, right. Philippians. Got it! Katie told me about that one. I'm writing a verse for Katie and then one for me."

"Todd! Bro. You remember the passage for 'The clouds are the dust of His feet'?" Doug had left the back bedroom and was now sitting on the floor next to the picture window.

"Nahum, I think." Todd thought a minute. "I don't know the verse."

"Nahum?" Marti repeated. "That's not a book in the Bible."

"Sure it is," Todd said. "It's right before Habakkuk. Hey, Doug, it might be in Habakkuk. I don't remember."

"I'll look it up," Doug said. "Tracy, let me use your Bible for a minute."

Marti went to the center of the room where Doug now stood and looked with him as he flipped through the pages of Tracy's Bible. Apparently Marti was sufficiently satisfied when Doug pointed out the passage to her in Nahum 1:3.

"How is it that any of you know these obscure, poetic verses and even more obscure books in the Bible?" Marti asked.

Doug gave her another one of his side to side Doug hugs and said, "We can't stop reading this love letter." He held up Tracy's Bible. "This is God's Word. It's alive. It has changed our hearts and our lives." Doug handed the Bible to Marti and she quickly handed it to Tracy as if it were a hot potato.

Christy smiled to herself. She looked down at the first few words that Todd had written on the threshold of the resuscitated house and her smile widened. Todd was writing the first verse in the Psalm of Moses that Todd first quoted months ago when their lives started down this bumpy trail.

"Lord, You have been our dwelling place throughout all generations."

Christy got up to get another marker from Tracy and found her friend writing on the floor in the corner of the living room that led into the open kitchen area. Her letters were straight and easy to read, like the handwriting of a first grade teacher. The corner Tracy chose had the best sunlight that came through the window. Todd's dad used to have a plant in that corner.

The verse Tracy wrote was, "The righteous will flourish like a palm tree." As soon as she finished, Tracy said, "This verse always makes me think of you and Todd. You are two palm trees, bending with the unforced rhythms of grace and flourishing wherever God plants you."

"Thanks, Tracy." Christy smiled, but inwardly she was aching. Surprisingly, this blessing party had turned into something that was really hard for her. She loved the idea when she and Tracy had come up with it, but now that they were putting all these truths and blessings into the house she was reminded that it would soon be occupied by strangers. Would the new renters have any idea how much care and prayerful efforts had gone into this dwelling place?

Christy noticed that Marti had not moved from the center of the living room. She did something Christy never had seen before and never would have expected. Bob came over to her, spread out a beach towel and held her hand as she lowered herself to the floor.

Leaning over demurely, Marti balanced herself as if she were inventing a new yoga pose that she needed to hold for sixty seconds. She uncapped her marker and wrote quickly. Bob waited beside her and Marti put out her hand for Bob to help her up, which he did with steady gallantry.

Christy stepped over to the middle of the room to see what Marti had written.

"Someone else will have to find the reference for this," Marti said, dusting herself off. "But I know those words are in the Bible."

Christy read the three words her aunt had written across the heart, the very center of the house. In all its understated simplicity, Marti's verse said it all

God is love.

Bob looked up the reference in I John 4:8 and knelt to add

it to Marti's contribution. As soon as everyone had finished their verses Rick asked Uncle Bob to come into the kitchen and help him open a couple of bottles of Rick's favorite sparkling pear juice. They filled eight plastic cups with the bubbly beverage and passed them out to everyone. The group gathered in the center of the room, unknowingly forming a circle around the words, "God is love".

"I have a toast." Rick raised his red plastic cup and Christy could imagine what a difference this was to the many other moments when young men had gathered in this place over the last six months and drank from red plastic cups. This space felt fully redeemed.

"This is a toast that Todd gave on a night when I needed it most." Rick was standing next to Todd and put his arm around Todd's shoulders, giving him a brotherly hug.

Rick raised his chin and said, "To the King and His kingdom. To His mysterious ways and His perfect timing."

Christy felt a lump swelling in her throat.

Doug immediately added a few hearty words about how great it was to be back together again with this band of God lovers and said, "May we have many more times like this in the year ahead."

Tracy added a few sweet words about the gift of being Forever Friends and by that time Christy could hardly blink fast enough to keep the tears back. So much had happened in all their lives since Todd first offered that toast several months ago, and since they'd all met during their high school years. God's ways were as mysterious now as they had been then. His timing was still perfect.

She lifted the cup to her lips along with the others. Even though it wasn't yet midnight, and even though there wasn't music playing, Christy heard in her thoughts the line from "Auld Lang Syne" as clearly as if it were being sung in the background.

We'll take a cup o' kindness yet.

Christy let the tingly sweet taste of the sparkling pear juice roll over her tongue and swallowed it with her eyes closed, as if with the swallowing, she was taking into herself the hope that she and Todd would indeed "take a cup of kindness yet". That kindness would be the Lord's blessing on their renovated lives and marriage. What that looked like remained to be seen, but more than ever Christy believed God was going to take care of them. It was as her faith was a muscle and with all the exercising she'd been doing the past few months, her faith muscles were growing stronger. As Katie had said in a recent email, "You're getting buff, Christy. All this living by faith has toned up your heart nicely. I can practically see your muscles bulging."

Rick and Doug headed back to the kitchen and weren't shy about making themselves a second plate of food. Todd and Christy joined them and the three guys reminded each other of what it was like when they shared an apartment during their time in college in San Diego.

"You do know, don't you," Rick said to Tracy as she entered the kitchen with the emptied red cups. "That your husband was the most competitive when it came to apartment games."

Tracy grinned at Doug. "I've heard a few stories about how he managed to win all the little toys you guys got out of kid's meals."

Rick and Todd looked at each other and in unison they said, "Mr. Gizmo!"

It had been a long time since Christy had heard the deep chorus of the laughter from a shared joke of these three amigos. This was a rare treat; the wonderful sound of memory filled happiness.

For that one moment, the first time in months, Christy felt rich. So rich.

The contented feeling of being extravagantly wealthy in what really mattered in life lingered in Christy's heart the rest of the night and most of New Year's Day. It was a gorgeous day. The storm had blown through, leaving the sky and the beach in pristine condition and drenched in golden, California sunlight.

Todd and Doug got a short surf session in soon after first light on that first day of the New Year. By eight o'clock the carpet installer and his team were ready to get to work. Christy stayed in the kitchen and stood at the counter, typing a long email to Katie on their laptop. She had lots to update Katie on, including the news that Katie had nothing to worry about when it came to her wedding dress. Christy and Nicole had a shopping date planned for the end of next week and if Katie couldn't find a way to video call with them during the shopping trip, they'd video it anyway and send all the best dress options to her for approval.

Tracy called as Christy hit send on Katie's lengthy email.

"Is Doug still there?" Tracy asked.

"Yes, do you want me to go get him? He and Todd have been helping install the carpet."

"No, I left a message on his phone. Just tell him that I called."

"Is everything okay?"

"Yes. His parents wanted to know if we wanted to go see a movie with them this afternoon. It doesn't start until three thirty so I'm sure he'll see the message before then. You and Todd are welcome to come, too, if you want."

"Thanks. I'll let Todd know. The way they've been going with the carpet I wouldn't be surprised if they were finished in the next hour or so."

Christy's prediction was right. By noon they were vacuuming the brand new, gorgeous carpeting with Bob and Marti's high end vacuum. The windows were open again, letting out the thick, textile scent of new carpet.

Todd stopped mid task and turned off the vacuum. His eyes went to the patch of floor by the threshold of the front door where they had both knelt together last night. Todd's verse, Moses' Psalm, God's Word was hidden under the plush padding and tufted carpeting.

"Hey, did you write a verse last night?" Todd asked. "I know that Tracy went around and took photos of all of them so we could remember them and remember where they are but I don't think I saw your verse."

Christy led Todd over to the corner of the living room area. It was where she remembered sitting the first time she ever came to this house at Christmastime many years ago. She and Tracy had made cookies at Tracy's house and with her heart full of hope Christy had hand delivered the cookies to Todd here in this living room.

"It's right here," Christy said standing on top of her hand-written words. "Ephesians 3:20. 'Now to Him who is able to do exceedingly abundantly above all that we ask or think, according to the power that works in us, to Him be glory . . . forever and ever.'"

"I like that," Todd said. "I like that verse a lot. 'Exceedingly abundantly above all we ask or think.' Wow. That's pretty extravagant." He turned so that he could look Christy in the eye. "Do you believe that?"

She nodded a timid nod. "I do." Clearing her throat, Christy added with stronger resolve, "I really do. Last night I felt so rich. Rich in family and friends and so many unbelievable memories. That's why I wrote that verse. God has already done exceedingly abundantly above anything I ever dared to dream for."

Todd smiled at her just as his cell phone began to buzz. "It's my dad." Todd quickly took the call. "Hey, Dad."

Christy went into the kitchen to where Todd had left his

backpack on the counter. She wanted to see if he had tossed in the phone charger because his call reminded her that she hadn't plugged her phone in last night and the battery was depleted.

Unzipping the crusty, old backpack, Christy hunted through all the pockets in search of a phone charger. She didn't find a charger, but she did discover a large, red envelope that looked like an unopened Christmas card.

Christy pulled out the card and remembered where she'd seen it before. Mr. Stanley had given Todd the card when they had gone to The Ark so Christy could say her good-byes to her co-workers. He was the ringleader parent who had wanted Todd to stay at the church. Christy paused and thought about how different their lives would be right now if they had stayed in Murrietta Hot Springs. They would have been caught up in the routine of coming and going and doing, and would have missed all the sweet times they'd had with their friends last night as well as the time they had with David, and even with Bob and Marti. Most of all they would have missed the times they'd had together, and all the ways that God knit them even closer to himself and to each other.

Christy quietly thanked God for their losses; Todd's job, her job, their apartment, money in their bank account. All that was gone. But they had everything they needed. Not everything they wanted, but everything they needed.

Christy heard Todd say, "I'll tell her. Okay. Yeah, we will. Thanks, Dad. I'm . . . yeah . . . thanks. We'll call you tomorrow."

He dashed into the kitchen and took Christy by the hand. "What? What's wrong?"

"Come on. I need to go put my feet in the sand. Right now." Todd pulled Christy out the front door and picked up the pace as they strode toward the beach.

Christy was dying to find out what was going on but she

knew better than to waste her words. Todd was furiously processing something and he wouldn't start to disclose anything until his feet were in the sand.

They got to the edge of the long sidewalk that ran parallel to the beach for several miles. Lots of sun seekers were out on this fresh New Year's Day afternoon. Some were riding bikes down the sidewalk. Some were pushing strollers as they jogged.

Christy and Todd slipped off their shoes and nestled their bare feet into the cool sand. The beach, the sky, even the ocean seemed to be welcoming them after the deep, dark rumblings from the past few stormy days.

Todd trucked right down to the water's edge and put his feet into the water. Christy trotted along beside him, feeling the invigorating surge of the cold ocean water on her bare feet.

With an equally exuberant rush, Todd suddenly scooped up Christy and spun her around.

"Wait! I dropped it. The envelope. Get it before it goes out to sea."

Todd put her down and waded into the foaming, receding wave. He picked up the red envelope, shook off the salty water and laughed. "Why did you bring a Christmas card down to the beach?"

"It was in my hand when you grabbed me and we dashed out the door. I found it in your backpack. I was going to tell you that you never opened it. It's from Mr. Stanley, remember?"

Todd gave the soggy envelope another shake and handed it back to Christy as he headed toward the sand and found a place for them to sit down. "Go ahead and open it if you want. They probably did one of those family Christmas photo cards. When he gave it to me, I think I wasn't ready to be reminded of any of the families from the church."

"Are you ready now?"

"Sure. Go ahead. Open it. Quick."

"Quick?" Christy looked at Todd. He was wearing his eight year old boy grin.

"Yes, quick. I brought you down here because I have something to tell you."

"Okay, I'll be quick. There." The soggy envelope nearly dissolved in her hand and revealed an elegant Christmas card that had the words, "Immanuel, God Is With Us" on the front. She opened the card and something fluttered out and onto her lap. It wasn't a family photo. It was a check.

Todd reached for the check before the breeze could snatch it and send it into the ocean for a dunk as well.

Christy read the handwritten message on the inside of the card.

Dear Todd and Christy,

Several of us got together as families and wanted to express to you our appreciation for the impact you made over these past few years on our teens. You have no idea how much your consistent, godly, caring efforts have affected our children and changed their lives. Thank you from the bottom of our hearts. We will miss you very much. Our own kids and many students in the youth group contributed to this small token or our appreciation. We hope this will help make the transition time a little smoother for you both. Wherever you go next, whatever the two of you do, we believe the Lord will bless you abundantly for all the ways you both have been such a blessing to us.

Merry Christmas from all of us.

Christy turned to Todd, her eyes wide. She didn't want to say, "How much is it?" because that felt garish on the heels of such heart-felt, affirming words. She didn't have to ask. Todd turned the check so she could see the amount.

Her hand flew to her mouth. She gasped. The amount on the check was equal to what Todd's salary would have been for six months. Six months! Right now, at that moment, to both Christy and Todd it was an astonishing amount of money.

Christy's eyes welled with tears. She felt her shoulders begin to shake. All this time the check had been hidden in Todd's backpack. But in God's crazy perfect timing, she had stumbled upon it and pulled it out now. She wanted to laugh when she thought about how the card had almost been taken out with the tide and eaten by sea turtles.

"Don't start crying yet," Todd said in a wobbly voice.

Christy blinked and saw that he was crying.

She nudged him with her elbow and laughed. "How come you can cry and I can't?"

"Because," Todd wiped his eyes with the back of his hand. "I know something you don't know."

"What?"

Todd turned to Christy. He folded the check and placed it securely in his pocket. With both hands he cradled Christy's face and looked deep into her eyes. She tried to read his expression with no success. Christy hadn't seen this look on her husband before. She'd seen many looks, but not this one. Todd seemed jubilant and humbled at the same time. He squinted his tear-filled eyes, looking like a miner who had been doing the best work he could in a dark place and was now coming out into the full sunlight.

"What is it?" Christy asked in barely a whisper. Her heart was pounding.

"My dad wants us to stay in the house. . ." his voice broke. "At no charge."

Christy's mouth opened as Todd pulled his hands away and wiped his eyes again.

"But we can pay him now," Christy said.

Todd shook his head. "He said he wouldn't take any money. He and Carolyn talked about it and they don't need the income right now. He'd rather have us there taking care of the place until we leave for their wedding.."

Christy felt the tears skimming down her cheeks and tasted their salty touch on her lips.

Exceedingly, abundantly above. . .

Todd kissed Christy's salty lips and then kissed her again. "This is God's doing. His fingerprints are all over this. The timing is . . ."

"Perfect," Christy whispered.

Todd rose to his feet and pulled Christy up with him. He twirled her around and they laughed out loud. They had a dwelling place for the next three months and they had more money than they needed at the moment. It felt so extravagant.

With one arm around Christy's waist and the other brawny arm lifted to the sky in a position of praise Todd called out to the heavens, "To the King and His kingdom! We praise You, Father, for Your mysterious ways and Your perfect timing."

Before Christy could add a whispered "amen", Todd's lips found hers. She lingered in the golden moment as he kissed her with all the exuberance of a surfer boy who had caught a perfect wave. The ocean answered for her with a knowing rumble as a frothy wave met the shore and receded on the unseen command of the One who holds all things in His hands. The next season of their life in Newport Beach was about to begin.

And Christy was ready.

Ritzy Chicken

4 boneless, skinless chicken breasts cut in bite sized chunks
1 can cream of chicken or cream of mushroom soup
15 to 20 Ritz crackers, crushed
½ cup butter, melted (more if you desire a more golden crust)

Place chicken in casserole baking pan, cover with soup. Top with crushed crackers and pour melted butter over the top. Bake at 350 degrees for 45 minutes.

For a complete collection of Christy's Favorite Recipes visit Robin's Online Shop at www.robingunn.com

• To find out how Katie ended up in Africa and how her relationship with Eli started, read the 4-book Katie Weldon Series.

• You'll find an update on Sierra Jensen and her current love life in *Love Finds You in Sunset Beach, Hawaii.*

• Want to know more about how Bryan and Carolyn reconnected and how their romance started? You can read the whole story in *Canary Island Song.*

Here is where it all began

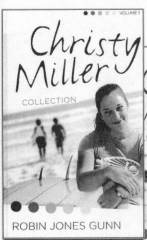

Christy Miller Collection

Vol 1: Books 1-3
Vol 2: Books 4-6
Vol 3: Books 7-9
Vol 4: Books 10-12

Follow Christy and her Forever Friends on an unforgettable journey through the ups and downs of high school.

The Friendship Continues

Sierra Jensen Collection

Vol 1: Books 1-3
Vol 2: Books 4-6
Vol 3: Books 7-9
Vol 4: Books 10-12

Christy and Sierra meet in England and the adventures pick up speed in the Sierra Jensen Series.

Christy & Todd the College Years

As Christy and Todd grow closer during their college years one question remains -- will their love lead to marriage?

ROBINGUNN.COM

More Stories about the Forever Friends

Take a peek into Christy's private thoughts in Christy Miller's Journal. Read about Christy and Sierra's overlapping summer adventures in Departures. Catch up on Sierra's love life in Sunset Beach.

Love Finds You in Sunset Beach, Hawaii

Christy Miller's Diary

Departures

Katie Weldon Series

#1 Peculiar Treasures
#2 On a Whim
#3 Coming Attractions
#4 Finally & Forever

Katie Weldon

Join Christy's best friend, Katie, as she takes the world by storm during her final year of college.

List of Robin's Books

The Christy Miller Series Vol: 1, 2, 3, 4

The Sierra Jensen Series Vol: 1, 2, 3, 4

The Katie Weldon Series
#1 Peculiar Treasures
#2 On a Whim
#3 Coming Attractions
#4 Finally & Forever

More Stories about the Forever Friends
Christy & Todd: The College Years
Love Finds You in Sunset Beach, Hawaii
Christy Miller's Diary
Departures

Glenbrooke Series
#1 Secrets
#2 Whispers
#3 Echoes
#4 Sunsets
#5 Clouds
#6 Waterfalls
#7 Woodlands
#8 Wildflowers

Sisterchicks® Series
Sisterchicks on the Loose
Sisterchicks Do the Hula
Sisterchicks in Sombreros
Sisterchicks Down Under
Sisterchicks Say Ooh La La
Sisterchicks in Gondolas
Sisterchicks Go Brit
Sisterchicks in Wooden Shoes

Stand Alone Novels
Under a Maui Moon
Canary Island Song
Cottage by the Sea

Non Fiction / Women's Studies
Praying For Your Future Husband
Victim of Grace
Spoken For

Visit Robin's online shop at
shop.robingunn.com

ROBINGUNN.COM

home of our hearts

*C*hristy was happy.

Happier than she remembered being in quite some time. She sat across from Tracy at their new, favorite Newport Beach café and scrolled through the photos on her phone. With a shy smile, Christy turned the screen around and told her friend, "So, apparently, it's a girl."

"Really?" Tracy leaned closer and tilted her head to get a good look at the image. She didn't seem convinced. "Is Todd still set on the name?"

"Yes. He's definitely set on the name."

Petite Tracy scrunched up her nose. "'Gussie' isn't exactly the best name, if you ask me. But then, this is your baby, not mine."

"I know. Trust me. Gussie wouldn't have been my choice either." Christy took one more look at the image on her phone before putting it back in her purse and picking up her over-sized mug to enjoy a sip of her English Breakfast tea latte.

"It does make sense, though," Tracy said. "I mean, to Todd's way of thinking, I can see where he came up with that name."

"He's so excited. I hate to douse his enthusiasm." Christy leaned back. Her long, nutmeg brown hair was folded into a loose braid that fell over her left shoulder.

"Lots of changes are ahead for you guys," Tracy said.

Christy nodded and grinned. "I know. Lots of good changes. Amazing changes. So much has been happening so fast."

"Doug and I feel that way, too. Tell me again . . . when do you guys leave for Africa?"